One for the Hooks

Also available by Betty Hechtman

Crochet Mysteries

Hooks Can Be Deceiving
On the Hook
Hooking for Trouble
Seams Like Murder
Knot Guilty
For Better or Worsted
If Hooks Could Kill
Behind the Seams
You Better Knot Die
A Stitch in Crime
By Hook or By Crook
Dead Men Don't Crochet
Hooked on Murder

Yarn Retreat Mysteries

Knot on Your Life
Inherit the Wool
A Tangled Yarn
Gone With the Wool
Wound Up in Murder
Silence of the Lamb's Wool
Yarn to Go

Writer for Hire Mysteries

Murder Ink

One for the Hooks

A CROCHET MYSTERY

Betty Hechtman

CROOKED
LANE

NEW YORK

Copyright © 2021 by Betty Hechtman

All rights reserved.

Published in the United States by Crooked Lane Books, an imprint of The Quick Brown Fox & Company LLC.

Crooked Lane Books and its logo are trademarks of The Quick Brown Fox & Company LLC.

Library of Congress Catalog-in-Publication data available upon request.

ISBN (hardcover): 978-1-64385-732-9
ISBN (ePub): 978-1-64385-733-6

Cover illustration by Jesse Reisch

Printed in the United States.

www.crookedlanebooks.com

Crooked Lane Books
34 West 27th St., 10th Floor
New York, NY 10001

First Edition: August 2021

10 9 8 7 6 5 4 3 2 1

For All the Lindas

Chapter One

I felt my breath stop as I turned into my driveway. Why were the lights on at my house? Nobody was supposed to be home. My son Samuel was on tour with his grandmother and her girl singing group, the She La Las. Barry Greenberg had a key to my place so he and his son could come by to spend time with their dog, but I didn't see Barry's Tahoe parked out front or his son's bicycle in the driveway. Besides, they hadn't been over for months. Mason Fields, the man in my life, had a key as well, but he was out of town.

I pulled my vintage Mercedes next to the garage and cut the motor, feeling uneasy. I looked back toward the street and saw several unfamiliar cars parked along the curb—though they could have been connected to my nearby neighbors, who often had a lot of company.

I considered whether I should call the cops. But what would I say? I was concerned because the lights were on at my house. As if burglars turned on lights. Didn't they use flashlights?

The only thing to do was to face whatever it was on my own. My backup was my smartwatch. All I had to do was push down a side button, and it would call 911. I got out of the car and walked to the chain-link back gate. The sight that greeted me didn't make me feel any better. Cosmo, the small black mutt, and Felix, the gray terrier mix, started to bark and whine as soon as they saw me. They weren't supposed to be outside. I rushed into the yard, and as I looked across the stone patio that ran along the back of my ranch-style house, my worst fears were realized. The outdoor floodlights weren't on, but I could still see that the French door that led to the kitchen was wide open, which meant the two cats were outside too, lost in the semi-dark yard.

Now I was angry. The intruder was going have to deal with my wrath. I wasn't being rational, but then rage never is. I stopped in the garage and grabbed a baseball bat and marched across the patio, ready to do battle.

I walked through the open door, rushing through the dark kitchen and into the living room. Ready for anything, I was still stunned to see a strange woman sitting on the couch. She was staring down at something and didn't look up. I did a quick appraisal of her and decided the gray tank dress and designer sandals didn't seem like burglar attire.

The sound of sirens growing louder barely made an imprint until I heard the pounding on the door as someone yelled out, "Police!" I knew what would come next and rushed to open the door before they battered it in.

Two uniformed cops gave me a quick once over. "Drop the bat," one of them ordered.

"Mother, what have you done now?" a voice behind me said.

I closed my eyes, realizing there was one other person I hadn't considered. My older son, Peter. But in all fairness, he had distanced himself more and more from my life. And when was the last time he'd come over?

It took a few minutes to straighten things out. I might have gone on a bit about the cats being lost in the yard, before Peter took over and told the uniform that I was a widow and was given to overreacting. My son saw the smartwatch on my wrist. "She must have panicked and pressed the button without realizing it would make an emergency call. You know—oldsters and technology." He and the cop traded knowing glances.

Maybe that's why Peter and I didn't spend that much time together. *Oldster?* He had to be kidding. I was barely past fifty, and everybody knew that fifty was the new thirty. But by the same token, I couldn't really blame the cop for choosing to listen to my son. I was probably a little wild-eyed, and there was that matter with the bat. Peter, on the other hand, seemed collected in his fancy casual wear.

Just as the cop was about to leave through the open door, a dark sedan pulled up behind the cruiser. A figure got out and rushed through the dark yard.

"Not him too?" Peter groaned as Detective Barry Greenberg came up the two steps to the front porch.

The two dogs had come in by now, and Cosmo, seeing Barry, rushed up to him and put his paws on the leg of Barry's dark suit. Felix seemed upset by all the commotion

3

and ran back outside. Without even looking, I was sure Blondie, who was a terrier mix in name only, was hiding out in my bedroom.

"The cats," I said rushing back through the kitchen and into the yard. Barry was right behind me. He knew the two cats only went outside when someone could watch them and make sure they didn't leave the yard, which was always during the day.

Barry had the presence of mind to turn on the floodlights, illuminating the yard. Mr. Kitty, as the black and white cat had come to be known, was sitting in one of the outdoor chairs, waiting to be rescued. I heard rustling in the bushes and knew it was Cat Woman, or Cat for short. Despite being ten years old, she was always on the hunt. Barry, ignoring the fact that he was wearing a suit and dress shoes, pushed through the brush growing between the redwood trees that ran along the fence in my backyard and grabbed her. I heard some residual noise, and I was pretty sure she'd already caught something when he grabbed her. But by the time he brought her to me, whatever it was had gotten away.

I shut the kitchen door and locked it when we came back inside. Peter rolled his eyes when he saw us. And he gave Barry a dirty look. It didn't matter that we were long over as a couple; my older son didn't like him. Honestly, I think the whole idea of me "dating" didn't sit well with him, but he definitely preferred my current plus one, Mason Fields.

Barry peered at Peter and then at the woman sitting on the couch. "Are you all right to take it from here?" he said, turning to me. Just then the woman stood up, and I think my mouth fell open when I saw that she was very obviously pregnant.

I saw Barry's lips curve into a smile, and there was the slightest shake to his head as he took it all in. I assured him that everything was fine. I thanked him for his help with the cats.

"Anytime," he said as I walked him to the door. "You probably figured that when I heard there was an emergency call to this address . . ." He shrugged. "I had an automatic reaction. Old habits die hard."

"Thank you," I said.

His gaze flickered back toward the living room, and he cracked a smile. "You're welcome, Grandma."

* * *

Once Barry had left, it was time to find out the story from Peter. Of late he'd been wrapped up in his new career as a TV producer, and I'd barely seen him. Or talked to him. I didn't want to meddle in his life and had left it to him to pick up the phone. He hadn't.

Peter had always been closer to my late husband. It was like he knew in advance that someday I'd be an embarrassment. Everything I'd done since Charlie died had irked my son. I'd gotten a job and developed a social life. And maybe I'd solved a few murders and gotten some attention for it. What did he think I was going to do—sit in a rocking chair and watch my life go by? No way. I was too busy living.

"Maybe we should start with introductions," I said, looking at the woman. No way would I call her a girl. She looked too focused for that. "I'm Molly Pink, Peter's mother. And you are . . .?"

"Gabby Alter," Peter said, answering for her. I noticed he didn't fill in exactly what their relationship was. "I'm sorry about the cats. I forgot you had them," he said. He shook his head. "I don't know what you have all these animals for, anyway."

"You can talk to your brother," I said. "The cats came with him when he first moved back, and Felix belonged to his last girlfriend. She lost interest in both of them."

"That's right, and the black dog belongs to the cop. If you broke up with him, why hasn't he taken his dog?"

"It's not your concern," I said. I didn't feel like explaining that with Barry's work and his son being a teenager, the dog was more assured of consistent care with me. And I loved the little black mutt.

"About that," Peter began.

My son, with the perfectly styled hair and Lupedo Renaldi sports shirt, appeared uncomfortable, which was unusual for him. Ever since he'd been a kid, he'd had a sort of a cocky sense of confidence. Something about his manner put me on edge, and I felt an uh-oh coming.

"This is just a temporary setback," he began and then took a deep breath. "We had a commitment from the network for two years of shows." He stopped, and his expression grew grim. "And then literally overnight everything fell apart. The family sitcom starred Billy Boxmeir. He was the head writer, and it was based on his life." He looked at me to see if I understood.

You had to be dead not to have heard about the scandal. Twenty women had come forward accusing him of sexual harassment. After decades of shoving that sort of thing under the rug, the whole Me Too movement had pushed it out in the open. Overnight, men in power had tumbled. Entertainers like Billy Boxmeir saw their careers collapse, taking everyone involved with them. It hadn't occurred to me that the situation might be connected to anyone I knew.

I nodded and Peter continued. "Gabby was one of the line producers. With a commitment like that, we went ahead and made plans." There was a slight pause as he looked at me, reading my thoughts that I'd been completely left out of the loop. "I was going to tell you when everything was settled. To cut to the chase, we had to back out of the house we were buying, and lost the deposit. We'd already sold our condo." He glanced around the living room. "I thought we could stay here."

I was about to say something to the effect that it would have been nice if he had *asked* if it was okay instead of just announcing they were moving in, but he continued.

"It would give us a decent address while I put something new together. Tarzana isn't Encino, and it is in the Valley," he said with disdain, "but at least it's on the right side of Ventura Boulevard."

There was a whole hierarchy of areas in Los Angeles. Any place on the city side of the Santa Monica Mountains had it over the San Fernando Valley. If you had to be in the Valley, the communities that ran along the base of the mountains were considered the most desirable areas, and it was always best if you were south of the Boulevard.

"I'm happy you approve," I said with a touch of sarcasm. I looked at Gabby, and she was nodding in agreement with Peter. Great: two snobs were moving in.

"Is there something else you'd like to tell me," I said, glancing down at her belly. The tank dress stretched across her midsection.

"I was so focused on getting a place for us to stay." He shrugged. "It's all kind of new. We already know it's a girl. We have a name and everything, but it's supposed to be bad luck to say it."

"What about her last name?" I asked. I was still of the old school that thought babies were supposed to have married parents.

"You mean are we married? Not yet. But the baby's last name will be Alter-Pink."

"I'm glad you have that worked out," I said. "So when were you thinking about moving in?" I asked.

"Our suitcases are in the car," Peter said.

Chapter Two

The next morning I tried to go on with my usual routine. I let the dogs out, made myself coffee, and drank it in the yard, but everything felt different. They were still asleep, but I was ultra-aware of their presence.

It was a relief to go to Shedd & Royal Books and More. Once I'd adjusted to Charlie's death and realized I needed to start a new chapter in my life, I'd gotten the job at the bookstore. I'd been hired as the event coordinator. One of the events I coordinated were the meetings of the Tarzana Hookers—that's hookers as in crochet. I ended up joining the group. Now I was the assistant manager of the store and in charge of the yarn department too. I really didn't think of it as work anymore. It was more like my second home.

As soon as I dropped off my things that morning, I went to set up the chairs for the book club meeting that morning. We had a book club for just about every niche. Mrs. Shedd loved book clubs because it brought a bunch of book buyers into the shop. This particular one was called

Be the Best You and centered on self-help, positive thinking, meditation, and the like.

I put out plenty of chairs since we were having a guest author, which always drew extra people. Merry Riley was local and a familiar actor. She'd been a side character in a long-running family show, *The Van Winkles*, playing an older cousin who'd come to stay with the family while she went to a nearby college. Pretty in a girl-next-door sort of way, she always seemed to have a sunny expression. When that series ended, she moved over to the Junior channel, which was devoted to G-rated programing for older kids, and played the mom on a program called *Shoot for the Stars*. She had written a book called *Coming in Second*, which maintained that you didn't have to come in first to be a winner. She was still married to her first husband, who also functioned as her manager. They had fraternal twins, a girl and a boy who were just the age their mother had been when she began her acting career. I knew all this because I'd written up a bio of her for the book club event.

The regular moderator couldn't make it, and one of the members had volunteered. I handed the guest leader the bio and hung around until Merry arrived. I walked away as the moderator was reading my little piece, and headed for the bookstore café. I was taking my break, and Dinah Lyons was coming in from teaching a summer school class at the local community college. Teaching freshman English was always a challenge, but the summer group was particularly difficult. We both needed a fix of caffeine and girl talk.

I ordered for both of us. Actually, all I had to do was walk in the café and tell our barista, Bob, that Dinah was meeting me, and he got both our drinks ready, along with some sweet treats.

She, as always, got a café au lait, which came as a pot of steamed milk and one of coffee, and I got my usual Red Eye, the menu name for a cup of coffee with a shot of espresso.

I was bringing the drinks to a table by the door when Dinah came in. Her trademark look was a long scarf. Today's was one that she'd crocheted out of a very fine yarn that was called thread. Any kind of scarf you were going to wear in August had to be made out of something light. The heat hadn't wilted her hair, and the salt-and-pepper spikes were gelled to attention. Dinah was older than I was, but had never been specific, just that she was in her fifties, but now that I'd joined her in the fifth decade of my life, the difference seemed negligible.

I took a quick look around the bookstore to check on the book club, then gave all my attention to her. "Have I got something to tell you," I said, giving her a hug.

"I've got news too." As soon as she sat down, she began to pour the steamed milk and separate pot of coffee into a mug. "I need this café au lait. This summer's group is the worst. The kids never read over their papers and see what presumptive type has done. But I got them," she said. "I made them read their papers out loud. I had to bite my lip to keep from laughing. Really, it was like compositions written by Martians." She looked stricken and then glanced around to see if anybody had heard her. "That can't be upsetting to anyone, can it? You never know anymore. Some science fiction fans might be offended." She finished pouring the two liquids into the mug. "That's not my news, but why don't you go first. I need to get this drink in me to revive myself." She clutched the mug.

I told her about my unexpected guests, and the whole story seemed to surprise her, but when I got to what Peter thought the arrangements should be, she couldn't hold it in anymore.

"OMG, he didn't really say that," she squealed.

The *that* she was referring to was Peter's suggestion that I turn over the master suite to him and Gabby. The master suite was like a separate wing of my house, complete with a sky-lit dressing area, closets, luxury bathroom, and a spacious bedroom with a fireplace, which I totally enjoyed inhabiting. "His thinking was that there were two of them and one of me," I said, rolling my eyes. "I told Peter they could have Samuel's room while he's on the road with my mother and her girl group. And when he returns, they can have my crochet room. I'll just have to find someplace else for all the yarn and partially completed projects. And the books and all the other stuff."

"So tell me about Gabby," she said, "and the idea of being a grandmother."

"The whole grandmother thing is going to take some getting used to. Gabby is going to take some getting used to too," I said. "She seems the ambitious type—she was one of the producers on the sitcom before the whole thing fell apart. She didn't seem very friendly, and I think she's not happy with the accommodations. I'm sure Peter assured her they'd have my room." I drained the last of my drink. "He dropped that they're going to tell everyone that the whole house is theirs."

"I hope he's not planning to entertain," Dinah said with a laugh.

"I didn't think of that," I said, and sighed. "I guess I'll deal with that when I have to."

"You could have said no," she said.

"How could I when his brother is already living there when he's not on the road? I probably should be glad that at least Peter didn't bring any pets with him. Just a pregnant woman who seems a little hostile." I looked at my friend. "Now it's your turn."

"My news seems pretty paltry after that. It's just Cassandra." She managed to say the name so it came out as a groan.

"It's not easy dealing with adult children," I said.

"At least, Peter is *your* adult child."

I got it. Cassandra was technically Dinah's stepdaughter. My friend had recently married Commander Blaine. She was long ago divorced, and he was a fairly new widower. Cassandra looked at Dinah as an intruder and made no attempt to keep it a secret.

"I thought she lived someplace back east." I said.

"'*Lived*' is the key word there. Commander didn't want to upset me, so he didn't tell me that she moved to Woodland Hills and that he gave her a job at his Mail It Quick shop. I only found out when I went in there to get some stamps. Now that the cat's out of the bag, he wants us to have weekly family dinners. I think I better hire someone to taste my food first," she said with a smile.

I took a sip of my Red Eye and willed it to give me a jolt of alertness. I hadn't slept well the night before, for obvious reasons, and I had a full day ahead of me at the bookstore, along with the Hookers' get-together later that day. "I might need another one of these," I said, holding up the almost empty cup. "I just heard from Mason. He had some sort of emergency and flew in this morning. He said we'd get dinner."

"Oh," she said, her eyes lighting up. "I'm sure he'll whisk you off to someplace wonderful."

As I said, Mason Fields is my plus one. I hated the word "boyfriend," but there weren't a lot of better alternatives. "Significant other" didn't work for me. It sounded forced. "Partner" was confusing—were you lovers or in business together? "Main squeeze" sounded like a tube of toothpaste. Whatever his title, he'd recently gone through a huge change in his life, almost like a rebirth. He was a high-powered attorney who mostly dealt with naughty celebrities and people with a lot of money. He spent as much time hand-holding as he did defending them. He had all the vestiges of a high-profile legal career, like a corner office in a Century City high rise that gave him a view of Santa Monica Bay, and custom-made suits. His Encino house was a mini mansion surrounded by beautiful landscaping, and he drove a deluxe Mercedes SUV.

But when he'd looked back over his career, he'd begun to regret that he'd used his highly skilled legal talents to basically do nothing more than help guilty rich people get off. It had all suddenly seemed hollow and without meaning, and had caused him to want to change his life. He connected with the Second Chance Project, a group of lawyers who helped innocent people in prison get new trials. Mason was still a partner at his regular law firm and still dealt with his celebrity clients, but he was spending more and more time traveling around, tracking down new evidence and working on appeals for people who'd never gotten a fair trial.

It meant we were apart a lot, but when I saw what it had done for his life, I could only be happy for him. Our relationship was on the casual side anyway. He was divorced and wasn't interested in getting married again. I'd been married for a long time before Charlie died, and was very comfortable being single. The best way to describe our relationship was the adult version of going steady. Mostly we had fun together. I missed him when he was on the road, but seeing the change in him more than made up for it. It was like a youth serum. He looked and acted years younger and was brimming with passion, which spilled over nicely into our time together.

"Yes, I can't wait to see him." I debated getting another Red Eye, but when I leaned back and looked into the bookstore, I was troubled by what I saw. "They should be winding down by now," I said, shaking my head as I got up. Dinah followed me through the magazine racks before we reached their gathering spot.

I stopped on the edge to wait for an opening to step in. One of the women was in the midst of asking a question. I recognized her as one of our regular customers. She had short brown hair, tinged with a little gray, and a forth-right manner. I couldn't remember her name other than it reminded me of mayonnaise. "Why don't you ever talk about the first movie you were in?" she asked.

Merry's smile barely faltered. "You mean *Eels*? It was so long ago and not exactly a shining performance." Her eyes moved over the group. "For those of you who missed it, it was a low-budget horror movie. Think a cheap version of *Jaws*, but with slithery, black snake-like fish that can zap you with an electric charge." She paused to let them all chuckle. "I still have a souvenir from the film." She glanced over to where a man was lounging against one of the book-cases, looking at his phone. "My husband, Mick, was the eel master. He created all the mechanical eels."

He looked up at the group and did a solemn bow before his face broke into a grin, and he used his arm to imitate a swimming eel. Then he pointed at his watch.

"I didn't realize how late it was. The discussion with all of you was so inspiring, and I hate to have to go," Merry said, turning to me. "I could come back in a few days." She glanced back toward the group, and they all nodded enthusiastically.

By this time, her husband had come over to join her. "That's not a bad idea," he said. "We didn't have any books to sign this time, but I'm sure something could be arranged for next time." He looked out to the group. "You could bring your friends."

"I'm sure we could make that happen," I said, putting an arm around Merry and attempting to separate her from the group, but Ms. Mayonnaise stuck next to her. I started to escort Merry and Mick to the front, when there was a shriek and the blur of a red cape as Adele Abrams flew out of the children's department, waving her phone on a selfie stick like it was a magic wand. When she stopped moving, I saw she was wearing a silver crown that was askew. She seemed ready to latch onto Merry, and I tried to stop her.

"Can you give me something for my vlog," Adele said, reaching around me. She quickly caught her breath and straightened her crown when she saw her image in the phone. "Going live," she said in a false bright tone. "I have a special guest, Merry Riley. Tell my followers what you're doing here."

Mick appeared ready to step in, but even though Merry had no idea what was going on or who Adele was, she rose to the occasion and brightened her smile.

Before Merry could say a word, Adele continued, "To all my many, many followers. I know my vlog started out to be about crochet and yarn, but it's become so much more. I'm sharing the adventures of my life with you all. And the exciting people that I meet." Then she finally let Merry talk about her book.

Ms. Mayonnaise realized she'd been squeezed out of their interchange and joined me. "You shouldn't let that woman with the crown bother Merry," she said in a scolding tone.

"They seem to have worked that out on their own," I said, doing my best to sound friendly.

Ms. Mayonnaise let out a harrumph and went back to get her things.

"You have to deal with a lot," Dinah said, catching up with me. "Force-of-nature Adele and people like that woman telling you how to do your job."

"It's not the first time she's made a *friendly suggestion* and probably not the last. I don't think she can help herself. We talked a little once, and she told me she was retired from an administrative job at a private school and felt it was her duty to step in when something didn't seem right to her." Dinah laughed when I explained the issue with her name.

"Ms. Mayonnaise is probably more exciting than her real name anyway," Dinah said as we continued to the back of the store. I surveyed the yarn department to see if there were any early arrivals for the Hooker gathering, but the wood table was empty. We dropped our tote bags on it before going back to where the book group had met, then started putting everything back the way it was.

We were just finishing up when a woman stepped in front of me.

"Just the person I want to see," she said in a bright tone. Without waiting to see if I recognized her she said, "Sloan Renner," and held out her hand.

"Of course, I know who you are," I said. She was a regular customer and had come to a lot of our events. We'd gotten talking after a demonstration a cook book author had put on. There was something stylish about her—the collar was popped on her shirt, and the cuffs rolled up, but somehow she managed it so it looked completely natural. I saw she was holding some hardbound books from our bargain table. She noticed me checking the titles and moved them so they were too far away for me to read. "They're just for show. I'm working on a house, and I wanted to have some books stacked next to a chair. I saw Martha Stewart do it and thought the look was fabulous."

I introduced her to Dinah. "Sloan wears a number of hats and all very well," I said. "Let's see, she's a set designer for one of the studios. When she's not doing that, she's a real estate agent, stages houses before they go on the market, and clears houses so she can stage them." I looked at Sloan. "Isn't there something else?" I said.

"I have a new service setting up backgrounds for online group meetings, and there's the occasional odd job," she said with a friendly smile. "I like having a number of professions. So when one starts to ebb, I can find one that flows. Besides, I have to keep my sister in designer shoes." She said it like it was a joke, but I remembered something about her having a sister she was helping support who had a lot of health issues.

"You're in charge of the yarn department here, right?" she said. I nodded and she continued, "I'm working on a emptying out a house, and we found a bunch of yarn. It seems like it's high quality, and I'm trying to figure out how to dispose of it. Do you suppose you could have a look at it? Maybe you could add it to your inventory."

I wasn't sure how to answer her. It was true, we had bought up yarn from a shop going out of business, but I wasn't so sure about something from someone's house. "We have a lot of stock right now," I said as an excuse, but Sloan persisted.

"Why don't you look at it before you decide? I'm sure my client will let it go for cheap, and you could make a tidy profit," she said.

"I suppose there's no harm in having a look," I said.

"Then come tomorrow," she said, and pushed a business card on me. "Got to run. I left my dog in the car." I immediately felt concerned since it was summer, and started to say something. "Don't worry—she's in the shade. I love that pup and wouldn't let anything bad happen to her." She pointed to the card. "I wrote the address on the back."

I waited until Sloan left. "Before we waste any time going over there, I'm going to check with Mrs. Shedd and see if she's even interested." I went looking for the bookstore co-owner. She was in her office, pouring over a book catalog.

"Sorry to interrupt," I said. Pamela Shedd had honey-blond hair without even a strand of gray. The texture was smooth and shiny, though she was well into her sixties.

"No problem," she said.

I explained about the yarn that Sloan had mentioned. "She's claiming the owner would sell it for a low price. What do you think?"

She shrugged. "You know more about yarn than I do. Have a look and tell me about it; then we'll decide."

Dinah had gone back to the yarn department, and I headed to join her.

"I found this on the floor," Dinah said, handing me a silver bangle. "What should I do with it?"

I picked up my tote bag off the table and held it open. "Drop it in here. It probably belongs to someone in the book group. I'll put it in the lost and found."

"So what did Mrs. Shedd say?" Dinah asked.

"She was okay with me having a look. It's probably going to turn out to be a lot of cheap stuff or wool that moths have gotten into."

"It doesn't hurt to have a look," Dinah said.

"I'm glad you feel that way, because you're coming along. But for now it's Hooker time."

Chapter Three

"Did I see you talking to Sloan Renner?" Elise Belmont asked as she pulled out her chair and dropped her crochet things on the table in the yarn department. Elise was one of those women who looked like a gust of wind could blow her over with her slight build. Her bird-like voice added to the image that she was ethereal and kind of out there. But it was all false. Elise had a laser focus on whatever she was interested in at the moment. Now, it was real estate, and Sloan Renner was competition.

I nodded as Dinah and I took adjacent chairs at the table. "What were you talking about? Are you selling your house? Did she try to get the listing?" Elise asked with an edge in her voice.

I heard Dinah laugh at the idea of me selling my house now that Peter and Gabby had moved in. "Actually, she was talking to me about yarn. She's emptying a house, and there's some yarn she thought we might be interested in for the bookstore."

"Emptying a house?" Elise said. "What do you mean?"

Just then Ms. Mayonnaise wandered into the yarn department, looking a little lost. Despite her reprimanding me just a few minutes earlier, I knew the attitude in the bookstore was the customer was always right, so I excused myself and went to help her.

"I'm just looking around," she said. "I've never come back here before." Her gaze took in the inviting area. The back wall was lined with stacked cubbies filled with yarn. A selections of crochet hooks and knitting needles hung from a rack next to the cubbies. In addition to the table and straight-backed chairs, we had several more comfortable chairs in the area for anyone who wanted to sit and work on a project or check out the many craft books we had.

"I heard you have a group that meets here." Her attention moved to the table as more of the Hookers arrived.

"You're welcome to join us," I said, but she held back.

"The book club was enough for today," she said. "Merry was a great guest. Her book is so inspiring. I had no idea that she was a neighbor."

Just then I remembered her name. "Anastasia," I blurted out rather abruptly, and she gave me a funny look before she turned to go.

I caught Dinah's eye, and she nodded with understanding. "Anastasia—mayonnaise, I get the connection," my friend said.

Rhoda Klein had just found a seat. She was a solid sort of woman with a thick New York accent. She had short dark hair and dressed for comfort. Sheila Altman took the seat next to Rhoda. They were like night and day. Sheila's round face always seemed on the edge of an anxiety attack. She'd learned to keep herself from going over the edge by pulling out something to crochet, and kept a small ball of string and a crochet hook in her pocket for an emergency. She was the youngest of the group, barely out of her twenties, and for now working at the lifestyle store called Luxe that was located down the street.

I saw Eduardo Linnares striding across the bookstore. It always amused me to watch people react to him. Some people recognized him from his model days. His image had been used on countless romance novels, where he was dressed as a buccaneer, pirate, firefighter, or one of the various renegade royals. But when the publisher had asked to use him as the model for the pirate's father, he decided it was time to hang up the flowing shirts and move on. He'd been a spokesperson for a while and finally bought an upscale drug and sundry shop, called The Apothecary, in Encino. What was he doing with a crochet group? He'd learned the art from his grandmother when she realized there weren't any granddaughters to pass her knowledge on to. He had large hands but could manage the most delicate thread crochet. He was a totally nice guy, and we all accepted him as one of us.

I had to laugh when I saw that Anastasia had followed him and come back to the yarn department. "He's one of your group?" she asked, watching him intently as he sat down. "I, uh, have a lot of your books," she said. She sounded kind of gushy, which seemed at odds with the way she'd been before. Her expression changed to one of embarrassment. "I read all different kinds of books," she said, sounding suddenly defensive.

Eduardo shot her a charming smile. "I'm afraid I can't take credit for what's between the covers of the books, but I'm glad you enjoyed them. We all need to get away from it all for a while, and there's nothing better than a good love story."

"You're so right," she said, sounding a little dreamy. The set of her face had softened, and she let out a sigh. "I'd stay, but I have an appointment." She gave him a last wistful look and left the area.

We all looked to Eduardo. "It's nice to be able to make somebody's day with a smile and a nice comment," he said.

"You should have given her a card for your shop," Elise said. "Why not get some business from being so nice." She swiveled her head toward me and brought up Sloan and the yarn. "You were going to tell me about her emptying a house and you buying some yarn."

"I'm here at last," Adele said as she swept up to the table. She'd lost the crown and the cape, but not the dramatic manner. "It's hard being a successful influencer. My fans keep wanting more and more from me. She dropped into a chair at one end of the table and put her phone on the selfie stick on the tabletop. "At last I have a few moments of a normal life, hanging out with all of you." She fluffed up one of the crocheted flowers that covered her sweater.

CeeCee Collins was the last to arrive. Someone always stopped her when she was coming through the bookstore and asked for an autograph or to take a picture with her.

There were people who knew her from the long ago *CeeCee Collins Show* and some who recognized her from her role as Ophelia in the movie about Anthony, the vampire who crocheted to control his blood lust. She had been nominated for an Academy Award and now in her sixties had a restart in her career.

She was a little self-absorbed but had a good heart and a musical laugh. She was the leader of our group and the one who came up with all the charity projects we frequently worked on. For now, we were all working on our own things.

As everyone was greeting CeeCee, Adele started grumbling. "Pink, you almost ruined my interview with Merry Riley," she said.

Adele called me by my last name because she knew it annoyed me. It was her lame way of getting back at me for getting the job that she wanted. She was already working at the bookstore when I was hired, and she'd hoped to get promoted to the position of event coordinator, but I had experience working in my late husband's public relations firm, which made me more qualified. As a consolation, she'd been given the children's department to run. It actually worked out for her because it gave her a reason to dress up in costumes for story time. And despite her not really liking kids, they seemed to adore all her drama.

Adele always wanted to be in the spotlight, and she'd finally found her way into it through her vlog. It had made her even harder to deal with now, if that was possible.

All eyes went to me. "Her husband was trying to get her out of there," I said.

"Well, if you noticed, she seemed fine talking to me," Adele said in a defiant tone.

"He's her manager, and I'm sure he was just trying to protect her," CeeCee said. "She's what you'd call a working actor. Her whole career has been playing background characters. Personally, I'd rather have a career like mine with its highs and lows. Hers seems kind of flat."

"I wouldn't call it flat," Rhoda said. "It seems pretty nice to me. She's been doing what she loves for all these years and has a couple of kids and an adoring husband. I bet they never have to wait for a table at the Cheesecake Factory either."

CeeCee's expression darkened as she took Rhoda's comment personally. "I could have had all that too, if I'd wanted. And I get seated right away wherever I go," she said. "I like to keep challenging myself. That's why I'm doing live theater for the first time ever."

We all knew about her new venture. She was starring in a play at one of the equity waiver theaters. They were in rehearsal, and she had gone back and forth from being excited about it, like she sounded now, to terrified.

"Who cares about Merry Riley," Elise said. Her chirpy voice had a surprising edge as she turned to me. "You never finished talking about Sloan and her 'emptying houses,' whatever that means.

Since the whole group was now listening, I had to backtrack. "Sloan is a set designer for one of the studios, but the work ebbs and flows, so she actually has a bunch of careers that all sort of work together. She's a real estate agent but also stages houses to make them look super saleable. Now, she said she's helping someone empty a house, and she said there was a bunch of yarn she thought the bookstore might be interested in. I'm going to look at it tomorrow. She thinks we could buy it and sell it here."

"I know more about yarn than you do," Adele said. "You better let me come with." It was true that Adele knew more about yarn and crochet than I did, but I suspected she had another motive. There was just the hint of a smug smile. Adele was looking for material for her vlog.

"I better come too," Elise said. "I'd like to see this house she's emptying, and I'll make sure you get the best deal on the yarn—that is, if you want it."

I looked at Dinah. "I hope Sloan agrees with 'the more, the merrier.'"

Chapter Four

O nce again I was in for a surprise when I got home. There were boxes and plastic bins stacked on the stone patio, and when I looked in the garage, I saw some unfamiliar furniture. I should have known that the suitcases Peter and Gabby had shown up with weren't everything. I heard the clang of the metal gate and started to tense, thinking, *What now?* I was pleasantly surprised to see Mason Fields coming toward me. He was beaming a big smile and inspired the same from me.

"I thought you wouldn't be here until later," I said as we hugged each other in greeting. I'd seen his text that morning to let me know of his last-minute trip. He'd been gone for over a week, and I was happy to get the surprise visit.

"I pushed everything up so we could have the evening." He looked at the stuff in the yard. "I'm sure there's a story to all this." Then he shrugged. "Whatever it is, let me take you away from it all." He put his arm around my shoulders. "I couldn't wait to see you. I didn't even change." He was dressed in his work clothes. The tan suit had the fit of something custom made, and the cream-colored dress shirt had the sheen of a high thread count. His dark eyes were bright, and he seemed full of energy. A lock of his hair had fallen across his forehead as it always seemed to do. I don't know why, but somehow it always gave him the look of someone hardworking and earnest. I had long since given up trying to brush it away.

He seemed impatient to go but knew I had to take care of the menagerie first. While I put out everyone's dinner, he looked around the kitchen. A fancy espresso maker was next to my coffeepot, and a box of groceries sat on the counter.

"More mysterious additions," he said, pulling out a package of fancy coffee. "You can tell me all about it as we go," he said.

"You seem pretty energetic after dealing with an early morning flight and then whatever it was you came back here for," I said.

"It's seeing you, Sunshine," he said with broad smile. He called me Sunshine because he said I brightened his life.

"I think there's more to it than me," I said. Much as I would have liked to take all the credit for his new lease on life, I knew it had a lot to do with his work with the Second Chance Project.

"Maybe you're a little right," he said. "I hated to have to leave and break my momentum, but one of my clients here required my presence and, well, they pay the bills so I can do the other work." The dogs and cats had finished their food, and the dogs got their outside run. Then Mason waited while I rounded them up. "We can talk about it while we drive."

He took my hand and led me back to the driveway. His black Mercedes SUV was in the driveway behind the Green-mobile. That's what I called my 1993 Mercedes. I used to refer to it as vintage, but decided classic sounded better.

Before we took off, Mason leaned over and kissed me. Somehow it was playful and passionate at the same time and left me a little breathless.

"The rest will have to wait until later," he said with a twinkle in his eye. "For now we need food and atmosphere."

I knew better than to ask him where we were headed. Mason loved to keep our destinations a surprise. It was rarely just a restaurant somewhere. Always romantic and a little fun. He got on the 101, and we joined the traffic headed into the sunset.

"So are you going to tell me what's going on at your place?

We generally talked every night while he was gone, but the previous night he had texted me to tell me of his unexpected trip home and said he'd fallen asleep trying to organize his work. "It's Peter," I said. "He's moving in with his . . ." Then I faltered, wondering how to describe Gabby. Was she his girlfriend, his fiancé, my soon-to-be daughter-in-law, or should I just call her his baby mama? Finally I just said "with Gabby" and left it at that.

"Peter?" Mason said. "What happened?"

I started to tell him what Peter had been working on, and he nodded with understanding. "It's terrible for Peter and for everyone working on the series. They thought they were set for two years of work and probably made plans accordingly. And then overnight it all disappeared, all because Billy Boxmeir couldn't keep his hands and other things to himself," he said.

"There's more," I said. "Gabby is pregnant. It's a girl."

Mason looked over at me and chuckled. "So you're going to be a grandmother."

"I know I should be happy about that part of it, but it's all so sudden. I didn't even meet Gabby until last night. I can't help it. When I think of a grandmother, I imagine someone in a shapeless housedress, stirring a steaming pot of something on the stove before she retires to sit in her rocking chair."

Mason laughed. "Maybe some grandmothers, but not you. You'll be reading her Nancy Drew stories when she's a toddler. I'm sure she'll have a cool name for you, like Golly." He laughed again. "Get it? 'Grandmother' mixed with 'Molly.'"

As we passed through the hills just outside of Calabasas, I figured he was heading for Las Virgenes Road, which was a scenic route to Malibu. But we flew past it and kept going.

"Anything but 'Granny,'" I said. "But enough about me. What about what you're working on?"

"Here or there?" he said. Before I could respond, he went ahead and dismissed the clients he'd come to see quickly. "It's all because the DA's son didn't get into Worthington University, and he's poking around, hoping to find some fraud involved with some kids who did get into the school."

Mason reminded me of the "Varsity Blues" scandal that involved connected wealthy parents getting their kids into elite schools by masquerading them as football players and rowers. "Careers were ruined, and people who never thought prison was in their future ended up doing time," Mason said. "I had to calm my clients. But the case I'm working on in Topeka is much more interesting. We're talking about giving a kid his life back." Mason sounded passionate. "I wish you could have seen his face when I visited him in prison and told him we were getting a hearing. He'd been convicted with shoddy evidence. It didn't matter that some-one else had confessed to the murder and that my client had an alibi." Mason shook his head in disbelief at how the first trial had been handled. "You have no idea how hard it is to get a chance to go before a judge. There's a bonus to having all my celebrity clients. Even judges in Kansas have seen me on TV talking about one client or another, and, well, they think I'm hot stuff and seem to listen to me a little more." I glanced over at him and he beamed with pride.

It was all regular freeway for a while, with car dealers and businesses on either side. Then the view changed as the roadway ascended, twisting through a mountain pass. As we rounded the last curve, the road ahead descended into an area of strawberry fields and citrus groves mixed in with the town of Camarillo. In the far distance, the sun was hanging over the ocean, about to drop in.

"I'm sorry we're going to miss the sunset, but there will still be the soft light of evening for a while," he said. Already the sky above us had turned a soft haze of pastel colors.

"What about you? What's up with the Hookers?" he asked. Even though he knew it was connected to a crochet tool, he still laughed at the name.

"The Hookers are fine," I said. "Adele is driving everyone crazy with her vlog." I started to say that it was mostly the same old, same old, and then I remembered Sloan and the yarn.

"One of the bookstore customers is trying to sell me a load of yarn from a house she's helping to empty." I took a moment to explain Sloan's many professions, and he asked for her name.

"Sloan Renner." I looked over at him, and he surprised me. I thought he'd shake his head and say he'd never heard of her, but instead he seemed deep in thought. "Then you know her?" I asked.

"Not really, but I've heard the name. You said she's a set designer. That's probably it." A lot of Mason's paying clients were in the entertainment industry, both in front of and behind the camera. "Why do I sense there's some kind of problem?" he asked.

"It's just that it was only going to be Dinah and me going over there. Then Elise got all huffy because Sloan is competition for her as far as real estate goes, so she insisted on coming too. Then Adele . . ." I let out a sigh. "It doesn't matter what reason she gave; it's because she's trying to get content for her vlog."

"Sounds like fun," he joked. "Maybe I should come too."

By then we'd reached Ventura Harbor. The streetlights were coming on, but as Mason had promised, the sky was still a dusky blue. We left the Mercedes in the parking lot and walked across the street to the beach. We climbed the small dunes just inside the fence and surveyed the area. The sand was soft and silky, and the beach extended a long way before meeting the water. A few die-hard surfers were catching their last waves of the day. Santa Cruz Island loomed off in the distance.

My stomach rumbled and Mason laughed. "I heard that. Let's eat." We went back across the street and followed the walkway along the harbor, full of commercial fishing boats, to a place that sold fish and chips.

"You're in for a treat, "Mason said as he carried a paper bag full of food to an outdoor table. The air had a bite to it, but a sweatshirt was enough to keep away the chill.

"Nice, huh?" Mason said as we sat down at a table with a view of the boats. "If you're not up to your elbows in a mystery, you probably haven't seen Detective Barry," he said. There was just a hint of something in his voice.

"Actually, I saw him last night. I wasn't expecting anyone to be at my house, and when I saw the door open, I freaked and accidentally made an emergency call on my smartwatch."

"And what? He automatically responds when he sees it's your address?"

"Something like that."

"But he didn't stay? You didn't feed him." Mason looked at me in the darkness. I had fed Barry a few times when our paths crossed. Just because we were done didn't mean that I didn't care about him as a human being. What was the big deal if I made him a few scrambled eggs, anyway?

"Nope. He just called me 'Grandma' and left."

We enjoyed the view and the food, but now that it was completely dark, the breeze had a chill, and Mason suggested we head back. The ride home wasn't nearly as scenic except for the few moments of seeing the moon hanging over the barren mountains as we drove up the grade and through the winding pass between Camarillo and the Conejo Valley.

"Spike will be so happy to see you," Mason said as he pulled into his garage. He'd left the toy fox terrier with a pet sitter the first couple of times he went on the road to work on one of his pro bono cases, but had ended up taking the dog with him after that.

Mason had kept the Encino house in his divorce. It was a large ranch style built in dark wood and surrounded by several old California oak trees Encino was named for. The front yard was landscaped with rolling hills and a plethora of interesting plants.. Spike was yipping at the door when we walked in. Then he danced around both of us. I saw Mason glance at his watch and thought it was a sign he was tired, but it actually turned out he wanted to watch the news.

The room he used the most in the house was a den that looked out onto his backyard. The furniture here was comfortable and felt lived in. He turned on the TV and directed me to make myself at home. "I'll make us a couple of cappuccinos."

He came in with the drinks and put them on the wood coffee table just as the news was starting with a tease of the upcoming stories. Mason's face appeared on the screen. "Oh, look who's on TV," he joked. "I'm not really that into watching myself. But I want to see how they present the story." He handed me one of the coffee drinks. "As you probably figured, it's about the clients I came back to see."

"Could it be happening again? Another scandal with powerful parents finding a side door for their children to get into a prestigious school?" the news anchor said.

Mason came on the screen as reporters pushed microphones in front of him. He was used to talking to the media and he came across as friendly and approachable. "It's all just saber rattling," he said. "Lindsey Bagatti got into Worthington University on her own merit. She is absolutely a legitimate croquet athlete." Mason looked at the reporter. "My hope is that the district attorney will not waste any more of the taxpayer's money pursuing a case where there is no proof of any wrongdoing."

Mason was grinning as he turned to me. "Was I great or what?"

"So that's what you came back for?" I said. "A *croquet* athlete? For a moment I thought you said a *crochet* athlete."

"That would be pretty funny. You better not mention it to Adele or she'll take it seriously. But yes, Worthington does have a croquet team. It's a collegiate sport with a national championship put on by the United States Croquet Association. It's not that common, but a number of schools have teams. Worthington wasn't one of them until the Baggati family donated a large amount of money to organize one. Having a team meant that students could get admission to the university as croquet athletes." He looked at me. "This is probably all very boring, but I have spent a lot of time going over it. Because it's not that common a sport, the proof that a student was actually a croquet athlete is different." Mason shrugged. "Basically, they need to satisfy the coach that they've played in a championship." He chuckled. "Who knew that croquet was a game of skill and strategy? The DA is making a fuss about the family donating the money and then having their two kids get admission to the school as athletes." Lester Bagatti has been a client of the firm for years. I came back to calm him down and talk to the media. Quite a switch from meeting my other client in prison. By the way, there's a vending machine in the room at the prison where we meet, and I always make sure he's gets some food. I just hope I can take him out for a steak dinner when I finally get him sprung."

He took my hand. "But enough about work. It's time for us, and I have a surprise for you."

Chapter Five

"You have me puzzled," Dinah said. "I'm trying to read your expression, but I can't tell if you look happy or dazed. It must have been quite a night with Mason."

It was Wednesday and we were standing outside Shedd &Royal, waiting for the rest of the crew who were going to accompany me to check out the yarn that Sloan had talked about. I realized that I had been staring off into space, probably with a strange expression.

"It was definitely a hot time with Mason. This work he's doing has given him a recharge in all aspects of his life." I knew I was blushing a little, and glanced at Dinah out of the corner of my eye. "And then in the midst of *everything*, he said we ought to bet married. Of course, typical Mason, he made it funny, offering to get on bended knee and do a formal proposal. I laughed it off, but I wonder what he would have come up with if I'd said I wanted the whole show."

"What?" Dinah said, her head jerking up straight. "When were you going to tell me?"

"Now," I said with a laugh.

"But didn't he always say he didn't want to get married again? And I know you told him you felt the same way."

"I'm telling you, he's like a different person. He said he feels like a young crusading attorney."

"What did you say?" The wind caught Dinah's long scarf of the day, and she had to pull the white silk away from her face.

"It was a total surprise and caught me completely off guard. Though I have been thinking about what it would like to be a grandmother, which feels like being side-tracked from the action somehow. I could see how the idea of a new beginning could be appealing. But it was way too much to deal with at once. I never understood how people could say they had to think about a proposal, but now I get it. I guess when I was younger, I never considered the consequences. And that's what I told him—that I'd have to think about it."

"How'd he take it?" Dinah asked.

"He's a lawyer, so he tried to argue his case." I chuckled. "He presented a pretty compelling argument. He wasn't just proposing marriage but asking me to join him so we could work as a team on the Second Chance Projects. A lot of the work is hunting down evidence and talking to people. Mason said I was a natural for that with my detective skills. He said once I worked on one case, I'd be hooked. He's probably right. The cases he's worked on were people who had no means to defend themselves and were convicted with faulty evidence. He said we'd be like Nick and Nora Charles, or the *Hart to Hart* couple."

"Were either of the men lawyers?" Dinah asked with a laugh. "Sorry for being picky."

"I think his point is that we'd be legendary." My expression dimmed. "But as appealing as it sounds doing something so meaningful, it would cause a total upheaval of my life. I couldn't come and go the way he does and keep my position at the bookstore, though Adele would probably be thrilled about that. Then she could finally get the job she thought she deserved. And I'd be only a sometime visitor to the Hooker gatherings." I looked at my friend. "And if I was gone so much, there would go all our girls' nights and playing Sherlock Holmes and getting into trouble."

"You wouldn't be gone all the time. I'm sure we'd manage to keep having our girls' nights. We'd just have to make the most of it when you were here."

"He suggested I move in with him while I thought about it since Peter is staying at my place."

"What did you say to that?

I shook my head in answer, maybe a little too vigorously. "A big no. To me that would be like saying yes. I'm old-fashioned that way. I'm not going to live with someone unless a wedding is in the works, and Mason knows that."

"Too bad—you and Peter could have a double wedding," Dinah teased. Then she got serious. "You should think about it, though."

"I will. I'm sure Mason will keep pleading his case—at a distance. He went back to Kansas early this morning."

Just then Adele came out of the bookstore. She seemed full of purpose and was talking to the screen of her phone.

I elbowed Dinah and put a finger to my lips to shush her. The last thing I wanted was for Adele to know there was a chance I might be leaving the bookstore.

She was still talking as she reached us. "Friends, I'm taking you along on a yarn adventure," Adele said in a melodramatic voice. She was really stretching it. It was hardly an adventure; we were just going to check out some yarn which was probably moth-eaten, had a bad smell, or was so out of date that nobody would want it. It was funny how tastes changed. Colors that looked so good at one time seemed dated and garish at another time.

Adele continued talking while modeling her tank dress made out of granny squares, but instead of the usual black yarn around the colorful sections, she'd used white yarn. Adele was known for her outfits. They were either heavily crocheted or actual costumes that she wore for story time. Her height and ample size made everything she wore even more of a standout.

Elise was the last one to join us. No matter what she'd said about helping me make a deal for the yarn, I knew she was really going along in her position as a real estate agent. The giveaway was her briefcase.

"I thought we could all go together," I said, but Adele objected.

"I'll drive with Elise. Give her the address," she said. I quickly scribbled it on a scrap of paper and handed it to our yarn buddy.

"I know that house," she said, her wispy voice rising in interest. "It used to belong to a family named Perkins.

Elsie Perkins was the last one and lived there alone. She died recently and her niece inherited it. I'm sure I sent her a postcard expressing interest in helping her sell the house, but Sloan must have gone there in person. Some people think that's too pushy." Elise sounded defensive.

"I don't know what arrangement Sloan has with her," I said.

"So then you don't know if it's on the market already?"

Adele started walking to her car and waved for Elise to follow.

"It's easier without them," Dinah said as we got into the Greenmobile. I told her where we were headed.

"Just keep your eyes out for Starlight Court," I said. I knew basically where we were going, which wasn't that far from my house. The topography of Tarzana was varied because of the proximity of the Santa Monica Mountains. Even in the more level areas, ridges appeared like fingers making steep hillsides and streets that were a mystery to me after all these years of living in the San Fernando Valley community.

Starlight Court turned out to be a cul-de-sac. Up close it appeared to be level, but just behind it the ground rose up into a steep ridge ribboned with houses.

I pulled to the curb of the short street and looked around. A man and a boy were sitting on the curb, racing remote-control cars. The man looked up at us and offered a cold stare that made me feel uncomfortable.

"What's that about?" I said, trying not to stare back.

"People on cul-de-sacs feel like they own the street. He probably views us as invaders in his space," my friend said.

As if on cue, the man and boy grabbed the toys and went into the house at the end of the street.

"I'm sure you're right, but I'm glad he's gone," I said, letting out my breath. "It's silly, but I felt like he was going to come up and pound on the window, demanding we leave." I looked at the address painted on the curb and saw that we were parked in front of the right house. "We might as well wait in the car for Adele," I said. In the meantime, we can play our Sherlock Holmes game. Let's see what we can deduce." I gestured to the five houses in front us. We eliminated the very first house since that was the one we were going to. I pointed to the one next to it. "What do you think?"

"You go first," Dinah said. I looked over all of the houses again and thought of them as a whole. "They were probably built at the same time." I gave all my attention to the house we were starting with. It was a pale blue ranch style and seemed well kept up but plain compared to the other houses.

"I'd call that one the Original," I said. "I bet that is similar to the way they all looked when they were built. And I bet the original owners live in it."

"Which means they're older and their kids are grown," Dinah said. She turned her gaze to the next house, located at the end of the street. "We already know something about that one since that's the one that Mr. Friendly and the boy went into. I'm assuming the kid was his son." This house was painted bright white. A second story appeared over the roofline and had clearly been added on. Black shutters decorated the front windows, and the front walkway was made of bricks.

"I'd call that one the All-American," I said, then realized I'd stepped on Dinah's turn.

"And the family has a daughter." She pointed to the pink bicycle lying on the front lawn.

"I hope she's friendlier than they were."

I took the next house. It was a softer white, as if not so newly painted. "I think an addition was put on the front," I said, pointing out that, unlike the other houses, it had an L shape in the front. "And by the four cars in the driveway, I'd deduce it's a family with older kids."

"And your name for it," Dinah asked.

"The Parking Lot," I said with a chuckle. We both looked at the last house, which was directly across the street from the one we were going to. It was stucco, painted a soft mustard color, with a dark tiled roof. A portico had been added to the front door. A number of advertising flyers lay in front of the door.

"I'd call it Colonel Mustard," I said. "And my guess is that nobody's been home for a while." I heard a car turn into the street. "Finally," I said. We opened the doors and got out.

Adele and Elise were sucking on smoothies as they joined us, making it obvious why they'd taken so long. "Which house is it?" Adele asked.

I pointed to the yellow wood frame house in front of us. Instead of a lawn, it had ivy growing in the front. A wooden sign stuck in the ground said "Holiday House."

"What's that?" Dinah said, looking at a cardboard sign attached to a street sign near the house. We hadn't been able to see it from inside the car.

"It's probably a lost dog," I said. I always checked lost dog signs so I could be on the lookout. But when I got closer, it wasn't a lost pet sign at all. It said: "This is a street for families. Short-term renters aren't welcome here." As I glanced around at the houses on the short street, I had the feeling we were being watched. I wanted to look at the yarn and get out of there.

I led the way up a stepping-stone path to the house. I could hear Adele talking into the camera on her phone about the great yarn mystery she was about to uncover. "Listen to her," I said to Dinah. "She's trying to make it sound like Al Capone's vault.

"Maybe she doesn't remember how that turned out," Dinah said, shaking her head. I chuckled to myself, remembering the big hype and how, when the vault was opened, there was nothing in it but some trash.

Just as I was about to ring the bell, another car pulled to the curb and Sloan got out. She raced up the walkway to catch up with us, doing a double take when she saw how many people I'd brought with me. Adele got the longest perusal. The granny-square dress was eye catching, and it seemed like Adele was talking to herself while admiring her image in her cell phone. It was always a mistake to let Adele come along.

"These are my yarn experts," I said by way of an explanation. Sloan took the lead. I followed her, with the rest of my crew straggling behind me.

Sloan knocked on the front before opening it with a key, and we trooped inside. We walked into an airy open space with a vaulted ceiling. It ended with several sliding glass doors that led to a patio and an expanse of lawn. A guesthouse sat near the back of the yard.

The furniture was ornate and didn't look very comfortable. There was a lot of it, and it had all been pushed together into the middle of the room. I noticed a table lamp with a curved shade, and several glass cases filled with figurines. A woman who looked to be in her twenties appeared from somewhere and came to stand with Sloan. She had curly dark hair and sharp features.

I smiled and put out my hand. "I'm Molly Pink and this is Adele Abrams, Dinah Lyons, and Elise Belmont." I pointed to each of them as I gave their names, and they gave her a nod.

"You here about the yarn, right?" she said, and I nodded. "I'm Miami Wintergarten." I couldn't help but do a double take at her name. She threw me a pointed glare.

"When you have idiot parents who give you a loser name like Bertha, which sounds like sleeping quarters on a train, you have to take matters into your own hands."

Elise pushed her way to the front of the group. "Are you the owner?"

The young woman seemed surprised by the question. "Yes. I am now." Her lips curved into a pleased smile.

"But you're selling it?" Elise asked. Out of the corner of my eye, I saw Sloan's expression darken.

"That's really not your concern," Sloan said.

"I just wondered," Elise began. "I thought if you were, I might have a buyer for it." It was a quick save on Elise's behalf. I knew she was trying to find out if Sloan was the listing agent.

"Well, it's not for sale or going to be for sale," Miami said with a lift in her voice. "Thanks to Sloan."

Sloan smiled at the praise and patted the young woman on the shoulder. "Once I understood what Miami wanted, I helped her come up with a solution."

The young woman interrupted. "I really want to keep this place while I build my career."

"Maybe we should just let them look at the yarn," Sloan said.

"Let me guess," Elise said with a knowing expression. "You want to be an actor."

"Ha," Miami said. "I already am. Perhaps you saw me as the girl on the bus in *Everybody Loves Bob* or the caterer in *Mila's Wedding*. I added my own touches to the parts. I blew a kiss to the bus driver, and I threw in my own catch phrase when I played the caterer. I made my characters memorable even if they only had a line or two."

I'd heard of the show and the TV movie but had no memory of the characters she mentioned. I smiled and nodded anyway.

"Those were just stepping-stones to my real goal, but it's thanks to Sloan and her entertainment business contacts that I found a more direct route." Sloan tried to dissuade her from continuing, but the young woman had an audience and seemed determined to perform.

She started laughing and waving her arms around. "I want you and you and you all to have yarn." Her voice was emphatic and loud before her expression abruptly grew somber and her delivery changed. "I know you will find a positive use for that yarn, saving it so it doesn't end up in a landfill." Then she walked up to each of us. "I will fight with the last of my strength to see that that yarn will go on to be part of something great." She stopped and looked at us expectantly. I could only speak for myself, but I wasn't sure what she was doing. She must have picked up on our collective blank looks.

"I want to be a personality. I was demonstrating my abilities. Didn't you get it? I did my impression of Oprah giving cars to her audience, then I was showing my crusader side, and finally I was being an inspiration. There's so much work for personalities now with all the game shows on. I could be a host or on the celebrity panel. Sloan came up with the idea of me trying out to be a contestant on game shows to get myself in front of the right people. Being a contestant would give me a chance to show off my personality."

She started jumping up and down and yelling "I won! I won!" and then rushed around, hugging each of us. When she got back, she turned off the enthusiasm like a faucet. "In no time I'll be able to afford the mortgage on this place, but Sloan showed me a way I can live here now and get the place to be a cash cow."

She looked to Sloan. "Tell them."

Sloan seemed uncomfortable with all the attention. "You probably can't tell from here, but the house has a C shape. One wing has four bedrooms, and there's a guesthouse in the back, all of which could easily be used for short-term rentals. There's a wing coming off the kitchen that has a full bath and a large room that Miami has kept as her private living space. I'm helping her get the place cleared out, and then we'll furnish the rental spaces."

"She's going to make them look so great," Miami said. "Sloan's a genius set decorator. It was her idea to put up the sign in the front so we can get photos and put up "Coming soon" postings on the apps we're using. She knew just the way to do the sign so that it would give the impression it's a fun place to stay." She looked over the group of us, and her gaze stopped on Adele.

"Don't mind her. She's a crochet influencer and gathering stuff for her vlog."

Adele realized we were talking about her and stopped taping. "I'm afraid Molly didn't fully introduce me," she said. Do you know how many followers I have?"

Adele had my interest because I was curious about her answer. I was a little stunned when she said it was in the five figures.

"Feel free to tape anything you want to," Miami said. "Just be sure to mention Holiday House and that we will have rooms available soon."

"Let's get to why you're here," Sloan said, directing us to follow her. "The yarn is in the guesthouse." She opened the sliding glass door, and we all went outside. Once we crossed the covered patio, I saw what she meant about the house being a squared kind of C shape. I checked out the yard, trying to orient myself, and noted that it was wider than I expected, but not as deep. The side fencing was hidden behind tall bushes, and just beyond the guesthouse a wood fence ran along the back of the property.

I was looking at the lawn, thinking it looked a little thirsty, when I heard a buzzing sound, and something big and black came into my peripheral vision. I thought it had to be a monster insect, but then I saw that it was a drone. It flew around the yard and over all of us. Then made another pass, getting lower as it neared us.

"Not that again," Miami said. She looked up and started yelling at it. "You might as well get over it. I've already started taking reservations. It is totally within my right to rent out rooms." The drone made another trip around the yard and then took off.

"I'm sure they'll get tired of harassing me," Miami said, "when they realize there's nothing they can do to stop me." She seemed to be talking to Sloan, who nodded in agreement.

"Ignore all this," Sloan said to us. "You're here about yarn." The guesthouse was a large room with a loft over one end. I did a quick survey and noted that there was a counter at one end that had the essentials to serve as a kitchen. The only furniture was a few chairs and a lot of stacked boxes.

Sloan pulled one of the boxes off the top and set it on the counter "Feel free to touch or take out any of the yarn you want."

Adele had just caught up with us and was sharing the view of the guesthouse. "And now we get to see the mysterious yarn we were promised," she said in her most dramatic voice and then pointed the phone at the top of the box filled with skeins. Adele stopped recording and joined me in pulling out the skeins of yarn and examining them.

I had a ball of turquoise wool yarn with the label still on it. I gave the strand a tug to see if the yarn would come apart, and I checked for any signs that moths had laid eggs in it. Then I gave it a sniff to see if it had a bad smell. The skein passed muster in all three areas. I checked the label and recognized the high-end brand, though I imagined the line of yarn was probably discontinued. As I looked through more of the box, I saw that while the yarn was all fancy stuff, there seemed to be just a single skein of each kind. I checked the labels on the skeins and noted they were on the small side; each one was only around 100 yards.

Adele looked at Miami. "So, what, are you a knitter or a crocheter?"

Only Adele could ask it like a threat, but then Adele had a thing about knitters. She didn't like them. She thought crochet was the only important yarn craft, and it annoyed her that knitting seemed to get more attention.

Miami ignored the question and moved away, letting Sloan step in.

"Nobody here knits or whatever. Miami's aunt worked for a local yarn company up until a year ago, and I believe these are samples You can count up the balls of yarn if you want and we can talk price."

I saw that Adele was fidgeting and had a storm cloud face. I knew a tirade about the *whatever* comment was coming, and I wanted to avoid a confrontation. "I don't know if it would work for us," I said quickly, noticing that Dinah had stepped in and was leading Adele toward the yard. "We usually have inventory of each particular yarn and color." I debated if I should explain why and decided to go for it. "You mostly have a single skein of each kind of yarn."

Sloan took my comment as a negotiating tactic and said they were willing to sell the lot of it really cheap. "It's all fancy yarn." She picked up one of the skeins and showed me the original price sticker still on the yarn. "You could offer it at a reduced price and still make money."

It was obvious that Sloan knew nothing about creating something with yarn so I explained again that most projects took more yarn than was in one of these skeins.

"It's not my money to spend," I said finally. "Let me talk to Mrs. Shedd."

Sloan seemed disappointed. "When do you think you'll have an answer? I was just giving you first look." She gestured back toward the house. We're going to have an estate sale, and I'm giving some select people an advance look."

"How about tomorrow?" I said.

She agreed and started to herd us to the door, then took us through the house back to the street. When we got back outside, the Holiday House sign had been knocked off its mooring.

"Did you notice that Starlight Court is a crooked street?" Dinah smiled when she realized what she'd said. "I mean the street itself isn't straight. But between the stare we got from that guy, the drone flyover, and then the sign vandalized, maybe it's the other kind of crooked too," Dinah said when we were back at the bookstore.

"I don't think Miami's neighbors are happy with her plan," I answered. "Thankfully that's not our concern. Just the yarn."

"It looked like good stuff. There were all kinds of textured yarn, and the colors were beautiful," Dinah said. Adele and Elise came in as Dinah was talking.

"Maybe it wasn't such a pot of gold at the end of the rainbow," Adele said. "Lots of pretty yarn, but not enough of any one kind to crochet even a scarf." When I looked over at her, she was talking to the camera again. I started to wonder about all of Adele's followers. Did they really watch everything she put out there? Were there really that many people who had so little going on themselves that they wanted to hear Adele go on about crochet?

"I wish she'd given us a tour of the place," Elise said. "I'd have liked to see the rooms in that wing she's planning to use for the short-term rentals and the room she's going to keep for herself. She says she's not selling, but I bet she changes her mind. Who knows what the neighbors will do to try to stop her. They could cause problems. The success of short-term rentals is all about reviews." I chuckled to myself about how Elise was always thinking about "the deal." It was so at odds with the image she gave off.

"The yarn was nice," Dinah said, "but how many people want to buy single skeins of yarn." I nodded, thinking she was probably right, but there was something in the back of my mind.

I suggested we finish the outing with a drink. We crowded around a small table in the corner, and I took everybody's order. Bob, our usual barista was behind the counter. He smiled when he saw me. "One Red Eye coming up," he said. "Let's see. It'll be a café au lait for Dinah, Adele always gets a half-caf latte with almond and coconut milk mixed." He eyed Elise. "I think she's a straight black coffee." He looked at me for confirmation. Had we really become so predictable? Not me anymore. "Right, except for no Red Eye for me. I'll have . . ." I looked over the menu for the most unlikely thing for me to order. "I'll have a frozen espresso Blur with an extra shot," I said.

Bob jiggled his head in surprise. "Wow, a party drink for you. You never order them."

"It's time for me to kick up my heels. Change, do something different. Who knows what I might do," I said. The Blur was the name that Bob had recently given to the list of frozen drinks I called party drinks. They were delicious and full of calories that I usually avoided. He asked if we wanted any treats and showed off the lemon bar cookies he'd made. I ordered one for everybody.

All eyes went to the tall beige slushy drink when I returned to the table.

"Who got the Blur?" Dinah asked. I pointed at myself and they all sucked in their breath in surprise.

"It's time to shake things up," I said. "Have new experiences. Taste different drinks. See things in a different way."

Dinah shot me a knowing look. She knew I was thinking about Mason and his offer. There was something else too. What had been in the back of my mind had moved forward, and I remembered a project I'd monkeyed around with. "I have an idea of what I could do with that yarn."

Chapter Six

"What if we deliberately don't have the same yarn for a whole project?" I began. "We could mix colors, textures, and types of yarn. It could be a scarf worked the long way so that it would seem like there were stripes."

Adele had her phone out and was back to taping. "I want to get this down for my followers." She pressed something and began talking. "I was just in a high-level meeting," she said. "We were discussing a top-secret plan for the yarn I showed you before. One of the things we've discussed is how difficult it is for knitters to work the long way. All those stitches crammed on a needle, just waiting to fall off and have stitches going haywire. But that would never happen with crochet." She cocked her head at an angle. "And that, my Adeleites, is your ammunition when someone tries to tell you knitting is the superior craft. The Adele is over and out." She clicked her phone off and set it on the table, leaning back in the chair. "Being a yarn star is a lot of work."

"Back to your idea," Elise said. "You'd have to create kits with the yarn. If you let people pick their own, they'd

never decide. You'd have to include a hook and the directions," she said. "I've made up kits for the bookstore before. I could do it again." We all remembered her kits from the days when, instead of being focused on real estate, she was fascinated by Anthony the crocheting vampire and had created what she called "vampire crochet." She'd made up kits for different projects, and they'd sold very well.

"It would be nice if the project was easy to make," Dinah said. "Something a beginner could do."

"And we could kick it off with an event. We could give a crochet lesson to anyone who wants one," I said.

"I'm sure you'd want me to be the chief teacher." Adele said. "Having The Adele would bring a little excitement to your mundane event. Of course, I'd talk it up on the vlog," she said in the snooty tone she'd recently adopted.

After that, we all went our separate ways. Elise had an appointment to show a house; Adele was meeting her motorcycle-officer husband, Eric, for lunch; and Dinah had office hours at the community college. And after a short stop in the yarn department, I went to talk over the idea for the yarn with my bosses.

Mrs. Shedd and Mr. Royal were in the office they shared. They had been partners in the bookstore forever and now were partners in life, though she chose to continue to go by Shedd. The argument was that if she changed her name they'd have to change the name of the bookstore to The Royals Books and More, which she thought sounded like Duchess Meghan and Prince Harry had taken over the bookstore.

I knew her first name was Pamela and his was Joshua and, as assistant manager, it would have been perfectly acceptable to call them by their given names, but I just couldn't, even if Adele had begun to.

Mr. Royal was a perfect example of how unfair aging was. Though he was around the same age as Mrs. Shedd, he seemed years younger. He moved with agility and had an air of adventure about him. I suppose it came from the all the time he had been a silent partner and off experiencing the world. I didn't know everything he'd done, just that he had worked his way across the Atlantic on a ship and that he'd once had a job at Tivoli Gardens in Copenhagen.

Since they'd tied the knot, my two employers spent a lot of time in the office just enjoying each other's company as they read some of the new releases. Currently, they were deep into their respective books, and their lunch of a baguette, cheese, and grapes was sitting in a basket on the desk.

I observed them for a moment, thinking how a second-act marriage seemed to have worked out for them. Could it for me? I tried to make some noise as I came in so as not to startle them, but they were too deep in their books and it wasn't until I spoke that they noticed I was there. They both jumped in surprise.

"Sorry I startled you," I said. "I wanted to tell you about my field trip." I left out all the extra stuff about protesting neighbors and the details of the house and went right to talking about the yarn.

"I was going to recommend not buying the yarn because there was so little of each kind," I began. I didn't bother calling them skeins or balls; both were vague terms rather than an actual indication of the number of yards. "But we came up with an interesting idea."

During my stop in the yarn department, I'd rounded up some odds and ends of yarn and made a mini sample of what a scarf would look like. I brought it out and showed it to them and then explained the idea of making kits. "Each one would be unique. I thought we could call them Serendipity scarves," I said. "Elise would help with the kits, and I thought we could have an event to showcase them." The details of the event came together as I was speaking "The pattern we'd include would be simple enough for a beginner, and we could have crochet lessons available."

Mrs. Shedd looked over the tiny scarf. "I like the idea." She handed the piece of crochet work to Mr. Royal. "What do you think?"

He was far more effusive. "Molly, that's a fabulous idea. Anything one of a kind is always good. I give you a hearty yes. The event sounds like it would be a draw."

"I'm glad you like the idea," I said with a smile. "I just want to have another look at the selection just to make sure the yarn will work with the plan. Then I'll work out the deal." As I turned to go, Mrs. Shedd pointed to a box of books.

"Merry Riley is coming in to sign some stock. Once she signs them, I thought you could arrange them on a table with her picture and a placard about her return visit with the book club."

"Of course," I said.

Mr. Royal, always the gentleman, insisted on carrying the books into the store for me. I cleared off a table of beach reads, which, now that it was late August, seemed pointless anyway. I set out a stack of Merry's inspirational books and took the empty box back to the storage room. On the way back, I picked up a roll of "Signed by author" labels.

When I came back, Merry was standing next to the table with her pen ready. Several women had stopped to talk to her, and it had turned into an impromptu author event. Her husband was lounging against one of the book-cases, looking at his phone. They were certainly a close couple. I cringed remembering how I'd introduced him to someone as Mick Riley when his last name is actually Byrd. Merry was all friendly smiles with the women she was talking to. I wondered if I should go and apologize to him again for the snafu with his name. But I decided it was best left alone.

When I approached the table, I realized one of the women talking to Merry was Sloan. By now I realized the popped collar was her look.

"I see you found your books," I said to Merry with a friendly smile. "Let me get you a chair." I put down the roll of stickers. I'd put one on the outside cover of all her books after she'd finished signing them.

"I'm good," the actor said to me, reaching out to give my hand a squeeze. I envied her breezy manner—the way she seemed confident and comfortable in her skin. But then, why not? She had a nice career going, a couple of almost grown kids, and a husband who adored her.

As soon as she started signing the books, I turned to Sloan.

"Do you have an answer on the yarn?" she asked. "I gave you first dibs, but I've got other people to contact."

"I'd like to have another look," I said. I'd actually only looked through one box and wanted to check out the other boxes of yarn before I committed.

Sloan tried to hide her consternation. "Can we do it now? I'd like it settled. There's something else I need to focus on." I was surprised at how upset she sounded, and I felt bad about not being able to accommodate her.

"I'm sorry, but I can't leave now. How about tomorrow morning around eleven?" I said.

She seemed a little deflated but nodded. "That would work, but please leave that posse of yours behind."

"No problem," I said. As an afterthought I asked her if everything was okay.

She let out a sigh. "I made a mistake I have to fix," she said cryptically. She went to pick up a large tote bag on the floor, and I saw the puffy white head of a small dog over the top. "That's a wrap," she said to the dog. That's when I realized that the only reason she'd come in the bookstore was to ask for the order. She really seemed to want to get rid of that yarn. I was sure I'd get a great deal.

With that set, I still wanted to talk over the plan with the Hookers since I was going to need their help with the event. I was ready for a little crochet time and looked forward to the group's gathering.

Adele was back from her lunch with her motorcycle officer husband and ensconced at the table when I went back to the yarn department. I stayed at the edge of the area, watching her. She had a whole selection of hooks on the table and her phone on a tripod so her hands were free. I listened as she seemed to be telling a story about a favorite pair of jeans that had an unfortunate accident. She hardly sat still as she talked but gestured with her whole body. She got up and paced, looking like her world was ending. The next thing I knew she was tossing glitter confetti as she unfurled a pair of jeans on the table like it was a magic trick. I moved closer to see what she was up to and saw her indicating what looked like a vine with leaves and red flowers climbing up one leg of the jeans. "And just like that I had my favorite jeans back, and a one-of-a-kind art piece through the miracle of crochet." She hit a button on the phone and leaned back in her chair with a tired sigh.

Adele had turned her self-importance into an art form. Like it or not, one thing seemed true. Adele had charisma. I'd come to realize that people being fascinated with you didn't necessarily have anything to do with admiration. Sometimes they just wanted to see how far you would go. Between her wild crochet outfits and things like making a hole in a pair of jeans into a drama, Adele specialized in over the top.

For a moment I thought about what it would be like if I accepted Mason's offer to work with him and left my post at the bookstore. It was appealing to think of working on something so important and, of course, being with him, but I was torn about giving up the life I had. Even with her vlog, Adele would take over my position. She'd turn every event into the Adele show, and she'd probably put up a fence around the yarn department with a sign that said "No Knitters Allowed."

"What were you thinking about?" Dinah asked, looking at my face as she came up beside me. She saw Adele sitting at the table with her phone. "Let me guess. She did something outrageous."

"Nothing more than usual," I said. "I was just thinking about what would happen if I started working with Mason."

"And Adele was in charge?" my friend said, and I nodded before asking how her office hours at the community college had gone. She smiled. "Nobody showed up so I spent the time grading papers."

The rest of the Hookers arrived just then ending our conversation and we took our seats at the table. I waited until everyone was situated before bringing up the yarn.

"Some of you know about this already," I began. I explained about the yarn Sloan wanted to sell and the plan we'd come up with to use it. "I talked to Mrs. Shedd and Mr. Royal, and they like the idea." I looked around at the group. "I kind of volunteered your services as crochet teachers for the event. I'm going back for another look at the yarn tomorrow to make sure it will work for the kits. I wanted to run this idea by you before I committed to buying the yarn."

"Pink, you better let me come along," Adele said, popping out of her chair and speaking to the group, "since I'm going to be the chief teacher."

I started to tell Adele that I was going alone, but gave up the fight and said nothing. I would just slip away without her.

When it was time to go home, I was thinking about enjoying an evening by myself. Maybe watch a romantic comedy and eat the leftover lasagna I'd made a few nights ago. All those plans dissolved when I walked into my yard and remembered that an evening alone wasn't an option. Nor, apparently, was the leftover lasagna. When I walked through the kitchen door, Peter and Gabby were sitting at the built-in kitchen table finishing the last of it.

Chapter Seven

I was still feeling like an intruder in my own house the next morning. Peter and Gabby were in the kitchen, making espresso drinks, when I came in for my coffee. They seemed to be blocking my every move, so I finally unplugged my coffee maker, grabbed all the supplies and took everything across the house to the master suite. There were two sinks in the bathroom, and one of them had a long tiled counter meant to be like a dressing table. It now became my coffee station. I took my mug and let the dogs out through the French door in the den. The morning was still cool, and I sat at the umbrella table while they had their morning spin.

Mason had called the night before to tell me his return to Kansas might have just been temporary. He didn't go into detail, but just said it had turned out that the district attorney hadn't given up the investigation of the college admissions. He was glad to hear about my idea for the yarn and the event I wanted to put on. He was interested in hearing about the cul-de-sac and Miami's plans for her house.

"Be careful," he warned. "Who knows what those neighbors might do."

"I'm just going there about the yarn. Nobody's going to bother me," I said. The call ended with him telling me how much he missed me and me telling him the same.

"It doesn't have to be that way," he said.

"I know. I'm thinking about it," I said with a sigh, and then we hung up.

I thought about Mason's warning as I got ready to go look at the yarn again the next morning. I appreciated his concern, but whatever trouble there was had nothing to do with me and was really between Miami and her neighbors. Adele was tied up in story time, and I'd hoped to slip out before she finished. But as I was heading to the door, she came rushing after me. Thankfully, she was out of her story-time costume and back in regular clothes, if you could call anything Adele wore *regular*. Since she was always taping for her vlog, she had amped things up. Today, she wore another tank-style dress. The top was a cotton fabric, but the bottom third was crocheted in thread, giving it sort of a 1920s flapper look. She carried out the look with a cloche hat with a large red flower attached to the side—all done in crochet.

I drove this time and a few minutes later pulled into the cul-de-sac. I tried to ignore the feeling that there were eyes on us as I got out of the car. But I was sure that I saw someone half hidden behind a curtain in the house at the end of the short street.

It was not my problem that Miami's neighbors were unhappy with her. That might have been an understatement,

I thought as I noticed the Holiday House sign had letters painted over and now read "Ho House," and the sign had been knocked over again too.

Sloan opened the door, with Miami next to her. She looked out and saw the sign and made an annoyed sound. "Live with it, people," she said in an angry tone.

They both did a double take when they saw Adele with me. Sloan seemed about to object, but I said that Adele was my yarn consultant. She motioned for us to come inside, and shut the door quickly. Nothing seemed to have changed. The furniture pulled into the center of the main room was just where it had been. Sloan saw me looking at it. "It's all still available. The best pieces I've placed on consignment. We can make a deal on any or all of that," she said in a bright tone to me and Adele. It was lost on Adele as she'd already put her phone on a selfie stick and was preparing to record. As I followed Sloan and Miami through the sliding glass door, I heard Adele begin. She had made the yarn into a story and was saying she'd come back for another look because she had come up with an ingenious way to use it.

Adele got waylaid in the yard while the rest of us went into the guesthouse. I tried to hide my feelings, but I couldn't wait to have a look at the yarn. I poked through all of the boxes, checking for damaged strands, and then began holding some of them together, imagining how they would work up. Adele finally came in and got a shot of what I was doing and said something about how the secret plan would be revealed soon, and then she went back out into the yard, saying the light was better. Sloan urged Miami to follow her.

"Well?" Sloan said when we were alone.

I had seen enough to realize the plan for the yarn would work. Now it was a matter of the deal. We went back and forth a few times, and finally she made an offer I knew Mrs. Shedd and Mr. Royal would be happy with. I agreed to bring a check when I picked up the yarn.

I went outside to find Adele so we could leave. When I got out there, I saw that Adele was almost inside the house, and Miami was tapping something into her phone. I heard a buzzy sort of whine and looked up just as a drone flew over the grassy area. It was bigger than the one I'd seen before, and this time a shiny black bag hung below it, swinging in an ominous manner.

Miami heard it too and looked up. It took a second for it to register, and then she ran toward the drone.

"Not again," she said. She'd grabbed a broom and was trying to swat at it, but it was high enough to be out of reach. "I know what you're doing, and it isn't going to work."

It seemed like a futile move, and she was more likely to get hurt than damage the drone. I looped my arm in hers and pulled her toward the house. I could hear the drone making more passes behind us, but I didn't want to take the time to look back.

I let out a sigh of relief when we were inside. Adele had her back to the yard and seemed to have no idea what was going on outside until we rushed in. Miami was still yelling at the drone as if it would make a difference.

"They're going to drop whatever is in that bag," she said. "Did you smell it? It stinks."

I turned to look back into the yard and saw Sloan coming across it. Her attention was focused on her phone. I opened the glass door to shout out a warning. Just as she looked up, the drone flew over her and the bag slammed into her, knocking her to the ground. Whatever was in it poured out and all over her.

"We have to help her," I said, rushing out the door. As soon as I was outside, the drone turned and flew toward me, with the ragged bag hanging below. It dipped, getting low enough that I felt the bag brush my hair. The smell of rotting garbage was overwhelming, and I thought I was going to throw up. Undaunted, I tried to keep going, but every time I made a move, the drone flew at me again.

I was about to give up when it suddenly lifted and flew off. With the threat gone, I rushed forward.

Sloan was on the ground covered in something with a lot of red in it. I rushed to find a hose to wash it off her. I dragged the hose toward her and tried to direct the stream with my thumb. I didn't even hear the sirens or realize help was coming, until two uniformed officers rushed past me and pushed me out of the way. One of them barked at me to go inside.

A few minutes later a pair of EMTs wearing N95 masks and gloves came through the yard, pushing a gurney. More uniformed officers arrived at the same time, and a pair of firefighters. By now there was the thwack of a police helicopter flying low above us.

It was hard to tell what was going on with all those people, but then I realized something disturbing. Everything

seemed to have slowed down. The EMTs weren't loading Sloan onto the gurney. Nobody seemed to be doing
anything. It could only mean there was no reason to rush
because it was too late—she was dead.

It had barely registered, when two cops came inside,
and one of them shut the curtain on the sliding glass
door.

The other one took a look at the three of us. "We better
separate them," she said to her partner. She glanced back at
us. "We don't want any influencing of stories."

Miami's face had crumpled into dismay. "What's going
on?" she demanded. She looked at the closed curtain and
then at the cops. "Is Sloan okay?" They answered with
stone-faced silence, and after a moment she realized what
that meant. "No, this can't be happening," she wailed.

Adele seemed stunned, and for once she was speechless.
I considered explaining to the other two what was going
on, but I didn't think it would look good that I was so
familiar with the drill at a crime scene. *A crime scene? Oh
no—not again.*

I didn't resist when the male officer took my arm and
led me away. I just wanted to give them my statement and
get out of there.

I felt for the cop dealing with Adele. I couldn't hear
exactly what she was saying, just the tone, which sounded
argumentative. I imagined she was throwing around Eric's
name, saying she was a motorcycle officer's wife, expecting
it would get her special treatment or preferably get her out
of there altogether.

I was taken into the kitchen and told someone would be there to talk to me soon.

"Soon" was a relative term, which I took to mean *whenever*. The police helicopter finally left, but I could hear the steady sound of news choppers hovering in the air, replacing it. I was glad I'd been taken into the kitchen, as I'd been curious to see what it was like. I could tell that it had been made larger than the original design. It was all wood paneled, with a built-in booth. The counters were all a pinkish-toned granite, and a small island had been built into the middle. A hallway went off it and led to what I assumed was the private area that Miami was living in. I snuck a look and saw a bathroom with a skylight and a very large room with a vaulted ceiling. It had probably been meant as a den. I resisted the desire to check it out fully, and instead stuck to examining the kitchen. I coveted the stove with the eight burners. I had a weird stove top and a couple of built-in ovens that seemed meant more for show than real cooking. For example, when you opened the oven, nobody could walk by. The refrigerator had gizmos for dispensing ice and water. I had my hand on the handle and was pulling it open when I heard someone come in.

"Excuse me," an authoritarian male voice said in a tone that made me feel like I'd been caught with my hand in the cookie jar. I shut the refrigerator quickly and turned around.

I expected to see a uniformed officer with a clipboard, ready to take my statement. I absolutely didn't expect to see the person I was actually seeing.

I guess he wasn't expecting to see me either.

"Molly?" Barry Greenberg said in a tone that was hardly his usual cool, collected detective voice. "What are you doing here?"

"I could ask you the same," I said. "I thought they'd send a uniform in to get my information. I hardly expected to go right to the big cheese." I was keeping my tone light, but I wasn't sure how I felt having to deal with him. Even though Barry and I had been uncoupled for quite a while now, there was something I couldn't quite get rid of. I'd noticed it when he'd shown up at my house the other night, though I'd barely acknowledged the feeling. It was almost like a buzz went through my body every time I saw him, no matter the circumstance. I hoped I was a master at hiding it and that it would go away.

After the moment of surprise, he'd gone back to being his professional self. His dark eyes were flat, and his lips were set in total non-emotion. I thought of it as his "just the facts, ma'am" detective pose. Barry excelled at reining in his emotions. I suppose years of being a detective and having to deal with all sorts of things I didn't even want to imagine had left an imprint on him. And working crazy hours had taught him to ignore feeling hungry or tired.

There were hints when he was tired, like a five o'clock shadow on his chin and dark circles under his eyes. And as much as he was able to ignore his appetite, if food was mentioned or was in the vicinity, it woke up his hunger. I gave him the once-over. His suit and white shirt looked fresh, and there was no shadow on his chin, so I guessed he hadn't been up all night chasing down evidence. His dark hair looked neat, but then it was trimmed so close it was almost impossible for it to look messy. I thought about picking up the loaf of bread on the counter and waving it in front of him to see if I'd get a reaction, but it was like he read my mind: "I just had lunch," he said.

He looked at me directly. "How did you manage to get in the middle of all this?"

"Is that an official question, or are you just curious?" I asked.

He began to shake his head with dismay. "You never make it easy, do you?"

"You'd be disappointed if I did," I said with a smile.

"Maybe not. Why don't you try me? Just try answering my questions without any editorial comment."

"That's kind of boring," I said. "But okay. You wanted to know how I got in the middle of this?"

"That was really a rhetorical question." He had a clipboard and began to fill in information. "I'm assuming that nothing has changed." He glanced up at me and I nodded, and he went back to writing in my information. "You've been involved with so many crime scenes, maybe we should have sheets printed up with your information." He glanced up again, and I saw the hint of a smile.

"Ha ha," I said.

He stopped writing and the almost smile vanished as he went back into true detective mode. "Okay, you want to tell me what happened?"

I was tempted to say "no" just to tease him, but really I wanted to get this over with and get out of there. "A drone flew in the yard and dropped a bunch of stinky stuff." I was pretty sure of the answer, but I asked him anyway "What about Sloan—that's the woman who the stuff landed on?"

Barry let out something along the lines of a worn sigh and shook his head in answer.

"I was hoping I was wrong," I said, telling him how I'd noted that nobody was rushing. "How? What happened?"

Barry was in official mode now and gave me only standard answers. Yes, the paramedics had called it, and there'd have to be an investigation as to the how.

"You must have some idea. You know, your cop's gut instinct," I said.

He put up his hands in a helpless manner. "I don't know anything about that gut business."

"Yes, you do," I argued.

"But even if I did, I don't have to tell you. And it's a little too soon anyway—that is, if there even was such a thing." Then he went back to asking me what I was doing there.

"I'm going to give you a freebie. An answer to a question you didn't even ask," I said. He stopped writing and looked up.

"Okay, shoot," he said with a disbelieving expression.

"The woman who inherited this house is turning it into short-term rentals, and her neighbors seem very upset about it. Upset enough that they've already committed minor vandalism. I think the drone thing is connected."

Barry had a self-satisfied smile. "Thanks, but I already knew that. You were going to tell me why you're here."

There was no reason to hide it, so I explained the yarn acquisition. He seemed disappointed that it wasn't something more nefarious, and tucked the clipboard under his arm and unclicked his pen. "I guess that's it, then. You're good to go."

It felt anticlimactic, but I was glad to get out of there.

As I went back through the house, I looked for Adele. It was too quiet, and I was sure she was gone. Maybe they'd actually called her motorcycle officer husband, and he'd come and gotten her.

I saw that the curtains had been opened, and a white tent had been set up where Sloan had fallen. Somewhere underneath, she was still lying there. Barry was already out there, talking to a couple of what I assumed were investigators. Now that I wasn't verbally dueling with him, the reality of what had happened set in. Sloan was dead. Just like that. She'd gotten up in the morning like it was any day, and now she was dead. I thought back to when I'd seen her at the bookstore, and suddenly I remembered the small white dog. What if the police went to her house and found the dog? They'd probably have the pound pick it up.

The poor thing had just lost her owner, and to be put in a cold enclosure at the pound seemed too cruel.

Miami was leaning against the pile of furniture, staring into space. She had to be more shocked than any of us. I made sure that Sloan hadn't brought the dog with her, then asked Miami if Sloan had a purse with her.

Miami took a moment to collect herself. "The cops asked me the same question, and I couldn't think straight. I told them I didn't know. But she always carried a bunch of stuff. You know, canvas tote bags and those recycled grocery bags.

"Could you look now?" I said. "Before the cops ask to go through this place."

I knew I was breaking all the rules, but all I could think of was getting the dog out of there. She stumbled around and came back with a black canvas bag that had a small purse inside. I grabbed the keys, used her driver's license to get the address, and left. As I was going to the door, Miami came up behind me. "You still want the yarn, right?"

Chapter Eight

My plan was to grab the dog and bring the keys back before anyone noticed they were gone. Sloan's house was a few block from Dinah's. The houses were mostly two bedrooms and one bath and had been built as tract housing tucked south of Ventura Boulevard. But only a few of the houses still looked the same. Most had been remodeled, rebuilt, or replaced. It seemed like Sloan had waved a magic wand over hers and turned it into a cottage out of a fairy tale. But then Sloan's main profession had been as a set designer. The house had a steeply pitched roof and diamond-paned windows. The chimney and fireplace were made of stone. It was adorable and whimsical. The only reminder of reality was the garbage cans waiting for pickup at the curb.

I felt uneasy unlocking the door, as if I was an intruder walking into her private world. The dog, a little white puff-ball, raced to greet me with excited barks. It broke my heart to think she was a little orphan dog now. I did a brief tour of the place to make sure nothing was running. If I felt like an intruder when I walked in, now I felt like a voyeur. Sloan's decoration choices were eclectic, and all I could think of was that everything seemed unique. The red velvet divan was occupied by a teddy bear, a purple rabbit, and a soft-bodied doll in a knitted pair of overalls that looked as though they'd been loved and discarded when their owner outgrew them. The dining area had a small round table surrounded by mismatched chairs. One of them had lost a leg that had been replaced with one from a totally different style of chair.

The kitchen was old school, with yellow tiled counters over white cabinets. There was a mug in the sink with the remains of Sloan's morning coffee. So strange to think that when she put it there, she never guessed she wouldn't be coming back. I checked the backyard through the window over the sink. It was small, but with the right placement of trees and a spread of lawn, it looked like a park. The dog followed me as I checked the two bedrooms. One had a bed covered with a quilt made out of remnants of old jeans. The other appeared to be an office. The desk was an old weathered door covered with a pane of glass. I looked through the papers, remembering that Sloan had mentioned a sister and hoping to find a way to contact her about the dog. I hit pay dirt when I saw a phone bill. One number had been called much more than any other. I wrote it down and gathered up the dog's things. She had on a collar that said her name was Princess. She seemed to understand I was there to take care of her, or maybe she smelled all the other animals and decided I was a friend. I clipped on her leash and led her outside.

She got right in the car and settled on the passenger seat and stayed put as I drove to my house. Peter was in the kitchen when I walked in, holding the dog in my arms.

"You didn't. Not another one," he said, eyeing the dog.

"I can't explain now," I said. "But I need to keep her separate from the others for the time being." I heard the rumble of animals crossing the wood floor in the living room. I quickly moved out of the kitchen to the smallest bedroom off the laundry area. I put Princess in there along with some water and dog treats.

Peter was still in the kitchen when I returned. "Could you check on her a few times until I get home?"

He looked like he was going to object, but then he softened. "Sure."

"I have go," I said, rushing to the door. I went back to Miami's. A cop hanging around the front door tried to stop me from going in, but I had a story ready about having left something. I mentioned that I knew Detective Greenberg and suggested he check with him to see if it was all right. I knew he wouldn't bother, and the cop let me in, though he did trail me. Sloan's things were where they'd been, and I feigned having to tie my shoe when I was next to her tote bag and slipped the keys back in. I was getting entirely too good at sneaking around. I walked around the main room a few times as if I was looking for something, and then turned to the cop. "I guess it isn't here." He escorted me to the door and I was home free.

Or almost. Kimberly Wang Diaz, the reporter from Channel 3, was setting up at the end of the cul-de-sac. I had parked around the corner and was trying to slip away without her seeing me, but her cameraman pointed me out, and she came toward me with her microphone outstretched. "Molly Pink, what a surprise to see you at a crime scene," she said facetiously. "You must know all the details. I heard someone say you were like the Sherlock Holmes of Tarzana."

"No comment," I said, but then I felt compelled to add something. "You can joke if you want to, but I have a pretty good record of figuring out whodunnit." I rushed off before she could think of a comeback.

Everything was still rolling around in my mind as I went back to the bookstore. What was supposed to have been a short time away while I gave the yarn another look had turned into being gone the whole afternoon. Mrs. Shedd stopped me with a worried look as I came in.

"What happened? Was it something with the yarn? What took so long?" Mrs. Shedd asked. She looked around. "Adele's not with you?"

"Everything is still on with the yarn. Adele should be here soon," I said. "Something happened," I said, letting out my breath. I took a moment to collect my thoughts and figure out how to explain. Long or short, detailed or blurb? I decided blurb was best. "Sloan was hit by a drone carrying something that smelled terrible, in the yard of the house with the yarn, and she died." Mrs. Shedd was speechless. It wasn't the first time I'd been delayed because of a crime, but this one was pretty high on the weirdness meter.

I finally made my way back to the yarn department. It was nestled in the back of the store and always felt like a comforting enclave. The back wall had cubbies filled with skeins of yarn in a rainbow of colors. I hadn't realized how late it was until I saw the Hookers already gathered around the dark wood table and busy working on their projects. Dinah looked up with relief when she saw me.

"We all wondered what had happened to you when Mrs. Shedd said you'd gone to make a deal about the yarn and hadn't returned. I'm glad you weren't kidnapped," my friend said in a light tone. She checked the area around me. "I see Adele isn't with you, so what happened? They decided to keep her?"

I glanced over the table littered with yarn while I considered what to say. I decided it was better to get right to the point instead of softening it with a lead-up.

"No kidnapping. Adele ought to be along any minute. We're okay," I said, "but the woman who was showing me the yarn, Sloan Renner, is—well, there's no soft way to put it. She's dead."

"What happened?" Elise said to me. She turned back to the group. "I met her yesterday when I went with Molly."

"Dear, that's terrible. That's right. She was involved with selling houses now. She sent me a postcard about her real estate business," CeeCee said. "I thought about using her last year when I was considering selling my house."

"What?" Elise said. "I could have listed your house."

"I know, dear, and if I decide to sell it, I'll give you the listing," CeeCee said, trying to placate Elise. "You see, she offered to do so much more, like helping clear the place and then stage it. I understood her magic was that she staged it so it had perfectly arranged furniture, but with touches to make it seem like it wasn't staged. I can't remember what else she said she did, just that it wasn't something useful to me. She seemed like a lovely person, What happened? Did she have a heart attack?"

"When I tell you, you won't believe it," I said. I gave them the details that I had, and unlike Barry, I added my thoughts about what I thought had happened. Someone had used the drone to drop the stinky payload just like they'd put up notices and knocked over the sign in front of the house, to annoy Miami in the hopes she'd give up her plan. Or maybe it was a threat of what they'd do if she did go through with her plans.

"That's true," Dinah said to the group. "I saw the protest posters on the street signs.

"It's seems like a pretty open-and-shut case," Rhoda said in her matter-of-fact voice tinged with a New York accent. "Whoever flew that drone is responsible."

"But it wasn't deliberate, was it?" Sheila asked. She almost swallowed the last few words, and I knew, with her anxiety issues, that everything worried her.

"Deliberate in that someone wanted to cause a nuisance," I said.

"Not being in real estate, I don't know if Molly understood what the owner of the place was planning to do. I'm pretty sure she intends to rent out rooms like it's a hotel. You know, with one of those short-term rental apps. It's a cute little cul-de-sac that is suddenly going to have a bunch of strangers showing up who will probably park along the street, make noise, and leave trash. There are rules about how often you can rent, but there's no saying this woman is going to follow them. There doesn't seem to be a lot of oversight," Elise said.

"Maybe she was using that app called Tempstay," Eduardo offered. "They hook up people looking for accommodations in private homes.

"I thought I heard her say she was going to rent out four of the bedrooms and the guesthouse. There's a large room on the other side of the house for her to use," I said.

"That's a lot of rooms to rent out," Rhoda said. "And on a cul-de-sac probably surrounded by families—" She shook her head. "I can see where the neighbors might be unhappy about the plan.

"Just imagine if the neighbors dropped a stink bomb when she had guests," Dinah said.

"Then the owner would get a bad review," Eduardo said. "Those kind of rentals are all about reviews. So, whoever did it probably meant it as a warning of what they'd do when the rooms were rented, hoping it would make her change her mind. By the way, who is the 'she' we keep talking about? Is that Sloan?"

"Miami Wintergarten is the owner of the place. Sloan was just helping out."

"How tragic," CeeCee said. "That poor woman was just in the wrong place at the wrong time." Adele came in just in time to hear CeeCee's comment. She let out a frustrated harrumph, realizing the whole story had already been told without her input.

I had deliberately not mentioned going to get Princess. I didn't know how illegal what I'd done was, and I didn't want to make anyone an accessory after the fact. It was better if no one knew—not even Dinah when she stayed behind to hang out for a few minutes after the group dispersed.

"How awful for you," Dinah said. "You go there for yarn and end up at another crime scene."

"Have you been talking to Kimberly Wang Diaz?" I asked with a smile, then told Dinah about her trying to get a comment from me. "It was pretty awful." I shuddered at the remembrance of the smell. "I don't know what got dumped. I saw some red stuff."

"I'm assuming the police were called," Dinah said. "And if there was a death, probably a detective."

"I know where you're headed. Yes, Barry showed up and he ended up talking to me."

"It figures," she said, smiling.

"No, it was pure chance. Nobody had even taken my name. He could have just as easily gotten Adele."

"Poor him if he had," she said. "So, how was it? How'd he look?" No matter what I said, Dinah didn't believe that Barry and I were finished. It didn't even matter to her that Mason had suggested we get married.

"I didn't notice," I said, and she laughed.

"I don't believe that."

"Okay, he looked good, uh, I mean not too tired—healthy," I said, hoping she'd drop it. Barry had the tall, dark, and handsome thing going for him. "Handsome" was really the wrong word. To me that conjured up boring, even features. Barry's face had character. It was all about the expression in his eyes, that is, when he let it show.

"What did Mason have to say?" she asked.

"You mean about Barry?" I asked.

"No, about what happened. You texted him, didn't you?"

"I was going to wait for our nightly phone call, but you're right," I said, pulling out my phone and beginning to type with one finger. There was no immediate return text from him, and when I finally got an answer, it was a phone call and I was sitting in my car, about to drive home.

"I needed to hear your voice to know that you were okay," he said. There was no teasing in his voice this time. It was filled with concern.

I assured him that I was fine. "I wasn't even close to the action."

"That's what I was hoping to hear. I guess you're done with it. The cops will go after the drone owner and try to get a charge of involuntary manslaughter."

There was silence on my end as I considered what to tell Mason. He was an animal lover. He took Spike on the road with him, so I thought he would understand, and I'd barely done anything wrong.

I told him about Princess and the rest of it. "I could have been your cover," he said with a chuckle. "But that's all you're going to do, right? You're not going to do your own investigating."

I let out a sigh. I hadn't had a chance to collect my thoughts until he brought it up. Would I try to investigate it? Mason figured out what the silence meant.

"I wish I was there to be Nick to your Nora Charles," he said.

Chapter Nine

I was snapped back to reality as soon as I got home. There were more boxes of stuff on the patio, and Peter was talking to a man with a clipboard, who seemed to be evaluating the garage for some kind of makeover.

"How about including me in the plans for my house?" I said.

"Sorry. I'm trying to make it easier for you. You have a lot going on . . ." He left the thought hanging, but I knew in his mind he was thinking *at your advanced age*. Did he really think I was ready to wrap myself in a shawl and rock away the rest of my life in a chair on the porch? There wasn't even room on the small porch by the front door. It was really more of a stoop.

"I'm looking into making the garage into a guesthouse," he said. I was afraid to ask who he thought would be living there.

"By the way," my son said, "do you suppose you could make yourself scarce this evening? I put together a meeting with some people about a new project, and I can't have them thinking I moved home with mom."

"So, you want them to think this is your house?" I asked, and he nodded.

"I can't look desperate. It's important that I seem like I'm doing okay." It didn't seem like he was asking for so much, and I certainly wanted to help him get back on his feet, so I agreed.

"Great. They're going to be here soon. The animals are already in your room. All the animals. I let them out first. And put their food and water in your bathroom."

"Peter, you didn't. You can't just put a new dog in with a bunch of other dogs and cats. What were you thinking?" I started toward the kitchen door, which was my usual way of entrance, but he stopped me and pointed to the door that went into the den.

"Why don't you go this way. It's so much closer."

He was right about that. I walked in the glass door and was literally next to the door leading to the master suite. I rushed in, worried about the little puff ball. As soon as I pulled open the door to the hall that led to dressing area, bathroom, and bedroom, I heard my greeting committee. Cosmo and Felix were in the front, and the two cats trailed them. It wasn't until I got in the bedroom that I found the third dog, Blondie.

If ever there was a dog that was different, it was Blondie. She was the only one of the animals that I'd actually adopted. It was after Charlie had died, and I was feeling very alone. Blondie had been living in a private shelter. She'd been adopted once and returned, probably because they thought they were getting a feisty terrier mix and instead got a dog who I really should have been named Greta Garbo.

As usual she was in the orange wing chair that was her spot of choice. But then I saw that she wasn't alone. Princess was nestled next to her. As soon as the relief that no fur had been flying settled in, I realized there was a new problem.

Peter had thought of everything—except that I had intended to come home and make my dinner. I considered my options. I thought about ordering food. The windows in my bedroom faced the driveway. Maybe I could arrange to have the delivery driver hand it through the window.

My cell phone rang, startling me out of my reverie.

"Molly, you answered. Good."

"Barry?" I said tentatively. It wasn't that I wasn't sure it was him—more that I was surprised.

"I tried your landline," he said.

"I didn't hear it ring." I looked around the bedroom and saw that the cradle for the cordless was empty. I must have left the phone in another room. I waited for an explanation for the call.

"We need to talk about what happened today," he said.

"Oh," I said getting a sinking feeling. He must have found out what I'd done.

"I'd like to take care of it now," he said in a serious voice. Great, now I was starving and in trouble. I could not handle being grilled on an empty stomach.

"Okay," I said. "On one condition."

"Oh no," he said. "What is it?"

"There's a lot going on here right now. I'm stuck in my room with no dinner. Unlike you, I can't just ignore a growling stomach. Do you think you could pick something up for me?"

It sounded like he laughed. "That's a switch. Maybe I should give you a lesson in hunger suppression."

"I doubt the lessons would work," I said. "When I'm hungry, I'm hungry."

"Have it your way. I'll pick up something for you. What do you want?"

"How about Chinese? And bring a lot," I said. He'd deny it if I said anything, but I was sure that once Barry smelled the food, all his hunger suppression would go out the window.

"Chinese it is then."

"We'll have to talk in my room. I'll explain when you get here. So park on the street and call me. I'll let you in through the den," I said.

"A room's a room, he said in his professional voice.

I jumped when my cell phone rang a half hour later. "I'm here," Barry said.

"I'll let you in." I slipped out the bedroom door and glanced through the doorway into the living room. There were people on both of the couches. They were too busy having wine and talking to notice me as I slid along the wall to the door.

As soon as I saw Barry step onto the stone patio, I opened the door and motioned him in, putting my finger to my lips. I saw him glance toward the living room as he followed me into the separate area.

The pungent fragrance of the food floated up through the paper bag in his arms. "Sorry for shushing you," I said once we were inside with the door shut, and it was okay to

talk. "Those people aren't supposed to know I'm h
delicious smells arising from the paper bag made m
start to water. "The food smells heavenly."

"Let me guess. They weren't just dropping by th
night," he said.

"It's a long story, but basically his life fell apart, ar
staying here for a while."

Before we passed the closets and bathroom, Cosmo
Felix gave Barry a hero's welcome because they liked
and, well, he was carrying food.

"This isn't where I'd thought we have our talk, but I
I said, a room is a room." He glanced around the lar
space that was predominated by my bed, and I pointed hi
toward the sitting area I'd set up. I'd found a stool and
folding table and put them up next to the butterscotch-
colored loveseat against the wall. He was all Detective
Greenberg, and the only clue that he felt anything was the
slight sigh I heard as he stole another look around. Was he
thinking of other times when he'd been here under different circumstances? I realized I was, and felt my face get
a little flushed. I pushed away the memories and directed
him to put the food on the table.

He glanced back in the direction of the rest of the house.
"So your son has sent you off to your room," he said with a
subtle headshake of disapproval.

"He's meeting some business people. I don't want to
stand in the way of anything that will help him and his"—
I hesitated, still not quite sure what title to give her, and
finally just said—"Gabby move back out."

He put the brown paper bag of food on the folding table, and I started to take out the containers. The smell was wafting his way, and I watched him try to ignore it. "I should have gotten plates," he said.

"No problem. I'll make do." I grabbed a set of chopsticks and sat down on the stool before digging into the sweet and sour chicken. "Thank you. I'm starving."

"I can see that." He was still standing and trying not to look at the food. "Maybe we can get to why I'm here," he said.

"Why don't you join me?" I pulled out another pair of chopsticks and offered them to him.

He hesitated and seemed to be fighting with himself. "This isn't a social call." Then he let his breath out. "You win." I handed him the sweet and sour chicken and began to open the other containers. He finally sat down on the loveseat, and we passed the containers back and forth.

"See, no plates, no problem," I said. "There are a few kinks to work out with them staying here." I let out a sigh, relieved that the edge was off my hunger.

He looking into the container he'd been working on as he put it on the small table. "I'm sorry I ate so much," he said.

"That's why I told you to get a lot. I knew the smell would win out over your hunger suppression, as you call it. Thank you again for bringing the food. If I'd tried going into the kitchen, Peter would have probably tried to pass me off as the housekeeper," I said with a shrug.

"Sure thing," he said. He seemed to be making an effort to keep a noncommittal tone.

"Okay, we might as well get to why you're here," I said. I checked and Princess was still next to Blondie in the chair. Barry hadn't even noticed her. I wondered if it was better to just confess what I'd done and ask for forgiveness.

"It's about this afternoon," he said.

"Whatever I did, I had a good reason." I stole a look at the tiny white dog. Even if I got in trouble, it was worth it, knowing that she was safe and cared for.

"What did you do?" he asked in his interrogation voice.

"Why don't you tell me what you think I did," I said.

"I think you should tell me what you think I'm here about," he said, narrowing his eyes. "Have you been up to something?"

"I'm taking the fifth," I said.

"Hmm," he said. "You're making me rethink my idea. Maybe I should just go."

"No," I said. "You can't leave without telling me why you came."

"Okay," he said, "I'll tell you why I wanted to talk to you, but you have to tell me what you did. Deal?"

"I guess so," I said. "But you go first."

He rolled his eyes. "I was going to ask for your help. Like how you did before when you fed me information."

"I don't think I just fed you information. I did a lot of investigating and figuring things out too."

"Whatever. But this time is different," he said. "I was just thinking of asking you to keep your ears open since you seemed to be in the middle of whatever is going on at that house and with Miami Wintergarten. But now I'm not so sure." He had a stern expression. "I told you mine. Now it's your turn."

"I didn't break and enter. I just borrowed a key," I said.

"Could you start at the beginning?" he said.

I told him about the dog rescue. "I was afraid you'd take her to the pound." I gestured toward the orange chair, and he finally saw the dog next to Blondie.

"So you stole a key from a dead woman's purse, went into her house, and kidnapped her dog."

"It all sounds so much worse when you say it like that," I said. "I'm going to call her sister and tell her about the dog. She'll probably be grateful."

He shook his head in a scolding manner. "Unless she decides to press charges because you stole her sister's key and went in her house without permission and kidnapped her dog. Next time, talk to me first," he said. "We could have worked something out." He leveled his gaze at me. "Is that it?"

"Yes. Do you really think she's going to press charges?" I said, suddenly scared.

He shrugged. "Probably not, and I'm going to pretend I don't know anything about it."

"Does that mean you want me to help you on this case?"

"I hope I'm not making a mistake. It seems like what happened was intended to be a nuisance, and it was an accident that the victim got involved. Whoever did it probably feels guilty about what happened. I thought that you could keep your ear to the ground."

"And then I would tell you what I hear?"

"But you can't tell anyone we're doing this."

"Because?" I looked him in the eye and he seemed uncomfortable.

"You know why."

"Because you don't want anyone to know you need help."

He blew out his breath. "I don't really *need* your help. I could handle this just fine. It's just more expedient to have you talk to the neighbors."

"Not to tell you your business," I said with a smile, "but I heard drones have to be registered. Can't you check out who has drones in the area and then use your interrogation skills to find out who did it?"

"That's fine, if the drone is legal. But I guess you didn't consider that someone committing a crime with a drone isn't likely to use one that could be tracked. And for your information, we already looked for registered drones in the cul-de-sac."

"If I agree to this scheme, how's it going to work?" I asked.

"I think it's more a case of if I agree to let you do it," he said. "But assuming I do, you give me reports in person. It has to stay between the two of us." He hesitated. "You can't even tell Mason." His mouth eased into an almost smile. "You probably wouldn't want to tell him anyway. He might not understand." Barry looked around the room to make his point.

My expression must have given away something, because Barry trained his eyes on me. "What's going on?"

"What makes you think there's anything going on?" I said.

"Detectives excel at reading body language and facial expressions," he said. "So, what is it?"

I was usually good at twisting things around by answering his questions with questions, but I didn't have it in me this time. "Mason proposed," I said.

"What?" Barry said. "I thought he didn't want to get married. Wasn't that his appeal, since you didn't want any commitments. You didn't want to get married again." He was trying to keep up his professional mode, but there was hurt in his voice. I was caught off guard by the display of emotion, expecting that by now Barry would have gotten past it. There were a number of reasons things hadn't worked out for Barry and me, like the fact that his life was totally chaotic. At any time, he could get a call and have to leave. He needed to be in control, and well, being controlled wasn't my thing, but the bottom line, and what he seemed to think was the real reason, was that he wanted to get married and I didn't.

I told Barry about Mason's pro bono work and that he traveled a lot now. "I didn't say I said yes," I said in a light tone. I hadn't expected such a strong reaction from him, and it made me uncomfortable.

"But you're going to, aren't you?" He was trying to stay in cop mode, but whatever control he had was gone, and his eyes flared with emotion.

"I don't know," I said. My shoulders slumped. "I said I'd think about it."

"What's made you even consider getting married again? Is it that you're going to be a grandmother?"

My head shot up as I realized he'd touched a nerve. Was that why I was even considering it? Getting married and starting a new life came with a different image than being called Granny.

"Of course not," I said. This was getting too personal, and I wanted to get back to talking about the case. "So, we're agreed that I'll see what I can find out for you."

He seemed relieved about the subject change too. "Fine. I agree that you're working for me. Just like before, I will contact you and we talk in person. Agreed?"

"I can't call you if I get a hot tip?" I said.

"No. It all has to be off the record. I don't want there to be a chance anyone overhears. Why don't you start off by telling me what you already know that you didn't tell me this afternoon?" he said.

"Why don't you tell me what you know first?" I said.

Barry laughed. "I thought we agreed that you'd give me information."

"Maybe you agreed, but I never did. Don't you think it would be better if we shared what we found out?"

"No," Barry said. "I'm the detective. Can't you just play by my rules and stop answering my questions with questions?"

"I don't know if I can do it that way," I said. "Besides, it's more fun this way."

"So you like to watch me get upset?" he said. There was a flicker of light in his eyes.

"Well, not really. I guess I like to know that I can hold my own."

"Don't worry. There's no doubt about that. Getting you to give a straight answer is always a challenge."

I threw him a teasing smile. "I'm just trying to keep you on your toes."

"You do that and more."

"Really?"

He shook his head with mock regret. "I have an easier time getting a straight answer out of a suspect. They're too intimidated to fool around."

"But this is more interesting."

Barry was silent for a moment, and I thought he was going to renege on the idea of us working together, but then he shrugged. "It's certainly something."

When Barry left, I turned on the TV to catch the news. I was only half listening until I heard Kimberly Wang Diaz's voice. I turned to look at the screen directly. She was standing in the cul-de-sac talking to a woman. I did a double take when I realized it was the woman from the book club whose name I'd forgotten again. She kept saying no comment, trying to get away. I bet she had just the kind of information Barry was looking for. And another thought passed through my mind. *What if she was involved?*

Chapter Ten

The next morning I brewed myself some coffee, glad that I'd thought to bring the pot to my section of the house. I stared at my phone as I sipped from my cup. I hadn't wanted to call Sloan's sister until I was sure she'd been notified of the death. It wasn't a comfortable call to make. I doubted she would accuse me of what Barry had suggested, but who knew for sure? By the same token, I wanted to let her know that Sloan's dog was being cared for.

I was onto a second cup before I finally picked up the phone and dialed the number I was pretty sure belonged to Sloan's sister. The phone rang a long time before a woman finally answered. I realized I didn't know Sloan's sister's name.

"My name is Molly Pink," I began. "Are you Sloan Renner's sister?"

"Are you calling from the police?" the woman asked.

"No. It's about Sloan's dog."

"Oh, dear, is she all right?"

I assured her that Princess was fine.

I heard the woman let out her breath. "We didn't even think about the dog." She took a breath. "My name is Marge Fairway, and I'm Sloan's sister's caretaker. By the way, her name is Donna Renner." She dropped her voice. "It's been a lot," she said. "Donna never expected to get a call from a police detective about her sister. She's in shock, and she's just recovering from another surgery."

"First, please tell her how sorry I am for her loss," I said. "I was calling to tell her that I took Princess to my house, and I'll be happy to take care of her for as long as necessary." I heard the woman relay the message to Donna. Then there was a lot of rustling, and someone new took over the call.

"What's your name?"

"Molly Pink," I answered. "Is this Donna?"

"Yes," she said. "Marge said you have Princess." She sounded agitated, and I worried that she didn't understand the situation.

"I'm so sorry for your loss," I said.

"I don't know what to think," she began. "The police person said she was hit by a drone. Do you know anything about it?"

"I'm sure the police will investigate what happened and will be able to tell you more." I decided to come clean with her and tell her exactly what I had done, hoping she would understand and not decide she wanted to see me in handcuffs. "I hope it's okay, but I used Sloan's key to get in. It was kind of breaking the rules, but I was afraid the cops would take the dog to the pound once they went to her place."

"Thank you. Sloan loved that dog. It would have been terrible if she'd been taken to the pound. You'll have to forgive me if I seem scattered. I'm on a bunch of meds and I'm in shock about Sloan. It feels like my mind is going in circles. My big sister was everything to me."

"Please let me know if there's anything I can do to help," I said. "Meanwhile, you don't have to worry about Princess. She can stay at my house for as long as necessary or forever."

"Thank you. I wish I could say I'd take the dog, but I'm living in a place that doesn't allow pets. You sound like you have a kind heart, and I'm sure Sloan would want you to keep Princess. If you could keep an eye on Sloan's house, that would be wonderful. I'm in San Diego and I can't travel. There's a key under the flower pot with the petunias," Donna said.

"Of course," I said. "Just take care of yourself for now."

"God bless you," Donna said before she hung up.

I let out a huge sigh of relief. Donna didn't want to see me in a striped suit behind bars. I went over and gave the small white dog a snuggle. "It looks like this is your home now."

When it came time to leave for the bookstore, I left through the den door instead of going out through the kitchen, which was my habit. I could hear Peter and Gabby talking in there, and I wasn't up for being treated like an intruder in my own home.

Mrs. Shedd caught me as I came in. "I hope this doesn't sound cold, considering that someone died," she began, "but what's going to happen with the yarn?"

"I don't think anything has changed. The homeowner still wants to sell it. I thought I would go there later today and pick it up."

Mrs. Shedd seemed concerned. "Joshua and I were taken with your plan for the kits and the event, but should we rethink it? Do we want yarn that's associated with a death? What if the connection comes out? The death was all over the news last night. But then I guess it's not every day that someone gets hit with a drone."

I hadn't heard the news and asked her if there were any other details. "Well, actually that Kimberly Wang Diaz did a report from out in front of the house, and I thought I saw you running away from the camera," she said, looking at me expectantly. I admitted that it was me, and she assured me that all that showed was my back.

"You certainly get in the middle of some unusual things."

"Not intentionally," I said before assuring her the yarn would be fine. I'd gotten caught up in the plan to create the kits. I loved the idea and that they would be something unique to us. My boss told me she'd have the check ready to take along when I went. I ran the idea past her of having the event the following Saturday, and she sparked on it.

I went back to the yarn department to start working on everything connected to the kits. Elise had said she would handle putting the packages together, so I concentrated on writing up some copy about them for the store signs. Mr. Royal was in charge of social media, and I was sure he'd get the word out. I found the pattern using assorted yarns I'd told the group about and made some corrections to it.

Dinah had texted me that she'd meet me in the café. She lived barely a block from the bookstore and often met me for my break. I was looking forward to spending time with her as there was so much to talk about.

We both reached the entrance of the café at the same time She wore a pale yellow linen tunic and pants and looked as refreshing as a glass of lemonade. I noticed her usual long scarf was tied loosely around her neck. The ninety-something temperature was normal for August and not really the kind of weather where you wanted anything too tight around your neck. We hugged each other and grabbed a table by the entrance to the bookstore so I could keep an eye on things. I waited until we'd gotten our drinks to start talking. She expertly poured the coffee and steamed milk into her mug simultaneously, creating the perfect mix of the two hot liquids. I took a took a generous sip of my Red Eye I always said the coffee with a shot of espresso was like a windshield wiper for my brain, which I seriously needed that morning. So much had happened the day before, and I hadn't slept well. If ever there was a time I needed something to clear my mind, it was now.

I started off by telling Dinah about the dog, since I felt confident I was off the hook. "I'm sorry for not telling you yesterday," I said. "I wanted to keep it quiet until I talked to Sloan's sister."

"And is she going to come get the dog?" Dinah asked. I explained the situation and the fact that Donna was in San

Diego. "I hope Princess realizes how lucky she is," Dinah said when I'd finished.

"You should have seen Peter's face when I brought her home." I explained handing the dog over to him because I had to return the key. "I told him to keep her separate from the other dogs, but he ended up putting her in my room with the others and then told me to stay there too."

"What?" Dinah said. "He sent you to your room?"

"Not exactly." I hesitated, trying to think of another way to describe it, but there really wasn't one. "Okay, yes, a bit. But not for being naughty," I joked. "He was having some business people over to talk about a project. The sooner he gets something going, the sooner they move out."

"If it happens again, you can always come over. The door to my She Cave is always open." When Dinah and Commander Blaine had gotten married, they'd opted to live in her house. He was a widower, and his place still had too many memories of his late wife. And Dinah didn't want to live with a ghost.

She'd discovered that she and her new husband had very different schedules. He went to bed early and she liked to stay up late. She'd worked out the situation by turning an added-on den into her "She Cave," as she called it. We'd spent many an evening there drinking tea and eating cookies while Commander slept peacefully in the other part of the house.

"There was a complication," I said. "Barry came over."

"What?" she said, her eyes widening.

"Calm down. It wasn't a social visit." Barry had told me to keep it quiet that we were working together, but I didn't think he meant to include Dinah in that warning. She was my best friend, and she knew that I had worked with Barry before. Besides, even if I didn't tell her, she'd figure it out. "He suggested we work together on finding out who was behind what happened to Sloan. Of course, Barry didn't exactly describe it that way," I said, taking another sip of my drink. "But no way am I going to be the information provider and let him be the one to do all the detecting."

Dinah let out a laugh when I finished. "Well, well, so he came up with a reason to see you," she said.

"That's not it," I protested. "He realized I have better access to some information than he does." Would Dinah ever accept that what Barry and I had was over?

"Admit it, you feel something when you see him," she said.

I hesitated. I didn't want to tell her about that buzzy feeling I'd noticed when I'd seen him at the crime scene. As an afterthought, I attributed it to a feeling of surprise when he was the one to take my information. I didn't want to admit the possibility that it might be something more, even to myself. "Sure I feel some concern for him, just like I would for any friend. You know, if he looks tired, or if I'm wondering if he's eaten.

"Yeah, yeah," Dinah said, rolling her eyes. "You can say it's just friendly concern, but it's more than that."

"It isn't." I shuddered to think it could be true. "It's so much easier with Mason. We're not always dueling. He's just fun and more easygoing."

"Then why don't you accept his proposal?" she said.

"I'm thinking about it. It sounds romantic and exciting to be a pair of crusaders looking to free innocent people, but I also like my life the way it is. The bookstore, the Hookers, even Adele," I said with a laugh. "And there's you. I love our girls' nights, playing the Sherlock Holmes game, and getting into mischief."

I had been married for a long time before Charlie died. It was a new experience being on my own, and I liked it.

"Maybe you can keep things as they are," she said. "He didn't give you an ultimatum like the whole package or nothing, did he?"

"Not exactly, but the way he's traveling now, I barely see him. And being part of what he's doing now would be exciting. He's become a hero and I'd be a heroine," I looked at my friend, feeling a little panicky about the whole thing. "I don't really want to think about it anymore right now. Besides, I need your help with the investigation."

Dinah laughed again. "Poor Barry, he's in over his head."

* * *

"We're going to get the yarn," I said to Mrs. Shedd. Dinah and I were both carrying plastic bins. Mrs. Shedd ducked into her office and came back with the check.

"You will check the yarn before you give her the check. The news said something about a stink bomb."

I promised my boss that I would give the yarn the smell test before I did anything.

"You don't think it'll be a problem that the yarn was part of a crime scene," she said.

I assured her there was nothing to connect them.

As Dinah and I headed to the door, Elise was about to walk into the bookstore. She looked at the plastic bins we were carrying.

"What's up?" she asked. Dinah answered before I could signal her not to, and said we were going to pick up the yarn for the kits.

"You should let me help," Elise said. I tried to dissuade her, but she insisted, and I finally welcomed her to join us. But there went my chance to talk to Dinah on the way over about what we might do to investigate. Despite Elise's claim she was just there about the yarn, I knew she had something else up her sleeve.

I parked the Greenmobile in front of Miami's. There were no police cars, and the Holiday House sign was lying facedown on the ground. Before we unloaded the bins, I pulled the sign up so Dinah could have a look at how it had been altered to read "Ho House." Dinah had to stifle a laugh. I glanced at the houses on the cul-de-sac, now that I knew Ms. Mayonnaise lived in one of them. While Dinah and I were each grabbing a bin, Elise was already on her way up the pathway to the door. We rushed behind her to catch up.

"Come in, come in," Miami said quickly as her eyes darted around the houses on the small street. I almost got the cuff of my khaki pants caught in the door because she was in such a hurry to shut it.

As we walked inside, I naturally looked toward the sliding glass doors along the back of the house. The white tent was gone, which I assumed meant that Sloan's body was gone as well.

Elise was stuck to Miami like glue. She gestured toward the backyard as she used her other hand to touch Miami's arm in a supportive manner. "What happened here was so tragic. Maybe you've changed your mind and would like to sell the place. I don't think we'd have to disclose what happened here since technically it wasn't in the house." She patted her arm again. "I'd be happy to step in and help you with the sale." I saw Elise reaching in her pocket and pulling out a business card. I knew that Elise was focused and single-minded, but she'd outdone herself this time, both with her timing and her directness. Dinah and I both blanched at her moxie.

Miami looked at the card in Elise's hand but didn't take it. "No, I'm not going to sell the place. I intend to go ahead with the plan. I don't care if the neighbors don't like it. It's my house, and I'll do what I want to."

"Have you considered talking to them?" I said.

"One of the neighbors stopped by the first time I came here. She wanted to let me know the street celebrated all the holidays. Next up is a Labor Day barbecue. Then she started asking me a lot of questions like if I was going to be living here, if I had a family and such. I kind of blew her off and told her I wasn't into neighborhood things and that it was my house to do what I wanted with. After that I made sure I drove into the garage and went directly into the house.

"Sloan suggested I ignore them. She was convinced that once I had some short-term rentals and nothing terrible happened, they'd back off. I never imagined they'd do anything like . . ." she hesitated and looked toward the yard with a sigh. "Would do anything like they did."

Now that she had opened that door, I stepped in. "Do you have any idea who did it?"

She shrugged. "Like I told you, I've avoided dealing with them. Sloan gave me their names once, but I lost the piece of paper."

"Poor Sloan," I said. "Did you know her very well?"

"Not really. She had access to some sort of list and found out that I'd inherited this place from my aunt. She contacted me and pitched me her real estate services. She said she was different from the other agents because she could help me clear the place out with estate sales and such. Then she'd do something she called staging to make the place look stylish. It sounded pretty good.

She explained her background and that she knew all about creating an image. I told her that I wasn't sure about selling. I needed a place to live, and there was just a small mortgage. She asked me a bunch of questions and she came up with a brilliant idea. I could use one of the temporary rental apps to rent out the bedrooms over there." She pointed to the area off to the side. "I could make the guesthouse a rental too. Still keep a private area for myself. We went back and forth about keeping the kitchen and the great room private or open to the guests." She did a half twirl, indicating the big open area we were standing in. "I voted to keep it for myself." She smiled at us. "I thought it was pretty cool how she'd figured out a way to make the house self-supporting and then some. The place was hardly set up for it, though. My aunt had a thing for fussy furniture and doodads." We all looked at the jumble of stuff in the middle of the large room.

"Sloan said she could clear out the place, taking a cut from the proceeds as her payment, and use the rest of the money to furnish the rooms for the short-term rentals. She said she knew how to decorate them so they would photograph well. I guess people pick the rentals from pictures. She was annoyed about what the vandals did to the sign out front because she was planning to take some photos of the sign and the house as sort of a 'coming soon' thing, so we could start getting reservations before the place was even finished." Miami sighed and looked around. "Now what?"

Elise didn't miss a beat. "I can definitely help you." She had her card out again. "I've learned a few things being in real estate, and I could certainly step in and take Sloan's place. Do you suppose we could have a tour?"

Miami didn't seem sold on hiring Elise, but she agreed to the tour. She took us through a door into the wing with the bedrooms. Elise checked the door handle as we went through. "We could put a lock on it, so you'd have options for whether guests could come in here."

Dinah and I followed Elise and Miami. Elise continued doing her pitch as we looked around. An exterior door could be added to the wing, so guests could go in that way. The doors to the bedrooms were open, and they'd mostly been emptied of furniture.

"We had to junk a lot of the stuff," Miami explained. "Sloan had a plan for the look of the rooms. It was all about how they would photograph for the listing."

Elise went on ahead to an open area at the end of the hall. "This could be a sitting area. Add some vending machines to give you a little extra money." She noticed a door leading to the yard. "We should add some lounge chairs and an umbrella table."

"Maybe you can put it on hold for now," I said to Elise. I hated to interrupt her pitch, but I needed to deal with the yarn and get back to the bookstore.

We went back into the main room and picked up the bins. Miami walked us to the sliding glass door and pulled it open. "The guesthouse is open," she said.

"Did the cops tell you anything about the stink bomb?" I asked.

Miami made a face, thinking about it. "They didn't have to. I saw for myself that it was garbage with disgusting rotting fish heads, lobster and crab shells, and that casing with the eyes and legs that are on the outside of shrimp."

I was holding my breath, expecting to get a shot of the stench, but when I stepped outside and took a tentative sniff, there was nothing, and I let out my breath in a gush. I understood why the smell was gone when I checked the lawn. The spot where the tent had been was dug up and had probably been shipped away as evidence. There was just an open space where the grass had been.

I had to admit that we kept looking up nervously, ready to duck if we saw a drone, but it stayed peaceful. I made another check of the yarn, and the only scent was a faint lavender odor. Sloan's work. She'd probably deposited sachets around the guesthouse to give it an inviting smell. We packed the yarn into the wheeled bins. Elise supervised as Dinah and I pulled ours across the lawn, and we went back into the house.

Miami was watching a game show on her phone, yelling out the answers while doing a little dance. She looked up when we came in. I offered her the check and was about to say goodbye, but before I could get the words out, Elise was on her like butter on toast.

"It just so happens I have some time now to work on this place," Elise said. "So, what do you think? Do we have a deal?"

"Elise, don't you think you're rushing it? Don't you think you should wait a little while?" I said. Sometimes Elise kept her eyes too closely on the prize.

But Miami shook her head. "I don't want to wait. The sooner I get things done, the sooner this house can start turning a profit."

"Then we do actually have a deal?" Elise said, sounding surprised.

"You're not worried about the neighbors . . ." Dinah said, letting her voice trail off.

"Not anymore," Miami said, and then I understood.

"Because whoever sent the drone doesn't want to do anything that could get them caught, and the others are afraid if they do anything and get caught, they'll get the blame for the drone attack," I said.

"Exactly," Miami said. She turned to Elise. "When can you start?"

"Now," Elise said.

"Remember, you're going to make the kits."

Elise looked at Miami. "I'm like Sloan; I can do a number of things."

"She better hope she doesn't end up the same way," Dinah said under her breath as we retraced our steps to the door.

Chapter Eleven

"I thought we could start on the kits," I said as I pulled into the parking lot behind the bookstore.

"Can't do it now," Elise said. She had the door to the car open before I cut off the motor. "I'm going to drive back over there. You heard Miami. She wants to start right now." She was gone a moment later.

"I guess that leaves you and me," I said to Dinah. We unloaded the bins and wheeled them in. I checked in with Mrs. Shedd, and then we continued on to the back of the store. The yarn department was deserted at the moment. Once we were situated, Dinah went to the café to get us our usual drinks.

"I have the small plastic bags to package the kits," I said. "I thought we could do the yarn and then add the hooks and instructions later." We spread out some of the yarn from one of the bins and I explained the plan I'd come up with. Some of the kits would have yarn that was different versions of the same color, but with a skein of something that contrasted or one that was a different texture and some would be a crazy salad mix of colors and textures.

"What are you going to tell Barry?" Dinah asked. She looked over the skeins of yarn on the table and picked out some that she thought went together.

"Nothing unless he contacts me," I said. "He said he'd be in touch, so who knows. I'm not supposed to call him. It's pure Barry. He wants to be in control." I gazed at the selection of yarn and realized the difficulty of making up the kits—each one required decisions.

"I hope Peter doesn't send you to your room again," Dinah teased. "Or you'll have to meet in your bedroom." She looked at the small pile of plastic bags, three skeins of yarn in each. "Elise is an expert at making kits. I'm sure she'll work much faster."

I agreed and began choosing some skeins in shades of rust and orange and threw in a kelly-green ball of yarn for contrast. "If I'm going to be spending so much time in there, I'm going to have to make some changes to my room. Make it into more of a She Cave." I made a face, thinking of my room. "Except with a bed in it."

"I bet Barry won't mind," she said.

"As a matter of fact, he seemed uncomfortable. He was there on police business, and that room's a little personal."

"And probably full of hot memories." Dinah drank some of her café au lait. Bob had premixed it for her this time, in a paper cup. "I bet he had trouble keeping his mind on police business," Dinah said with a laugh. "He was probably afraid that he'd lose that iron control he has over his feelings," she teased.

"I think it's only hunger and tiredness he keeps at bay," I said.. Dinah was convinced he was keeping *other* feelings under lockdown that had to do with me, but I wasn't so sure.

"Sometimes things are just what they are," I said. "The whole volcano churning inside him is probably just your imagination." I dropped some yarn in a bag and added it to the small pile. "I really think he's only after information. He saw me there. It's a weird case, and he figured out that I'd probably hear stuff the cops wouldn't. I wonder if Miami told the cops about her dealings with the neighbors." I had stopped working on the kits. "The contents of the stink bomb could be a clue. It would seem that with all that seafood garbage came from a restaurant or a seafood market."

"Or a grocery store," Dinah said. "And then there's the neighbor Miami talked to. It sounds like the neighbor was being friendly and Miami was being hostile. Finding out that Miami was turning the place into a short-term rental might have been too much."

"Could be," I said. "And I found out that woman from the bookstore, the one I call Ms. Mayonnaise, lives in one of the houses on the cul-de-sac. She made a point of telling me that she stepped in when she didn't think things were right." I stopped for a minute. "But I can't see her with a drone."

"You never know," Dinah said with a shrug.

Both Dinah and I realized we had other things to take care of and decided to put the kit making on hold. She began putting the unused skeins of yarn back in the bin.

"I don't really know much about how this short-term rental business works," I said, pulling out my smartphone and doing a search. I read over some material and glanced up to report my findings to Dinah. "The neighbors would have to have been notified of Miami's plan, but there isn't anything they could do to legally stop her."

"So, someone must have decided to do something illegal," Dinah said. We packed up the rest of the stuff in the bin and put a lid on it.

*　*　*

I was glad to see that the driveway was empty when I came home. Finally, I had my house to myself, at least as far as humans were concerned. The dogs and cats formed a greeting committee by the kitchen door as I came across the backyard. It was nice to have someone so glad to see me.

It was still light, so I let the cats in the yard for some outdoor time. Cat Woman went right for the bushes and went into hunting mode. Mr. Kitty found a spot to lounge where the stone patio still held the warmth of the sun. Cosmo and Felix chased each other around the yard. One of them found a ball and dropped it at my feet. I threw it, and they went off, racing each other to get to it. Before they had a chance to come back with it, I went through the house and encouraged Blondie to join everyone outside. Princess was still sticking with her, but once she got outside, she wanted me to pick her up.

"So you're a cuddler," I said, putting her in my lap as I sat in one of the chairs around the umbrella-covered table. I was considering what to have for dinner when my cell rang.

"Sunshine," Mason said in a cheery voice, "if I can't see you, it's nice to at least hear your voice." He asked about my day, and I mentioned going to the Miami's to pick up the yarn.

"There weren't any cops there this time, were there?" he asked.

"No, everything was gone. The tent, Sloan, and even the smell." I said.

"I'm sure the cops will hunt down whoever sent that drone, and that will be that. There's no reason for you to get involved, right?"

I wondered if he had some sixth sense that Barry had approached me, but I brushed it off. It was just my guilty feeling that I was keeping something from him. I didn't really want to talk about it, so after telling him that I had the luxury of the house to myself for a little while, I asked about his day.

It was as if I had pushed a "Go" button. He went on in an enthused voice about the progress they were making on the case. Then he stopped for a moment. "Any more thoughts about my proposal?"

"I'm thinking about it," I said. "I just don't know."

"Why don't you tell me your objections?"

"So you can overcome them?" I said in a light tone.

"Maybe. But seriously, talk to me. Tell me what's on your mind." He sounded open and caring.

I thought about what to say and simply went with the truth. "It's a lot to deal with. Getting married and working with you. It means upending my life. What about my job, my friends, the Hookers?"

"Let's take it apart," he said. "You're right about your job at the bookstore. Though maybe you could work part time. You could still see Dinah and spend time with the Hookers, just not as much." He stopped for a moment. "You know how I feel about you, and I just want us to be a team, companions. You'd be giving up some things, but you'd be getting something in exchange. Maybe it would be easier if you saw what you'd be working on." Princess snuggled closer and scratched at my hand until I began to pet her.

"I have an idea," Mason said. "You must have some time off coming from the bookstore. Why not take a week and come with me. Try before you buy."

I laughed. "I know what you're doing," I said. "You're betting that once I dip my toe in and see what it's like, I'll be hooked."

"Am I that transparent?" he said. "But you're right. I know you and how good you are at investigating. Working on these cases has given so much meaning to my life, and I want to share it with you."

I figured he meant some vague time in the future for this trip, but then he said, "I'm going to have to come back next week. The same clients again. The DA has nothing, and I think this is his last-ditch effort, but they want me there anyway. I was thinking that when I come back here, you could come with me. There's a good chance you'd be there for the hearing. I'm pretty sure what the outcome is going to be. When you see my client's face as the judge tells him he's free to go, and then see his family's joy, you'll understand. There'd be no strings, but there'd always be the option we could seal the deal with a stop in Vegas on the way back and have a silly wedding with an Elvis impersonator."

"You're certainly persistent," I said with a laugh.

"I guess I am. So what do you say, are you up for the adventure?" he asked.

"I hate to say this again," I said, "but I'll have to see. I'd have to get the time off, and it's kind of last minute. I have the event at the bookstore. And the animals. And . . ." I couldn't very well say *and what I'm working on with Barry*, so I just left it hanging.

"I get it," he said. "But if you decide you want to do it, I can help with the arrangements with pets and so forth. The whole point is that we'd be in it together."

He was good. How could I turn down his trial offer? More importantly, I didn't want to.

The animals were all hungry, so they came in quickly when I called them. Even Cat Woman gave up her hunt, for some canned cat food.

It was so nice not to have Peter and Gabby in the kitchen that I went through a repertoire of things to make for dinner. In the end, I made some marinara sauce from scratch and put on a pot of water for the spaghetti.

The kitchen smelled wonderful, and as I poured the sauce over the noodles, my stomach gurgled with anticipation. I was considering where to eat when my cell rang again.

I assumed it was Mason, wanting to add something to his pitch, but it was Barry.

"Just checking. Do you have anything?" he asked.

"Maybe a little," I said. I was about to continue when he cut me off.

"Only in person," he cautioned. Dinah thought this was his way of getting to see me, but I figured it was because he absolutely wanted to keep it off the record. "Can we do it tonight?"

I looked at the spaghetti and thought about my ravenous hunger. Then there was the potential of Peter and Gabby returning at any time. The last thing I wanted was for Peter to see me with Barry. I couldn't explain what I was doing. So, it would have to look as if it was a social visit. Peter didn't like Barry, and he'd been pushing for Mason all along. I could hear the lecture from my son now, telling me I was going to blow it with Mason.

"When were you thinking?" I said.

"Now. I'm in front of your house."

I went to the front window and saw his Tahoe parked out front. "Could you move your SUV down the street?" I asked, thinking Peter might recognize it. It was silly—after all, I was an adult in my own house. Still, it was better to just avoid trouble. I was at the front door when Barry walked up, and I let him in before he rang the bell, avoiding a rush of Cosmo and Felix to the door.

Barry was dressed in his work clothes, but his tie was pulled loose, and there was a shadow of a beard on his chin. He tried to hide it, but I noticed him sniffing the air, though he was working hard to keep up his business demeanor.

"We can't talk in here," I said. "I don't know when my housemates will return."

Barry nodded with recognition. "Right. It wouldn't be good if Peter saw me here."

He sniffed the air again.

"Have you eaten?" I asked.

"Don't worry about it. This isn't a social call," he said.

"But I owe you for the Chinese food," I said.

He seemed to consider it for a moment and then relented. "I guess if it was okay to eat that time . . ." He blew his breath out and acknowledged his hunger pangs.

"Go on into my room," I said. "I'm sure you know the way." I meant it as a joke, but he nodded without the hint of a smile. He was going full force with the official business attitude. He nodded when I asked him to grab two individual folding tables.

I came in a few minutes later with a covered dish of the spaghetti and a couple of plastic plates. I had the cheese grater in the pocket of my shirt. A parade of two dogs and two cats followed me. Blondie and Princess were already in the chair.

He had set up the small tables. I put the food down and we resumed our seating arrangement from the last time.

Felix and Cosmo huddled at Barry's feet. "I forgot to give them a treat," he said. "I missed last time too." He dropped the cop demeanor long enough to bend down and give each of their heads a rub.

"I came prepared," I said, taking some dog treats out of the pocket of my khakis. Cosmo was technically Barry's dog.

He and his son had adopted the mop-like black dog wh(
were a couple. It quickly became apparent that the dog
better off living at my place since I had a big yard and (
animals, and was used to caring for them. When we b
up, Cosmo stayed. Barry's teenage son Jeffrey had com
visit the dog, and Barry had stopped by to drop off food
him. But then the visits had gotten farther apart until t.
were mostly nonexistent. Cosmo had continued to play
part, though. Whenever he saw Barry or Jeffrey, he acted l
he belonged to them. Until they left. Then he was all min

I heard a car pull in. Two of the windows in my roo
looked out onto the driveway, and I rushed to close th
shutters.

"Role reversal," he said with a chuckle. "Now you hav
to hide who's in your bedroom."

Barry's expression had relaxed finally.

"It's so much easier with Samuel," I said, referring to my
younger son. "He just plays ignorant. Peter would give me
a lecture."

"Peter's still pushing for Mason, huh?" Barry said.

I nodded and thought about my earlier phone call. I
wondered if I should say something to Barry, but decided
not to for now. It was really of no concern to him except
that if I left, I might not be able to finish the case with him.

"Bon appetit," I said, grinding some fresh parmesan on
the mound of spaghetti I'd put before him.

Barry always seemed to go from zero to sixty in no time
at all. He'd show no signs of hunger and then practically
inhale food.

"This is so good," he said as he twirled more pasta on his fork.

"There's plenty," I said. "So eat hardy."

I had to agree with Barry. It was delicious. It always amazed me how something so simple could be so satisfying.

Once the edge was off his hunger, Barry asked for the goods. "So, tell me what you found out," he said.

"I guess we should start with Miami," I said. "Why don't you tell me what you know?"

Barry shook his head with a knowing smile. "Remember I asked you to tell me what you found out."

"I just thought it would save time if you told me what you already knew," I said defensively.

"I'm not in a hurry," he said. He leaned back in the loveseat to prove his point.

"Okay, then, here goes," I said with a shrug. "Do you know what her real name is?"

Barry rolled his eyes at me. "I thought you were just going to give me the information."

"I thought this way would make it more interesting. More like a conversation than an interrogation."

"And more difficult. If you're so worried about time, why don't you just get to the point?"

"Have it your way, but I hope it doesn't put you to sleep after that plate of pasta."

"I'll take my chances." He gestured with his hand for me to get going.

"Her real name is Bertha," I began. "And she's something of an actor, but she wants to be a personality." I

stopped and thought about it for a moment. "I don't think it's a very good plan. Sloan gave her some idea about becoming a contestant on game shows so she could demonstrate her winning ways."

I heard Barry blow out his breath in frustration. "Just the facts, please. I'm not concerned about Miami's future career aspirations."

"Sloan, or maybe she's better known as 'the victim' to you, told her how she could make the house pay its own mortgage and then some by setting up most of the bedrooms and the guesthouse as short-term rentals." I looked at Barry while I was talking, trying to read his reaction. but the best way to describe his expression was noncommittal.

I stopped and eyed his face again. "Dinah thinks you have this whole undercurrent of emotions that you keep zipped up."

He seemed startled by my comment, which made sense since it had come in the middle of talking about Miami. But he barely missed a beat before he answered.

"Tell Dinah that she's wrong. Yes, I am able to push off hunger and tiredness. It's a necessity of the job. And, well, when I have to tell someone that one of their loved ones has died, I try not to think too much about what I'm saying."

"Were you the one who had to break the news about Sloan?" I thought about her sister Donna.

He nodded. "It never gets any easier." His brows suddenly furrowed. "Did you tell Dinah about this?" he said, gesturing back and forth between them with his finger.

I suddenly regretted what I'd said. "I'm sorry. I didn't think you meant her, and besides she would have figured it out."

He nodded his head and rolled his eyes. "Since when does 'don't tell anyone' mean there are exceptions?" He looked at me with his best serious detective expression. "We got off topic. We should go back to where we were."

"And that was?" I asked. It wasn't me answering him with a question. I really had lost my train of thought. Had I really brought up what Dinah had said? Obviously I knew firsthand there was another side to him, but even then he'd always been reserved, like he was holding something back.

"You were telling me what you found out."

"Right," I said. "It's pretty clear from posters on the street signs and the vandalism on the Holiday House sign that the neighbors aren't pleased with Miami's plan." I had a hard time not laughing when I thought of the abbreviated name on the sign, but I managed to keep a straight face. "She had sort of a run-in with one of the neighbors when she first moved into the house. "It seems like they were friendly to her, but she wasn't very nice back, and that was before she had the plan to turn the place into a revolving-door rooming house."

Barry sat forward. "Which neighbor?"

"I don't know. Just that it was a woman. Miami didn't mention the name, and I couldn't exactly start grilling her."

"It would be helpful to know who it was," he said. "It sounds like this woman had an extra motive." He looked at me intently. "Anything else?" he asked.

"Just that Miami thinks the neighbors will stop the attacks. Whoever sent the drone won't want to do anything that might get them caught, since what was meant to be a nuisance caused a death. And no one else will want to do anything because if they got caught they would be implicated in the drone attack."

All Barry said was "Hmm."

"Well?" I said.

"Thank you," he said.

"That's all you're going to say? Was it helpful?"

"Here we go again." He put his napkin on his plate. "Remember, I said from the start I just wanted to hear what you picked up. There was never supposed to be a give-and-take of information. It's not up to you to find out who sent the drone in."

"That's not fair. Just for my own curiosity you should tell me what you know."

"I know what you're up to. This is all so you and Dinah can play your Sherlock Holmes game and get into trouble."

My mouth fell open in surprise.

"Yes, I know about the little deducing game you two play."

"Who told?" I asked, my eyes flashing.

"Commander Blaine," Barry said with a smile. "When I've had to ship something from his Mail It Quick place, we always talk. Turns out he's not so happy with Dinah's detective adventures either."

Now I was angry. I'd been successful a number of times at nabbing bad guys with Dinah's help. I didn't like the idea that Barry was making it out to be a game. And then I slipped.

"So you think what I do is a game?" I said. I didn't mean to, but I had my hand on my hip and my lips were probably pursed. "I'll have you know that Mason wants me to go with him as soon as I can get the time off, to help him on the case he's working on." I pushed a stray strand of spaghetti across my plate. "He's doing pro bono work for the Second Chance Project now. The plan is that I'd work with him on cases in the future."

Barry took a moment for the information to sink in, though his expression barely flickered. "I'm sorry. You know that I value your help. Why else would I be here?"

"For the food?" I said, trying to lighten the moment. I'd said too much.

Barry rolled his eyes at the comment, then turned serious. "You're not going with him, are you? What if this case isn't settled by then?" He looked down at the two dogs at his feet and the cats who had settled on the bed and finally to Blondie and Princess in the chair. "You can't just up and leave all of them. You're not going to trust Peter to take care of them."

"I wouldn't go unless everyone is taken care of. And no, I wouldn't leave them to Peter's care. I'll just work faster at getting information for you."

"Okay," he said with a grunt. "You wanted to know what Miami told us. She said she'd inherited the house and that she had hired Sloan as a consultant to help her set the place up for short-term rentals. When she was asked about the neighbors, she didn't seem to know anything about them. She said she drove her car directly into the garage and never saw any paper signs or even knew that the sign out front had been knocked over. She had no idea where the drone came from or why someone would want to upset her."

"Really?" I said in total surprise. "Wow, she lied to you."

His cell rang and he picked up the call, walking to the corner of the room to talk.

"You have to go, don't you?"

"Yes, but it's not what you think. I told Jeffrey I was bringing dinner."

"Bring him some pasta," I said. I had a soft spot for Jeffrey. He was an interesting kid and had totally different interests from Barry's. We'd been close when Barry and I were a couple, but had lost touch in the time since.

"If it's no trouble. I know he'd prefer it to another fast-food burger."

I made up a package of pasta for him to take home to Jeffrey and then helped him slip out the den door.

After he left, I played a little solitary Sherlock Holmes and deduced something I'd missed before.

Barry was driving the Tahoe, not a black crown Victoria like he did when he was working. He was coming to see me on his own time.

Chapter Twelve

I t was going to be a busy morning at the bookstore. I picked up a Red Eye in the café and went right to work. Adele had story time, and I'd arranged another get together for the book club so they could have more time with Merry Riley. It wasn't completely altruistic. I knew some of the members would bring their friends, who'd buy a copy of Merry's book. We'd decided to do it on a Saturday, thinking we might get more of a crowd.

Merry had an ulterior motive for her return engagement too. I knew she was hoping it would help launch the line of merchandise with her name on it that had come out of the book. I had arranged a larger display with a stack of the books and all the related stuff. There were journals, special chocolates for days when you had the blues, bath soaks, aromatherapy, and T-shirts that said "I'm with Merry." I added a chair for our guest with a circle of seats for the book club people.

I had to play traffic cop and arranged it so the book club people would be in their area before the arrival of the kids for story time. Merry and her husband, Mick, or M&M as I'd started thinking of them, were the first arrivals. There was something fresh and "girl next door" about Merry. She was wearing navy-blue capri pants and an untucked white shirt with a pair of flats. Her chestnut hair fell just past her shoulders. But all anybody really noticed was her smile. It seemed big and friendly and lit up her face. Mick gave off an easygoing vibe and was nice looking in a rugged sort of way.

"Thanks for coming in," I said to both of them.

"I'm always glad to accommodate—any chance to meet up with fans," Merry said. "If I don't have a public, I don't have a career." She glanced around the bookstore as if she was remembering something. "Didn't I see you talking to Sloan Renner?" she asked, and I nodded.

Merry shook her head sadly. "I can't believe what happened to her. How tragic to be caught up in a freak accident." She straightened one of the journals on the table. "I didn't hear all the details, just what was on the news."

Mick announced he was going to get her a cup of coffee, and I wondered if I should tell Merry that I was there when it happened. The decision was made for me when two women approached the table and greeted Merry, and our conversation ended.

Mick came back with Merry's drink and set the cup down where, even if it got knocked over, it wouldn't do any harm. *How nice to have someone so intuitive looking after you.* But maybe I had that too. I thought about Mason and how he had anticipated my needs and gone the extra mile for me numerous times.

Mick had moved off to the side and was looking at a book with fish on the cover. More people were coming in, and I was about to move on when I saw Ms. Mayonnaise. I really wanted to talk to her now that I'd seen Kimberly Wang Diaz interviewing her and knew she lived in the cul-de-sac. But I couldn't interrupt now. I would grab her when they were done.

I moved on to the children's department. It was a separate area set off by a row of bookcases. The carpeting changed to cows jumping over the moon at the entrance. Adele was fussing around the child-sized chairs arranged to face her. Adele lived for story time. It had all the things she liked: people—in this case little people, who hung onto her every word—and costumes. The more outlandish, the better as far as both she and the kids were concerned.

With her build and height, Adele stood out just being herself, but the costumes took her to a whole new level, which she adored. Today's outfit was actually low-key for her. She was dressed as Engineer Sal who drove the train in *Lewis the Caboose*. She had on the striped denim cap with a bandana around her neck. Her attire was the traditional engineer look of striped denim overalls and Engineer Sal's trademark red flower corsage. Adele had crocheted hers and made it even bigger than the book character's.

"Where are the juice boxes and cookies?" she asked, looking at the empty table near the entrance.

"I'm glad I came to check," I said and offered to go to the café.

My coworker gestured toward the entrance, urging me to go. "I need some alone time to get into character."

As I left, I heard Adele begin doing vocal exercises. Our barista, Bob, apologized profusely for not having brought the snacks to the kids' department and went to pack them up.

When I started back with the tray of treats, I saw that the kids had started to arrive, and Adele was already at her post. It was strictly kids only for the reading, not that the parents really wanted to come. They were thrilled to drop their kids off and have a few minutes to themselves. But they also had to pick up their kids when it was over. Adele had arranged a membership log that required parents to give cell numbers and addresses. It worked two ways for Adele. She could reach parents if they were slow coming back for the kids, and the bookstore could send them coupons and lists of special events. It helped sell a lot of books, which made Mrs. Shedd happy and more than willing to put up with Adele's shenanigans.

As I got closer, I saw that Adele was holding her clipboard and glaring at a woman dressed in yoga pants and a tank top. The little girl with her scooted into story time, but the woman didn't leave.

An alarm went off in my head. What had Adele done now? I headed toward them, expecting to have to smooth something over. They both looked up as I approached.

"Talk to her." Adele pointed at me in an accusatory manner. "She's the one who knows that woman and arranged the whole thing."

The woman turned her glare on me as I handed Adele the tray of goodies.

"Can I help you?" I said in my customer-service voice.

"It's not about the bookstore," the woman said.

"She recognized me from the other day," Adele said in a forced manner. She was making weird motions with her head, and I was sure she was trying to tell me something, but it wasn't clear what.

Finally, Adele couldn't take it anymore and groaned. "Pink, could you deal with this? Somewhere else. Story time is about to start."

I gestured for the woman to move away from the kids' department. I didn't want her too near the book club either. I took her over near the shelves with the animal books.

"Hi, I'm Molly Pink. What seems to be the problem?" I asked.

"I recognized Queen Adele going into one of my neighbor's houses, and when I asked her about it, she said it was your idea to go to that woman's house," she said.

I knew the kids called her Queen Adele, but I didn't realize she'd gotten the parents to do it as well. "Could you clarify who you mean," I asked, still sounding customer-service friendly.

"I'm not sure what her name is. It's Orlando or Sarasota or something."

"Do you mean Miami?" I asked.

"I knew it was someplace in Florida. Somebody needs to make her understand she's ruining our street with her plans. Nothing seems to get through to her, not even someone dying in her yard. My husband checked the Staythe-Night App, and the posting is not only still there but seems to have been updated. We've tried to talk to her, but she always avoids us. I thought that if Queen Adele knew her, she might have some influence. Or maybe you could talk to her, since it seems like you were there."

She didn't give me a chance to respond and by now wasn't even looking at me as she ranted on. "There are rules you know, but she's probably not going to follow them since there doesn't seem to be much oversight. Our cul-de-sac will be ruined. How can our kids ride their scooters or play ball in the street? There will be all kinds of cars and strangers in and out. My husband is livid." She took a deep breath, seeming to try to calm herself. "You should tell her that's she wasting her time. She can ignore the signs, but when the first guests show up, I bet they won't ignore the protests from the neighbors. If you have any influence with her, you should tell her she better cut her losses and sell the place."

That sounded like a threat.

"Do you have any idea who was behind what happened?" I asked.

"Why are you asking?" she said. Then her eyes narrowed as she looked more closely at me.

"You're the one Queen Adele was talking about when she read the kids one of the *Pixie Porter, Girl Detective* books. My daughter said Queen Adele told them there was a grown-up version of Pixie who worked at the bookstore. She meant you, didn't she?"

I remembered the day Adele had read the kids *The Case of the Missing Tiara*. Adele had gone full trench coat and fedora. Pixie Porter liked to think of herself as a super detective, but to everyone else she was just a nosy kid. It figured that Adele would liken me to her.

I answered with an uncomfortable smile.

"You don't think what happened counts as murder?" the woman said a little too loudly.

"Accidental homicide," I said, trying to sound professional.

The woman put her face in her hands. "I didn't think of it that way somehow. I just thought the woman died in the backyard all on her own."

I thought of what Barry and I had discussed about somebody having a guilty conscience, and wondered if she was going to blurt something out, but instead she pulled herself together and just repeated that I should advise Miami to sell the place, and I should not play Pixie Porter and get involved. Then she was on her way to the café, probably to meet up with the other mothers.

Too late I realized I hadn't gotten her name. Pixie would have been horrified.

"I deal with people like her all the time," Mick said, coming into my line of sight. "You did a good job of letting her vent." We both began to walk back to the book club get-together. "When in this shindig supposed to end?" he said.

"We had a beginning time but didn't mention a stop time, so you can end it whenever you like." I was checking through the clump of people now standing around the actor-author, looking for Ms. Mayonnaise, but she'd left.

How could that be? She was always the one who got there early and stayed late.

"How about now?" he asked.

I zapped back to the present and smiled. "Do you want to step in or should I?"

He smiled in a light, friendly way. "I think I'll let you be the one," he said.

As before, the group was hanging onto everything Merry said. I noticed quite a few of them were holding onto books or merchandise that she had signed. "We'd like to thank Merry for coming back," I said. "And now if you will all take your purchases to our cashier, Rayaad will take care of you.

The group reluctantly followed my orders, though one woman reached out and grabbed Merry's arm. "We love you. It's so refreshing to see that you are just as wholesome in person as you are on the screen."

Chapter Thirteen

"Without that woman's name, I've got nothing," I said to Dinah, feeling dejected. "Even though I'd bet she lives in the house we named the All-American." I fretted some more. "On top of everything else, how could I have let Ms. Mayonnaise escape the book club meeting?" I told my friend about seeing her on the newscast. "She's clearly a resident of the cul-de-sac. I'd bet the Original is her house."

It was hours later, and Dinah had come by the bookstore early for the Hookers' gathering. We were already sitting at the dark wood table in the yarn department. She'd taken out her latest project. Even though it was summer now, she was thinking of the winter and the drafty classroom where she taught, and was mixing furry-looking yarn with a strand of mohair and making herself a generous cowl that could go over her shoulders to keep out the chill. She was making it in black, which I thought would show off her spiky salt-and-pepper hair.

"You could just tell Barry what you think you know," she said. "I'm sure he'd be glad for a reason to come over."

I rolled my eyes at my friend. Did she really think Barry asked for my help just to see me? I highly doubted it.

"He'd probably be delighted to spend some more time in your bedroom," she teased.

"I told you, he seemed uncomfortable."

She laughed. "Probably because it was too tempting and he was afraid he'd lose his cool." I made a face and she continued, "I know, I know—he's a master of control."

"As a matter of fact, I told him what you said about him having a huge reservoir of bubbling emotions that he kept tamped down."

"You didn't really say that," my friend, said giving me a pretend swat.

"Okay, maybe I didn't use such dramatic words, but I did say you thought he kept more than just hunger and tiredness under control."

"What did he say?"

"He denied it. He agreed about the hunger and tiredness, and he said when he had to break the news of a death to someone, he couldn't show anything more than professional consideration. He didn't use those words, but that's clearly what he meant." I crocheted a few stitches. "The point is, without giving him the woman's name, the information is pretty useless. And, well, I already told him about somebody else I couldn't identify. I've been promoting myself as this super detective." I cringed. "I think even Pixie Porter would have done better."

"Who's Pixie Porter?" Dinah asked. She laughed when I told her about the kid detective.

"I get it," she said. "Can't you just ask Adele?"

"No way. I'd really never hear the end of it from her about what a lousy detective I was. Plus she's all secretive about her list anyway. She's always saying its classified information."

I knew what Dinah was going to say next. "And no, I can't go looking for it after she leaves. She takes it with her." I grumbled to myself. "If I saw the list I'd be able to figure out who she was right away. Adele lists addresses, and all I'd have to do is look for the one on Starlight Court."

"Good, you're here," Elise said, coming up to the table and interrupting us. She pulled out the chair next to me and sat. "I'm sorry, but I'm not going to be able to make the kits. When I said I could, I didn't have this gig with Miami. But I'm sure you can get the group to put them together."

"What?" I said, surprised.

"I tweaked the pattern you had." She handed me a pile of sheets with the revised pattern and a flash drive with it. "I'll bring you the hooks, and you have the bags. I'm sorry," she said with a slightly fake-looking regretful shake of her head. "Working with Miami is really important for me. I've helped clear out a place before and advised a few people on how to rearrange their furniture to make their place more appealing to a buyer, but designing rooms is something new. Even though"—she leaned closer to me—"it's probably a waste of time. Miami's neighbors are not going to give up trying to sabotage her plan."

* * *

Elise had taken out her work. She was working on an afghan that was basically a giant granny square. She made them all the time, and this one was for one of the rooms at Miami's. "I'm calling it Yarn Lovers' Paradise. I'll win either way. If she manages to go ahead with the short-term rentals, I'll help her manage them, as Sloan was going to do. I already updated the postings on the short-term apps, adding the lounge I suggested." She pulled up a loop of the yarn with her hook. "And if it goes bust, I'll help her sell the place." Elise's ethereal aesthetic and wispy voice didn't go along with her inner steel core.

The rest of the Hookers were starting to arrive, and we dropped the subject.

Eduardo took his seat and pulled out a filet crochet piece he was making in ecru crochet thread. The filigree pieces would be a display shelf lining in his drug and sundries shop he was calling The Apothecary 2.

"I have something for you," Rhoda said with a twinkle in her eye.

She leaned across the table and pushed a folder to me. "Now that you're going to be a grandma, I thought you might want to start making baby things." She noticed my surprised look and said that Dinah had told her.

I knew she meant well, but I imagined Peter's reaction to my homemade items. I knew already that Peter and Gabby would want everything to come from some trendy store.

He got it from his father's side. Charlie had had his own public relations firm that dealt almost exclusively with entertainment business clients. His whole business had been about keeping up an image for his clients, and I guess Peter had paid close attention. Too close.

I thanked Rhoda and put the folder in my tote bag.

CeeCee was the next to arrive. She took the seat at the end of the table, as the leader of our group. She had just come from a rehearsal and seemed concerned. "In all my years in the business, this is the first time I'm doing live theater," she said. "I know it's good to keep growing and trying new things, but what if I flop?"

She seemed genuinely worried rather than just fishing for compliments.

"Don't worry, the theater only holds fifty people," Rhoda said. "We'll all sit in front."

CeeCee thanked her but still seemed worried. "But, dear, what about the people sitting behind you?"

Sheila offered everyone a tense greeting as she pulled out a chair. I knew the source wasn't the anxiety which plagued her. This time it was something real. Sheila had created a style of crochet and knitting (Adele went nuts whenever Sheila brought in a knitting project and had been known to mutter "traitor" under her breath). She mixed mohair-like yarns in shades of blue, lavender, and green, which she turned into scarves, shawls, and small blankets. The mixture of colors was reminiscent of an Impressionist painting. She'd been selling them at Luxe for a while but now was getting orders as well and was having trouble keeping up. "I used to be able to get some work done at the store, but since the owner started taking in vintage pieces along with the new stuff, we've had more business." She shrugged. "But I guess that's a good thing."

"I can help you out. It's something to do when I wake up in the middle of the night," Rhoda said. "Just give me the yarn and the pattern."

Sheila let out a big sigh of relief. "Thank you," she said, going around the table to give the former New Yorker a hug.

Adele came in just as Sheila was hugging Rhoda. "What's going on? What did I miss?" Adele barely took a breath before she continued. She looked at CeeCee. "I'm sure you understand how hard it is being a celebrity. Everybody wants more of The Adele," she said.

"The Adele?" CeeCee said, trying to restrain a chuckle.

"I had to do something to differentiate me from that singer Adele," she said indignantly.

As Adele went on and on about how her followers wanted more and more vlog posts, Dinah and I exchanged glances. We both ended up shrugging. There was no way I was going to ask "The Adele" for anything that might even slightly make me seem lesser than. I'd just have to figure out another way to get that woman's name.

"There's something I need to run past you all," I said as soon as Adele took a breath. Without saying that Elise had dropped the ball, I brought up making the kits with the yarn. "I'll get everything together, and we can make up an assembly line," I said.

"Of course, dear," CeeCee said. "With all the bookstore has done for us, giving us a place to hang out, I'm sure we'd all be glad to give something back." I noticed that she looked at Elise and had clearly figured out what had happened. "Why don't you explain what you have in mind to all of us?"

"We want to do the event next Saturday to give the kits a push, and in addition to some or all of you being crochet teachers, I was hoping you'd be willing to make some of the scarves. We need them for a photo to put on the insert with the kits and as samples for the event. I know it's short notice, but they work up quickly."

I passed around the pattern for them to look over and said I'd print some up.

In the midst of all this, I saw Dinah quietly slip away from the table with a wink. I deliberately looked away from her so no one would follow my gaze. No one noticed when Dinah returned a few minutes later either. Success was written in her smile, and she slipped something in a folder and put it in the chair behind me.

I pointed to the covered bins of yarn and told them anyone who wanted to help could pick three skeins. As everyone got up from the table, I used it as an opportunity to take the file from behind me. I opened it to reveal Adele's clipboard. She had it organized weirdly, and I had to keep going back and forth to put names together with addresses.

"Stop," Adele said in a loud voice. I jumped and the folder flew out of my arms as I frantically tried to come up with some excuse why I had it. If I thought asking her for the name would cause a problem, it was nothing compared to having taken her sacred clipboard.

Sure that I'd been caught, I began to apologize, but before I could get out the words, Adele had added to her command. She wasn't even talking to me. "Rewind everything, please," she commanded. "Let me get this for my vlog." She had her phone out and started to film. "Here we are at Shedd & Royal as the Tarzana Hookers start on my plan of how to use orphan yarn."

I objected to her saying it was her plan, but I liked the term "orphan yarn." I went back to the clipboard and finally matched up a name to the only address on Starlight Court: Bitsy Jonquet.

Chapter Fourteen

I was packing up the Serendipity scarf I'd started during the Hooker gathering, getting ready to leave the bookstore, when Barry called. "Do you have a gift for me?" he asked. It took a moment for me to understand what he was asking. Technically, I had something on two of the neighbors and therefore could have given Barry an update, but I wanted to do a little more checking things out before I passed anything on to him.

"Nothing for now," I said, "but I'm working on something."

"Oh," he said. Was there a hint of disappointment in his voice? If there was, it quickly changed to disapproval. "What do you mean 'working on'?" he demanded. "Our agreement was you're the ears and I'm the brain."

"Really? Did you just say *you're* the brain?" As I said it, I heard background noise from his side. There was the sound of a voice and a car door shutting. His tone abruptly changed.

"Did I say that? A mistake, honey. I'm not in a good place to talk," he said. He was probably with his new partner.

"I get it. You can't talk, *honey*," I said with a laugh.

It was lucky I got a little laugh in because I went home to a nightmare. I knew something was up when I saw a big Mercedes sedan and a gold Porsche parked in front of my house as I pulled into my usual spot in the driveway. As I walked across the yard and looked toward my kitchen door, there were no cats or dogs anxiously awaiting my arrival, which meant that Peter had locked them in my room. I felt my anger rising, and I marched toward the kitchen door, ready to do battle.

I smelled cooking food as soon as I opened the door. Three people in cook's uniforms were moving around my kitchen. They turned and stared at me as if I was an invader. "I live here," I said. "Who are you?" I looked through the cutaway to the dining room and saw the table had been set, complete with cloth napkins.

A man who seemed to be in charge started to say something, but Peter rushed in and shushed me.

"It's a dinner party," he said. "These guys are loaded, and they could give me backing," he said. Gabby came in behind him. We'd had little interaction since they'd moved in. I think she was trying to will me invisible.

"Go on back in there," she said to my son. "I'll handle this."

I had to keep my mouth from dropping open. She was going to handle me in my own kitchen? "We want to get out of here as much as you want us to leave," she said as soon as Peter went back to his guests. I'm sure she'd grown up on the west side of Los Angeles or in The Palisades, as people called Pacific Palisades. Her voice had that slightly superior lilt I'd noticed in people from those areas. She was doing her best to carry on as if she weren't pregnant, but at the same time was dressed in a tight knit dress that accentuated her shape. Whatever happened to the loose jumpers and baggy tops that had been popular in my day?

"Peter is doing everything he can," she said. "Now, please just be helpful and . . ." she looked around. "Can't you go in the other door and go to your room?"

This time my mouth did fall open. *Really?* My not-even-daughter-in-law-yet and she was ordering me out of the way!

*   *   *

I could have made a scene. It was my house, and while the baby she was caring was family, technically she herself wasn't. I could have marched into the living room and introduced myself to my son's company and thoroughly embarrassed him. They'd taken over, brought in caterers, and had not even had the courtesy to tell me. But I didn't. I didn't want to ruin anything that would help him put his life back together, and while we didn't see eye to eye, he was my son and I would always support him. I peeked into the living room to see what his company looked like and was surprised to Merry Riley and Mitch Byrd having wine and appetizers with several Hollywood types. It would have been a lose–lose for both of us.

So, I went around to the den door and slipped into the master suite. I must have known something like this was going to happen and had left supplies for the animals. I was even able to give the dogs a little outside time in the enclosed patio off my bedroom, known as the spot where I'd once gotten trapped. The wall around it had no gate, and that time the doorknob had fallen off the door. This time I made absolutely sure I could get back in and took the pets out into the small garden. They'd never been out there before, and it was funny to see how confused they looked. Then I brought them all back in, grabbed my crochet work, and went to Dinah's unannounced.

"He *what?*" Dinah said as I explained my sudden visit. "Come in, come in," she said. Commander was sitting on the couch, watching the news. He looked up and gave me a wave. They were still having some adjustment to getting married, but he'd always been okay with our friendship. I felt a little uncomfortable now that I knew that he knew about our Sherlock Holmes game. I was afraid it made us sound too much like Nancy Drew wannabes.

"Caterers and everything," she said as she led the way to her She Cave. "What were they making?" she said before stopping herself. "What's the difference—they booted you out of your own kitchen." Dinah slid the glass door closed behind us. The room was an add-on to the two-bedroom house.

Before Commander had moved in, we'd lounged on Dinah's chartreuse couch in the living room, and this extra room had been mostly unused. Commander was an early to bed, early to rise sort of guy, but if Dinah went to bed before midnight, it meant she was sick. That's what had prompted her to turn the added room into her den.

"What can I get for you?" she asked. "Commander made dinner, and he makes the exact amount for the two of us, so no leftovers." I told her not to worry, that it was a business dinner and likely to be over early.

"At least I can give you cookies and tea." She had an electric kettle and tea fixings in the room, and she always kept a tin of butter cookies. She brought mugs of tea and the cookies to a small table in front of the chartreuse couch. Commander had since picked out a more sedate one for the living room.

"You did get the name you were looking for off The Adele's clipboard, right?" Dinah asked with a giggle. "Just when you think Adele can't top herself, she does."

"I got the name. But it didn't seem enough to give to Barry," I said.

"Why don't we see what we can do with what you know?" Dinah said.

"You mean the Sherlock Holmes game?" I asked, and she nodded. "You know Commander knows about it?"

"So what. Let's do it."

"Let's start with what we know." I looked at my friend expectantly.

"We know that Miami seems determined to turn the place into a cash cow, and the neighbors aren't happy about it. They put up signs; knocked over the house sign; and, last but not least, dropped a stink bomb in the backyard."

"Which would be viewed differently if someone hadn't died because of it."

"And she died because?" Dinah said.

"I guess I assumed that bag hanging from the drone hit her in the head and knocked her out before the stuff fell on top of her. Maybe it suffocated her."

"Did Barry tell you that?"

"No," I said. "We didn't talk about it."

"I wonder why," she said.

"Probably because he's so sure that it was supposed to be an annoyance to Miami."

"Sometimes it helps to look at things from a different perspective," Dinah said.

"You mean think about the victim," I said, nodding in agreement. "We've been assuming that it was an accident. That Sloan was in the wrong place at the wrong time. But drones have cameras, so whoever was operating it had to have seen she was there. They could have been in a hurry to dump the stuff and it was just bad timing." I stopped to think. "Or maybe she was the target."

We both heard some noise coming from the living room, and a moment later, Commander slid open the glass door and stuck his head in. "Molly, you have some company."

I had company? Who could have tracked me down? I went to the sliding glass door expectantly.

Commander Blaine stepped back and someone took his place.

"Mason," I said. It was probably more of a shriek. It took a moment for it to register, and then I rushed to him and gave him a big hug. He was dressed in the wardrobe style of his current endeavor—jeans and a T-shirt with a sport coat. The look was more casual, but the pants and jacket had a custom fit.

"What are you doing here?" I asked. The surprise hadn't worn off, and I'm afraid it sounded almost accusatory.

Mason laughed. "Looking for you," he teased. "Everything got messed up. My clients are in a panic because they heard they might be interviewed by the FBI, and they need major hand-holding. I had to drop everything and grab the first flight here. I'm going to be tied up with them all day Sunday, but I wanted to see you tonight." We were still standing in the doorway. Mason looked around the girly room. "Can I come in, or is it ladies only?"

"Of course you can," Dinah said, waving him in.

"You're a hard person to find," he said. "I called your cell, your landline, and there was no answer at either, so I went over to your place. Peter answered the door."

"And I'm sure he invited you in," I said. Mason was just the sort of person he'd want to impress his guests with. Everybody knew he was the attorney to the stars.

"He did, and I even got points from all of them about my pro bono work. I stayed for a drink just to find out what he was up to." He gave me a kindly smile. "I figured he didn't tell you much."

I laughed. "Are you kidding? All he tells me is to stay out of the way, and he dangles that he's trying to do something so they can move out."

He looked at the tea and cookies. "I hope that means you haven't had dinner."

"She hasn't, and she deserves something delicious," Dinah said. She started clearing away the tea and cookies as Mason kept his arm around me and escorted me to the door.

"I hope you don't mind, but I thought we could go someplace close and easy. I'd love to drive to the beach, but I don't think I have it in me." We'd gotten into his Mercedes SUV, and the interior was dimly lit by the street-lights. I could see the tiredness in his face.

"It's the company that matters, not the restaurant," I said.

He reached over and squeezed my hand. "I couldn't agree more."

He was usually the one to pick a place, but this time, I did. We parked at the Village, an outdoor shopping and dining destination in Woodland Hills, and went to a casual dining spot. We sat outside on their patio, next to a pond with fish and lily pads. At first, Mason and I were both too hungry to talk. As soon as the counter person brought out the food, we dove in. As usual we shared—this time it was quiche, chopped salad, and warm pita bread, glistening with melted butter. There were pieces of chocolate cake and cheesecake for dessert.

"I would have liked to have stayed there this weekend, but when the Bagattis call, I have to go," he said when he'd gotten the edge off his hunger. He took another sliver of the quiche. "I've been living on pizza and fried chicken. It's nice to have some vegetables."

"You lived up to Dinah's command and did take me someplace delicious," I said.

"It was your suggestion. You should get the credit." The food had revived him, and he reached across the table and touched my hand. "If something like that happens again with Peter, you can always go to my place," he said.

"Thanks, but I had to take care of my menagerie. Peter assured me they'd only been locked in my room for a short time, but who knows, really." I took another piece of the bread and broke it in pieces. "You started to tell me what Peter was up to."

"You'll be pleased to know that he really is trying to put something together. I don't think he wants to stay there anymore than you want him to. After what happened with that production he was working on, he's looking in a different direction. A group of people are interested in launching a channel with feel-good programming, and Peter wants to provide them with content. He's working on getting someone to be the host for some of the drama shows. In the old days of TV, they used to do that. Someone with the girl-next-door quality," he said.

"I get it. Merry would be perfect."

"If she wanted it. Though it was her husband who did most of the talking. He's working on his own project now. She's busy with her books and the other commitments she has. I'm sure if Peter waved enough money in front of them, they'd change their mind. But I don't think Peter has access to it. The reason they probably chose her is that she has a recognizable name, but since she's like a C-level celebrity, they thought she'd work cheap."

"Too bad," I said.

"Don't worry, Peter isn't giving up. Merry was just his first choice." He looked at the chocolate cake. "Maybe we should get it packed to go. We could take it back to my place. I'll make you a cappuccino. We could have a sleepover."

Then he let out a sigh. "I forgot—I have an early morning with my clients."

"And I have my animals, and who knows what shape my house is going to be in."

He put the desserts in to-go containers and offered them to me.

"You haven't said anything about coming with me," he said. "Last I heard you had details to take care of."

He'd caught me. That was what I'd said. "I'll talk to Mrs. Shedd first chance," I said.

"Good," he said, putting his arm around me as we walked to his car.

"We can talk about it tomorrow night over cappuccinos and whatever comes with them," I said, giving him a snuggle.

Chapter Fifteen

The house was better than I'd expected. The dining room table had been cleared and the dishwasher run. The caterer had packed up leftovers and put them in the refrigerator. Some furniture had been rearranged, and some entertainment industry award statuettes that Peter had won were on the mantelpiece.

Peter and Gabby were in their room with the door shut in a reversal of roles, which was fine by me. The animals were beyond happy to see me and to be released from the master suite. They let me know their displeasure at having been confined. I found a trash can knocked over and the contents spread around the room.

They went rushing across the house, and even Blondie and her new friend, Princess, joined in. The dogs all got yard time, and the cats got attention and a second dinner of their favorite wet cat food.

As much as they couldn't wait to get out of the master suite when I got home, they were anxious to go back in

there when I went to bed. I feel asleep being cuddled by their furry bodies.

I had to admit that I felt reassured by Mason's assessment of Peter. At least if he was taking over my house, he was on a mission. They were sitting in the backyard having breakfast when I came outside the next morning, on my way to the bookstore.

"Mason told me what you're working on," I said. "I'm okay with all the masquerading, but I do insist you not leave the animals locked up for a long time. They need their water and cat boxes." I considered what to say next. "I need advance warning and for you to ask, not tell me you are taking over the house.

"You don't have to worry about any people here tonight. You can do karaoke in the living room wearing that grass skirt you got in Hawaii," he said. For a moment I froze. Was that what he thought I did when I was home alone? I checked his expression and was relieved to see a good-natured smile. He was joking. "Gabby and I are taking a ride up to Santa Barbara. We're going to stay over a couple of nights." He looked at my attire—my usual work wear of khaki pants and an untucked shirt—and shook his head. "It's Sunday. Don't you ever take a day off?"

I debated what to tell him. Would he understand that the bookstore was more than a job? I didn't really *have* to go in, but I wanted to work on getting everything together for the event.

In the end, I just shrugged off his comment and wished them a pleasant trip.

I grabbed a Red Eye from the café. I'd considered ordering something different just to show Bob and myself that I wasn't stuck in a rut, but the Red Eye was what I really wanted. There was no story time, and the bookstore was quiet. I took the drink to the cubicle near the front of the store that served as my office. Each of the kits would have an insert, with the pattern on one side and the details about the kit on the other. I'd handed out copies of the paper version of my pattern that Elise had tweaked to the group. But I needed something more elaborate for the kits. I took out the flash drive that Elise had given me and put it in the computer. My plan was to fold the sheet in half, with the name and information about the kit on the half of the sheet that would show through the bag. I wanted to include a color photograph, but since each scarf would have different yarn, the best I could do was to have pictures of several finished scarves, to give an idea of what the kit would make.

I took out the one I'd started and was contemplating how long it would take me to finish it when I heard someone clearing their throat, a sure sign they wanted my attention. When I looked up, Rhoda was leaning on the counter that surrounded my little space.

"I didn't want to scare you," she said in her nasally voice. She held up a Serendipity scarf done in shades of red with a shot of royal blue. "I brought it over as soon as I finished it."

I thanked her profusely. Having two scarves to photograph would be better than one.

Sheila came up to the booth a moment later, also with a scarf. It figured that she'd chosen yarns in her usual color palette—a mixture of green, dark blue, and lavender. She dropped it off quickly, saying she had to get back to Luxe to open up the lifestyle store. I called out a thank-you.

"And thank you to you too," I said to Rhoda. I showed her my work in progress. "I'll finish this, and then I can take a picture of the three of them."

"It was fun to make. I'll grab some yarn and work on another so you have more samples for the event."

I picked up my work, and the two of us went back to the yarn department. Rhoda looked through one of the bins of yarn and pulled out three skeins. "This time I'm doing crazy salad," she said, showing me what she'd chosen. One of the yarns looked like it had confetti hanging off it, another was a ribbon yarn in shades of pink and orange, and the last was a glittery gold. She dropped them in her bag. "I better go. Hal's waiting in the car. We're off to brunch." I thanked her again, and she rushed out the door.

I sat down at the table and started to work on my scarf.

"There you are," Adele said, coming up to the table. "I just came in to drop this off." She was holding a pot of glitter and a wand. Thankfully she didn't feel the need to demonstrate how she planned to use them. As soon as she saw I was crocheting, she pulled out her phone. "Let me get this for my fans." She had me hold her phone while she held up my work. "This is being made the long way. Do you know what it would look like if you tried to knit like this?" Adele made a dramatic horrified face. "Stitches pushed together just waiting for a chance to jump off the needle just when you've done rows and rows. *Poof*—all your work for nothing as your project unravels into a pile of yarn."

I turned her phone so it was facing me. "I'm sure all your followers want to know what I'm making," I said brightly. "I'm Molly Pink, and here at Tarzana's own Shedd & Royal Books and More we are doing something special in our yarn department." I could feel Adele's eyes on me. She hated to have the spotlight stolen even for a few minutes, but she also realized I was giving her some much-needed content. Even so, she couldn't totally stay out of it.

"She's talking about the special kits I came up with. An exciting mixture of yarn curated by yours truly. To kick things off, there will be an event at Shedd & Royal," she said. She turned to me, asking the time and relayed it to her followers before logging out.

"And that's the way it's done, Pink," she said when she stopped taping. "In a single stroke of genius, I just made those kits into a super item. The Adele's followers will make the kits a sellout."

"I'm surprised you didn't tell your followers the story of where the yarn came from," I said.

"I considered it, but if I mentioned the stink bomb, they might think the yarn smelled." Adele made a face at the memory of it.

"You were there that time?" I asked.

"Of course, Pink, how could you not remember?"

I looked at the phone in her hand and had a sudden thought. "Did you tape anything for your vlog from there?"

"I suppose I did. I was in such shock after what happened that I didn't even think about it." Adele seemed to be reimagining the moment and, in one of her typically dramatic poses, bent her head and put the back of her hand on her forehead.

"Do you still have whatever you taped?" I asked.

"I don't know, probably. I was so disturbed by the whole circumstance, and then when the police wanted to talk to me, they totally ignored that I was a police wife." She let out a loud harrumph.

I really wanted to see whatever she'd gotten, but with Adele it was better not to be direct. "Don't you want to check?" I asked. "If it's too upsetting for you, I'd be glad to look." I reached for the phone, but Adele snatched it back. Actually, I was glad. I didn't have a clue how to find it.

"You'd probably mess everything up," she said. She looked at the screen and went through a bunch of swipes and clicks. "I did tape it. I guess the shock erased my memory." She was watching something, and she let out a gasp.

"Can I see it?" I said, taking a chance of being direct this time.

Adele held the phone close as she thought it over. Finally she handed me the phone. "It's cued up, just hit the arrow."

I took the phone and hit "Play." At first there were just shots of the inside of the house and Adele with her narrative about being on a crochet adventure, this time a yarn hunt. There were a few shots of the boxes in the guesthouse, then Adele was talking to the camera. It must have been after she had gone into the house. The sliding glass door and yard beyond were visible behind her. Sloan came out of the guesthouse, looking at her phone. The drone was hovering nearby and started to fly toward her. It appeared she was trying to move away, but the drone kept on her. The picture stopped just as the bag swung at her, and Adele grabbed her phone back.

It sure looked like Sloan was the target.

Chapter Sixteen

The rest of the day at the bookstore was very quiet. I took advantage of the peace to talk to Mrs. Shedd about taking a week off. She was a little concerned about how soon it would be, but when I explained the situation and the opportunity to be able to witness the culmination of Mason's case in Kansas, she understood. As long as I managed to hold the event first and left them with enough scarf kits, she was okay with it. When I finally went home, I didn't do karaoke or get my time with Mason. He'd texted me his apologies and said that he was tied up with his clients. Something about having to go out of town with them to a croquet tournament.

I knew how that went. Charlie'd had his own public relations firm when we were married, and a lot of his clients were entertainers. My late husband was expected to be there as part of the entourage whenever they performed. The only way we had a weekend night out was if I went with him.

The only other interesting thing that happened was I got a call from Miami, telling me she'd found two more boxes of yarn and requesting I pick them up on Monday.

I told Dinah about it when she came into the bookstore the next day. "Would you mind coming with me?" I asked as we stood outside the café.

"I need a drink first," my friend said. "It was one of those mornings." We got our drinks and found a table. "Before we talk about my morning, though, what's with you and Mason? You've been kind of radio silent about him," my friend said.

I told her about our phone call and his updated offer.

"He's good," she said with a laugh. "So did you take him up on it?"

"Yes, I finally talked to Mrs. Shedd yesterday and she agreed. I just have to tie up all the loose ends here before I go." I let out a sigh.

"What about the other night?" she said. She laughed at how we couldn't manage to get together.

"It was so much easier when we were all in our twenties," I said. "But enough about me. What did your students do this time?"

She taught freshman English at a community college that had open admission. They had year-round classes now, and for some reason, the summer session was always the toughest. I suppose they all really wanted to be at Zuma Beach instead of in a classroom.

"This group is outdoing themselves," she said. She'd had students who tried to include emojis in their papers and others who had tried writing in text speak. They were all out of touch with a world before cell phones and computers. I knew she'd just given her classes one of her favorite assignments. They had to hand-write a paper, so there was no presumptive type, no grammar check, and no smiley faces or eggplants. Just words that they had to write with a pen. Just getting past their handwriting was a challenge.

She held out a sheet of paper for me to see. The writing was printed in pencil. "Can you believe these kids don't know cursive writing?"

"I've got something to take your mind off it," I said. "We'll talk as we drive." As soon as I described Adele's video, Dinah understood.

"It sure sounds like Sloan was the target. But do you think they meant to kill her or just upset her with the stink delivery?"

"You mean like whoever did it knew that she was behind helping Miami make the place into a temporary rental," I said. "That's probably it. Her death was still an accident, but dumping the stuff on her was intentional."

I pulled the Greenmobile in front of Miami's. The sign that said "Holiday House" had been propped up, and the posters were gone from the street signs.

Miami motioned for us to come in as she glared at the houses in the cul-de-sac. She had circles under her eyes, and I noticed that she'd added a lavender color to her brown hair. "It's been a little much," she said. "It was stressful before, trying to get this place together, but then what happened to Sloan . . ." She let her voice trail off.

"But you've got me now," Elise said from inside the house.

Dinah and I walked into the main part of the house. Elise had a presentation book open on a table that was part of the mishmash of furniture. She began to thumb through the pages as the three of us looked on. It was impressive. She had used a design program to put together a bunch of themed rooms. The Glamping Room was made to look like it was inside a tent, the Tropical Breeze had walls painted a sky-blue, with carpet the color of sand, and a fake palm tree sitting in the corner. The furniture was all wicker, and the curtains and bedspread were covered in tropical flowers. There was one she called the Library that had bookshelves, a comfortable chair, and a reading lamp.

The Treehouse was meant for kids and had a loft held up by a fake tree stump, with a rope ladder.

"Wow," Miami said, "that's a lot different from Sloan's concept. Much nicer. But you said you'd take the same deal I had with her."

"What exactly was the arrangement you had with Sloan?" Elise asked.

"She was going to sell off the stuff in the house and use the money to buy beds and stuff to furnish the rental rooms. Her plans weren't as elaborate as yours. She wanted to make the bedrooms look like they'd belonged to kids who'd grown up and moved away, by using some of my aunt's stuff like that old sailboat." She pointed to something sticking out of a box.

"Then you weren't paying her anything," Elise said. She looked surprised and wary. "How was Sloan getting paid?"

"She was taking a cut on the stuff she sold, and I was going to pay her something out of the rentals so she could help me run the place." The three of us looked around the mostly empty room.

"It doesn't seem like there's enough to sell to make anything," Dinah said.

"Sloan had arranged things in a number of groupings. There were the good pieces she sold separately. My aunt had a lot of junk, but some really good stuff too. They were supposed to bring in enough to pay for the basic furnishings for the rental rooms. They've been out of here for a while. She put the things for an estate sale in the garage. She planned to leave a few pieces of furniture and some doodads in the bedrooms, and there was stuff she still had to go through."

"Who was keeping track of the money?" I asked.

"Sloan was supposed to take her cut and put the rest into a business account I'd set up for the place."

"So, then, you have access to it and know how much is in there?" Elise asked.

Miami let out her breath and seemed uncertain. "I have access to it, but Sloan was the one keeping track of it." Miami shrugged. "She just told me not to worry about it."

"I'd like to see what you have for the rental rooms," Elise said, her tone changing. "And I'm going to need some kind of retainer."

I didn't want to get in the middle of Elise's deal making and excused Dinah and myself to get the yarn. As we headed to the sliding glass door, I heard Miami offer to sign over the check I'd given her for the yarn.

"Do you think we should warn Elise?" Dinah asked, glancing back at the two women. "If these people went after Sloan, maybe they'll go after her too."

"I don't think so," I began, repeating what Miami had said before about no one wanting to do anything that might get them caught. "But it does seem like Sloan kept Miami in the dark about the pieces she was selling off." I shrugged. "It's Elise's problem now."

Dinah and I avoided looking at the spot where the stink bomb had been dropped as we crossed the yard. The guest-house was open as Miami had said. And two boxes of yarn were stacked against the wall. We'd brought trash bags to put the yarn in. My tote bag slipped off my arm and landed on the floor next to the counter that separated the kitchen-ette area. I left my purse on the counter and started to open one of the dark plastic bags. I glanced toward the open door.

"We've got the yard to ourselves, so we might as well have a look around."

There was nothing new to see in the grassy area between the guesthouse and the house, but I was curious about the area behind the guesthouse. The lawn continued around the small dwelling, but the strip of land between the guest-house and the wood fence that ran along the back of the property had a neglected feeling. There was gravel instead of grass, and a shed sat up against the fence.

"It looked like the drone came from over there." I pointed toward the top of the fence.

I tried to orient myself as I looked along the length of the fence, which seemed to curve before it was lost in greenery.

"I wonder what's on the other side of it." The fence was too tall for us to see over, and my fence-climbing days were long gone.

"Maybe there's a ladder in there," Dinah said, noting that the door to the shed was ajar. "Since it's open, it seems like it's okay to look inside."

"I'm not sure if Barry would agree, but he's not here, so why not." I felt an uptick in my heartbeat as I pushed the door open wider. Who knew what was in there?

Dinah had her phone out and turned on the flashlight, moving it around to illuminate the small space. The light must have stunned something, because there was a rustling sound. A folded up stepstool was resting against the back wall of the shed.

"If I can deal with those students of mine, I can certainly deal with a creepy shed. I'm going in." She marched in quickly, grabbed the stepstool, and rushed back out with a nervous giggle. "Look at this. A step stool built for two," she said as she unfolded it. There were steps on both sides of it. I moved it against the fence and we both climbed up to have a look. Instead of peeking into a neatly mowed yard, we were looking at a wild area filled with bushes and wild growth in a tangle of green. "It's like a secret garden," I said. "If no one tended it and it was left to grow as it pleased." I surveyed the area as I tried to orient myself for the first time realizing that the backyards of the cul-de-sac were at the bottom of a greenery-covered slope that rose up into one of the finger-like ridges. I couldn't see it, but I knew there was a street at the top. As I looked around the open area, I caught glimpses of fences that I assumed belonged to the other houses in the cul-de-sac. When I glanced the other way, there was some chain-link fencing covered in ivy.

"I've seen areas like this before," I said. "It looks like there's a small ravine that probably floods when it rains and can't be built on." I surveyed it again. "I'd really like to go in there and look around. Maybe peek into the other yards." We both looked over the fence and agreed there was no way to get over it.

"I guess that's it then," Dinah said. Reluctantly I agreed, and we folded up the stepstool and replaced it in the shed before returning to the guesthouse.

We packed up the yarn and I grabbed my purse. Instead of going through the house, we went through the yard to the street. We were just loading the bags in the car, when Elise came out.

"Miami showed me how much was in the account. There's not enough to even cover some mattresses. I wonder where all the money went?"

Chapter Seventeen

I pulled the car into the driveway, glad to see no other cars. Peter and Gabby were still on their trip to Santa Barbara. I was already planning to shed my slacks and shirt and change into a light dress. Now that it was close to evening, the temperature had started to drop to comfortable levels. I would eat outside.

I opened the gate, walked into my yard, and started across the stone patio. I was thinking about what I might cook, when I heard what sounded like a whine and sensed something moving. I looked at the ground and saw a toy SUV. "Toy" seemed the wrong word when I looked at it again. It was big enough to transport guinea pigs. The body was all black and kept making revving noises. With a final rev, it started to move toward me. It picked up speed and stopped short just before it reached me. When I tried to move away from it, it followed me. I made a run toward the two cement steps that went from the patio to the grassy part of the yard, sure the thing couldn't drive up stairs. I thought I was home free, but the SUV rolled up the stairs with ease. It would have been funny if it wasn't so creepy the way the SUV chased me around the yard. It would speed up and stop short just before it made contact. Then it started playing games. I took a step, and it didn't move. Another step, and still there was nothing. I looked longingly at the kitchen door. Taking a chance, I sprinted to the door, but as I fumbled with the key I heard the SUV roar up behind me, and it tapped my ankle ever so slightly. I felt the metal of the bumper press against my skin. How was I going to get inside without the SUV coming in with me? And then I had an idea. I turned abruptly and ran back across the stone patio to the chain link gate that led to the driveway. I pulled it open, went through it and slammed it shut before the SUV could get through. I heard it hit the chain links with a loud noise.

"Got you now," I said. I'd barely taken a breath when a menacing laugh came out of the creepy toy, and I heard it revving up again. The top flipped open and it sprouted a helicopter rotor and flew straight up and over the gate. I tried to follow it with my eye, but it flew over my neighbors' yard and disappeared. Sure that whoever was controlling it must be in the street that ran on the other side of my neighbor's house, I took off down the driveway, determined to see who it was. I ran past my neighbors' place and turned up the street. I kept going, looking for anything, anyone. And then I sensed someone running behind me.

I suddenly regretted that I hadn't been exercising much lately and I felt a stitch starting in my side. When it hurt too much, I stopped and bent over, trying to catch my breath and ease the pain as I felt someone grab me from behind.

Stitch or not, I wasn't going to go quietly, and I began doing what I could with my elbows and stepping backward, hoping to hit someone's toes.

"Hey," a voice called out just as the *someone* lifted me off my feet and stopped my elbow action.

"Barry?" I said, taking a look over my shoulder.

"I'll let you go if you promise to stop poking me."

I agreed and he released me. He noticed me holding my side.

"Got a stitch, huh?" he said, and I nodded.

"Take some deep breaths—walking should help." He looked down at my hip. "Massaging it might help too." I did all three things as we began the trek back down the street.

"Why were you running after me?" I asked, beginning to feel the stitch subside.

He took a moment to answer. "Who were you running after?"

"I asked you first," I said.

His face broke the hint of a smile. "Here we go again. Can't we just cut to the chase?"

"Sure, you first," I said.

We had rounded the corner and reached the entrance to my driveway. "Fine," he said with a disgruntled shake of his head. "I pulled up in front of your place and was going to call and ask if you had anything for me when

I saw you come flying out of the driveway." He stopped and smiled. "Maybe not flying—more like sprinting. You seemed like you were going after something, and I thought I could help."

I looked over at him, and I could tell by his expression that he meant it. "Then thank you," I said. "And I do have some information for you." I started walking up the driveway, and he followed.

"And now how about you answer my question," he said. "Who were you after?"

We'd gotten to the chain-link gate that opened onto my yard. He followed me in, but then I stopped short when I saw a piece of paper with some drippings of what I hoped was red ink that said *Stay out of it.*

"Do you want to explain?" Barry asked.

"Why do they always use red ink?" I said, shaking my head. This wasn't the first time I'd been left a threatening note. I answered my own question: "It's supposed to look like blood."

Barry stopped when we got into the yard. "I'm assuming that has something to do with your sprint. Remember, you were going to tell me who you'd gone after." His brow furrowed. "Is this about the case you're helping me with? Have you been up to something?"

"That's a lot of questions to answer," I said. "Any preference where I start?"

Barry rolled his eyes in frustration. "Start anywhere you want."

"Aren't you going to collect it for evidence?" I asked.

"Of course." He pulled out a paper bag from his pocket, picked the paper up by the edge, and slipped it in the bag. He wrote something on the bag and followed me across the patio. "And now can we get back to you?" he said. The animals had heard all the ruckus and were looking out the kitchen door.

"Maybe the first step is to go inside," I said.

Barry looked back to the door that led to the den and the shortcut to the master suite. "Is this going to be a repeat of me sneaking into your room?"

"No, I have the house to myself for now. Peter and his lady went up to Santa Barbara."

"Oh," he said, and I wondered if he sounded disappointed. "And you're not worried about Mason showing up?"

"He should be back in Kansas by now. He's running himself ragged going between his regular clients and working on the Second Chance Project," I said.

Barry made a face. It had to do with the natural antagonism between cops and lawyers. "What is he trying to get someone out of now?" he said with an edge to his voice.

"It's something stupid about a college croquet team and the district attorney being pissed that his kid didn't get into Worthington U. And then he's working on getting an innocent man out of jail in his pro bono work."

Barry made a disparaging noise. "So he's playing the hero now."

"You could say that." I finally opened the kitchen door, and Cosmo and Felix rushed out into the yard. I closed the door just in time to keep the cats from making an escape. Cosmo made a rush to Barry. The dog was a genius. Whenever Barry came over, the dog acted like he was seeing a long-lost friend, but as soon as Barry left, Cosmo reverted to his usual self and acted like I was his human companion.

I brought Blondie and Princess from the other side of the house. Blondie held back, but Princess joined the other two dogs. Barry had found a ball on the ground and was playing fetch. Felix and Cosmo were into it. The ball was as big as Princess's head and she went to join Blondie in a quiet corner of the yard.

After they'd all had their outside time, we rounded the dogs up and went inside. "Don't think I've forgotten all my questions," Barry said as he closed the kitchen door behind us.

"But first I have to take care of them," I said. The cats and dogs were at my feet, waiting for their dinner. Once they were all eating, I turned back to him. "Okay, I'm all yours."

Something passed over his face, and I thought he was going to say something, but as quickly as the look had appeared, it vanished.

"We could talk while we eat," I offered. "I was going to make some dinner for myself. Are you hungry?"

He laughed at the question. "You probably know better than I do, since you're so sure I never feel anything," he said.

I opened the refrigerator to check out the contents. With Peter and Gabby living here, I never knew what I'd find. They were good at eating, but not so good at going to the store. The caterer had packed up the leftovers from their dinner party, and I decided to leave that for them.

"How about scrambled eggs?" I asked, offering him the old standby. He nodded and I started to pull out the eggs, butter, and some leftover chopped salad.

"I can help," he said.

"Really?" I examined his expression to see if he was being polite or if he meant it. He seemed genuine. "Okay, do you want an apron?"

He made a face at the suggestion, though he did take off his suit jacket.

I handed him a bag of potatoes that could be cooked in the bag. "You just clip off the corner and put them in the microwave for four minutes," I said.

"I can do more than that," he said after taking the bag from me. "I'm seeing someone, and she likes to stay in and cook. We get those meal kits. You ought to try them. They're really convenient."

I was glad I was watching the butter melt in the frying pan and he couldn't see my face. I covered up my surprise, and maybe some displeasure, before getting out a benign, "Oh, I didn't know."

He shut the microwave door and punched in the time. "It didn't exactly come up in conversation before," he said.

I added a dollop of sour cream to the eggs and mixed it in as I waited for him to say more. He didn't, forcing me to have to ask him about her.

I had a million questions. Who was she? How did they meet? Were they serious? I knew he'd wanted to marry me. Did he want to marry her now? But I contained myself and stuck to the first question.

"She's an ER nurse, so she understands crazy schedules. She's divorced with two kids. Jeffrey likes her and her kids." He looked down at the floor. Cosmo was sitting next to his foot. "I told her about Cosmo, and"—he faltered—"she thought it would be nice for all the kids if he came home." He avoided looking at me. "You do remember that Jeffrey and I were the ones who got him at that animal fair." He glanced at the microwave timer. "Really, you should be glad to have one less animal to worry about when you go off crusading with Mason." He seemed to be overstating his case for taking Cosmo, and I imagined that he knew it upset me.

I managed to get out another, "Oh." It was a bit much all at once, and so unexpected. There was no reason that Barry shouldn't be seeing someone and thinking about marrying her. But to take Cosmo? I considered telling Barry about the black mutt's trick of making up to him when he was there but decided to say nothing about it for now. "What does she think about you being here?" I asked.

Barry shrugged it off. "She gets that you're just someone helping me out on a case."

I don't know why, but that made me even more upset. I suppose it was because of everything Dinah had said about Barry and me not being finished and the twinge that I felt when I saw him. A twinge he obviously didn't feel when he saw me.

I kept it all to myself and swirled the eggs in the pan; when they were fluffy, I poured them onto a couple of plates. The microwave chimed and Barry opened the door. I rushed to hand him an insulated mitt to take the potatoes out.

"What now?" he asked. "The meal kits come with directions and seasonings."

I took the bag and tore it open, pouring the tiny potatoes into a dish. I let some butter melt over the top of them before I poured on a sprinkle of seasoning. I added some capers and a generous blob of sour cream. I made up two plates of food. *Some people don't need a meal kit to make an interesting supper.*

We took our plates into the dining room. I didn't want to talk about any more personal business, so I brought up the case. "Now I can answer all your questions," I said. "Where do you want me to start?"

"How about we work backward. You tell me about that note and who you were chasing."

"The piece of paper was left by a black SUV." He gave me a funny look, and I realized he thought I meant a full-sized one. "Not a big one, a radio-controlled toy."

I told him how it had sprouted wings and that I'd thought it had flown to the street around the corner."

"Why would somebody be trying to scare you? Have you been sneaking around? Our deal was that you were just to pass along what you heard. Have you been made?" I knew from his cop lingo that he meant had someone figured out that I was collecting information.

I told him about Bitsy and that she'd more or less come to me. "She seemed angry at me for even going to Miami's house," I said. He listened with interest as I described my encounter with her at the bookstore, leaving out what I'd gone through to find out her name.

"Hmm, that sounds almost like a threat," he said. "You think she was behind the SUV and note?" He shook his head in disbelief. "You really attract a lot of strange stuff."

I couldn't really argue with that. In the past I'd been left a rat trap with a toy rat in it, a dead fish, and a threatening milkshake. Actually a note left by a toy SUV seemed rather mild in comparison. I was annoyed that he implied I'd given away that I was collecting information. "I wasn't made. Nobody has a clue I'm feeding information to you," I said. "Bitsy seemed upset that I had a connection with Miami, and maybe another neighbor saw me go to her place too. There's a good chance they could have recognized me from the bookstore. Somebody could even have followed me home when I left there."

"But the note said, 'Stay out of it,'" he countered. "Stay out of what?"

"Like I said, she seemed angry that I went to Miami's. She could think I was helping her with the short-term rentals and wanted me to stay out of it."

Barry seemed unmoved. "That seems like a stretch. More likely it's someone connected to the drone drop."

"I might have taken a look over Miami's back fence to see if I could see into any of the neighbors' yards. Maybe someone saw me."

"Well, don't do that again," he said, as if his words could make it so.

"There's something else," I said.

"Oh?" he said, giving me all of his attention.

"I think we need to consider that it might not have been a random accident. That Sloan might have been the target."

Barry let out his breath, and I could practically read his thoughts. He thought I was wrong and had gone off the deep end with my illusion of being a detective. His superior detective gut told him it was just what it seemed: something that had been meant to be a mean-spirited prank to get Miami to give up her plan. But even before Adele's video, I had mentioned to Dinah that I had a feeling it might have deliberately been aimed at Sloan. It was what my gut told me. But Barry would argue that his gut was superior to my gut.

He gave me a funny look. "What are you thinking? Your eyes are moving every which way, as if you're having a conversation with someone."

"You don't want to know."

"Yes, I do. Is it something about me? I hope I didn't upset you when I told you about Carol's cooking."

"Why would I be upset about her cooking?" I said, trying my best to sound like I couldn't care less. I wasn't sure what to tell him and figured, what the heck, I'd go for the truth. "I was thinking that you'd say that your gut was superior to mine."

"Huh?"

"You know how you're always saying detectives have a gut feeling about who did something. I have gut feelings too. This time it's that whoever flew the drone into the yard meant to hit Sloan."

He was shaking his head with disbelief. "My gut is based on years of experience of dealing with criminals. Do you have any backup for your gut?"

"There's a video," I said. "You know about Adele and her vlog. She's going by 'The Adele' now," I said with a chuckle. "She was taping when it all happened. She showed the video to me, and it looked like that drone was going after Sloan, and then all that stuff dropped on her." Barry had eaten all of his potatoes, and I offered him more, which he gladly took. "It's not really dinner conversation, but you've never told me what the cause of death was."

He seemed to be debating with himself. "I thought our deal was that I don't have to tell you anything."

I rolled my eyes at him. "C'mon, it's not fair that you have all the information."

"It's not really necessary for you to know anything in order to do what I asked, but okay. There hasn't been an autopsy, but since everyone but you believes it was a prank gone wrong, they have settled on the idea that she was struck on the head, either by the drone itself or the rocks that were in the bag of garbage, hard enough to knock her out, and she landed face first, so when the payload of garbage fell on her, it suffocated her."

I looked at my plate with sudden distaste. All I could think of was the stench. Barry seemed unconcerned as he finished off his potatoes.

He put his napkin on his plate. "Unless, you have anything else, I have to go." I offered him something to take home for Jeffrey.

"Thanks, but he's eating with Carol and her kids."

I forced myself to smile as I walked him to the door. "How nice."

"If you get me that video of Adele's, I'll look at it," he said.

"Really?" I said, surprised.

He smiled. "My gut isn't as closed-minded as you think."

Chapter Eighteen

"**B**arry's got a girlfriend," I blurted out when Dinah came up to the table in the yarn department Tuesday afternoon. We were both early for the Hooker gathering.

My friend surprised me by smiling at my announcement. "Well, finally," she said. "I thought the two of you would never figure it out." Then I got it. She thought I was being facetious.

"Not me," I said. When would she ever get that it wasn't going to happen? "He has a real girlfriend. An ER nurse named Carol. She probably keeps her emotions together just the way he does. The two of them are probably like two robots."

"You sound jealous," my friend said.

"Me? Jealous? Of course not. It's just that Barry really needs someone who could pry open his emotional safe."

"And who would that be?" Dinah said with a pointed look.

"Not me. Barry and I settled that a long time ago. Remember, he even told me that I should stick with Mason because Mason could give me what I need and he couldn't."

"And what was that again, that Barry couldn't give you?"

I gave her an exasperated sigh. "Remember, Barry is married to his job, and he's too controlling. He always has to be in charge. And that whole emotional thing too. It makes me crazy how he can keep all his feelings locked behind that blank face."

"Until you tempt him with food and his hunger surges forward." She got a mischievous glint in her eye, "Or you tempt him with something else."

"I don't want to talk about it anymore," I said decisively. "I'd rather tell you what happened after we left Miami's." Dinah seemed disappointed, but she listened to my story of being chased around the yard by the SUV and about the note it left behind. I was surprised by her reaction.

She laughed. "How scary could a toy be?"

"Pretty scary," I said. "Did I mention that it was big and it let out a creepy laugh just before it flew away." As I heard myself say the last part, it did seem more funny than menacing, so I added, "You had to be there to appreciate it."

"So I take it that you're going to ignore the warning," Dinah said.

"I don't like that whoever did it knows where I live," I said. "But I don't think it's anything serious and was meant as more of a nuisance, like dropping a bag of stinky garbage as a protest. I thought back to our time at Miami's. "I really wish we'd been able to go into that open area." I smiled thinking of it. "I think I was wrong when I called it a secret garden. It's more like a garden full of secrets."

Just then Mrs. Shedd came into to the yarn department. She was smiling, then her brows furrowed. "Where is everybody?"

"It's summer," I said. "Our meetings get more casual."

"I was hoping you could update me on how the kits are coming and about the event. There seem to be so many loose ends to tie up before your time off." She seemed frazzled.

"No worries," I began. I went and got a completed kit to show her. I'd taken a photograph of the three scarves I had and added it to the pattern that Elise had given me. The paper was folded in half so the picture and name of the kit showed clearly. I took out the sheet and showed her the other side before opening the bag so she could see the three skeins of yarn and a hook. "We'll have plenty of kits ready for the event, and I'll be sure enough are made up for the time I'm going to be gone."

She seemed impressed.

"There are already signs around the bookstore about the event, and between Mr. Royal and Adele, it'll be mentioned on social media. Our starting-from-scratch clinic should be a draw." I threw a lot of excitement into my voice, and it worked its magic.

The tension left her face and she smiled. "I know I can always count on you," she said before walking away.

"Let me know if you need any help," Dinah said.

"Thank you," I said before letting out a sigh. "What happens if Barry's case isn't settled before I go?"

"He'll have to finish alone." Dinah said. "Barry's a big boy, and I'm sure he'll be able to manage." Dinah pulled out the Serendipity scarf she'd started and began to crochet.

Our conversation ended as the other Hookers arrived. "I brought one of my daughter's friends," Rhoda said. "I'm always talking about the group, and she was interested in seeing what we're about. And we wanted to see how the crochet clinic idea would work on a real person."

As I went to introduce myself, I made eye contact, and we both froze. Now I knew her name was Bitsy, and she was the resident of the cul-de-sac who had vented at me.

She looked at the ground, as if she was hoping it would open up and offer her an escape. "I didn't realize that you were in the crochet group. I'm sorry if I went off at you. Obviously, you have nothing to do with what's going on in that house. We're just all overwrought from what she's doing and what it's already done to our street." She turned to Rhoda. "Thanks for bringing me, but I'm afraid I've made a very bad impression, and I think I should leave."

"Stay," I said. "We all have our moments."

"Yes, stay," Sheila said, pushing her hair back from her round face. Her eyes darted from side to side nervously. I hadn't realized she'd joined us and heard the whole thing. "Take it from one who knows, crochet will help you cope."

It took a little more coaxing, and Bitsy took a seat. Rhoda handled the introductions as Bitsy apologized again. "We were hoping a family would move in. We do something to celebrate every holiday. I put it together, but the whole cul-de-sac takes part. You can see how having a bunch of strangers wandering around ruins it. And her business has brought bad stuff to our block. We're all suspicious of each other now, wondering which one of us is behind what happened to Sloan." She bowed her head. The way she said the name made me think she knew her.

"Then she was a friend of yours?" I asked.

"She sold us our house. That's why I was so surprised that she'd help that woman do something that was so bad for the cul-de-sac. The reason we picked our house was because she pointed out that it was a little community that we could have barbecues with and sing Christmas carols with." Her expression dimmed. "But I guess she didn't really care, and she'd do anything for a buck."

I considered whether I should mention Sloan's sister, Donna, and how Sloan seemed to be supporting her, but I decided to just let Bitsy talk.

"Sloan did some work for my parents. They use Zoom a lot for their business and wanted to have the right backdrop. Sloan worked in set decoration, so who better? It was all about how it appeared on a screen. I doubt anyone my folks deal with realizes their office is really a bedroom. Sloan set up a pedestal to shoot them at the most flattering angle. She painted the wall behind them a dark blue-gray with white trim, and hung some shelves. She filled one with books she got from somewhere. But the most prominent shelf was filled with awards and trophies. She took anything they had, even my brother's old T-ball trophies. Anything to fill the space and make it look impressive. And it worked. They get compliments on their 'office' all the time."

Rhoda had taken out a hook and some worsted-weight yarn. Bitsy watched as Rhoda made a knot and started a chain. Then she did the same. She picked up single crochet with ease, but not much enthusiasm.

"I'm good at crafts. I make a lot of the decorations," she said. "It's really my husband who's the most upset. Darwin's worried about our property value. He might get transferred, and then we'd have to sell." Her cell began to ring, and she excused herself to answer it. "I'm afraid I have to go. My kids need to be picked up."

Something was nagging at me as I watched her walk away. I realized that Darwin was the man I'd seen that first day, with the remote-control car. Was he behind the SUV that had chased me around the yard? I wished I'd thought of it before Bitsy took off.

Rhoda took back the hook and yarn and shrugged. "I guess crochet isn't her thing."

Adele whirled in and flopped in her chair with a world-weary sigh, but at the same time making sure we all noticed the crocheted tunic she was wearing. It was made of mitered granny squares and was both over the top and stunning at the same time. She went on wailing about the trials of being an internet influencer. "The fans just can't get enough of The Adele. More, they want more and more. How much do I have to give them before they're satisfied?" Her late arrival to the group was odd, but then I understood. She hadn't wanted to be confronted by Bitsy in front of the group.

I urged everyone to work on the scarves so we'd have plenty of samples for the event. Once everyone was working,

I took advantage of the peaceful moment to approach Adele about the video of the drone. I was sure that once I showed it to Barry, he'd agree with me. I wasn't sure how I was going to get her to send it to me, but the first step was to see it again.

I tried being extra friendly, which was a big mistake, and she saw right through it. "What do you want, Pink?" she said as her hook moved the yarn, making a long strand of chain stitches.

"That video you showed me of the drone. Could you send me a copy?"

"What for?" Adele said, eyeing me pointedly. "Oh, I know. You're probably investigating." She gave a nod to Dinah. "You two are probably playing your detective act."

I endured her comments, hoping it would help me get the short scene.

"Sure I could send it to you, but"—she feigned regret— "I deleted it right after we talked."

Chapter Nineteen

I was thrilled when Dinah suggested a girls' night. An evening in her She Cave was preferable to being stuck in my bedroom now that Peter and Gabby had returned from their trip to Santa Barbara. I also thought we could work on the Serendipity kits for the event, since it was coming up and most of the yarn was still in bins or bags.

First, I went home to take care of the animals. It was so different when my younger son Samuel was at home. He always automatically took care of them all. Peter was too busy with his wheeling and dealing to even notice their presence except when he wanted them out of the way.

Gabby had remained mostly a shadow. I'd barely spent any time alone with her, and Peter seemed to do the talking for both of them. I didn't know who she was, what she cared about, etcetera. So, when she came into the kitchen while I was feeding the crew, I seized the moment.

I suggested we have a cup of tea and sit in the yard. By now the heat of the day was past, and the air was soft and a pleasant kind of warm. She agreed and I made a pot of tea, doing the whole routine of warming the pot and then using loose leaf tea. I brought the tea cups and pot out on a tray, and we sat down. She was pretty, I thought, if you liked uptight ambitious types.

"I'm sorry, I didn't ask you how you take it. Should I get milk and sugar?"

"This is fine," she said, looking at the amber liquid in her cup. Her tone didn't match her words, and I went in and got a little pitcher of milk and the sugar bowl. She used both.

I started the conversation the easy way, with a question. "Where's Peter?"

"He had a meeting at Fox," she said matter-of-factly. "He should have taken me with him. I have an impressive list of credits. I could have been a showrunner if I hadn't gone to work with Peter."

"I'm sure he'll include you when the time is right. It's great that he's trying to put something new together. I know neither of you want to be here." I left off the other part, that I didn't want them to be there either.

She stayed mute.

"I should get in touch with your mother. We can start putting together ideas for a baby shower." I glanced around the patio. "We could have something out here."

She didn't even try to hide her eye roll. "Don't worry about it. Mums has it covered. We're going to have it at my favorite restaurant on Melrose." The street was over the hill in L.A. and lined with trendy restaurants and shops. Her tone was icy cold, and I regretted suggesting the tea. It was obvious that she didn't like me, and I wanted to let her know she was making a mistake. I got along with everybody, even Adele. I was going to be G-ma, or Grand Molly or whatever version of grandmother that I got. I bet it wasn't going to be at "Mums's" house when they were looking for some place to drop off Baby Pink. (I was afraid to think what they'd chosen for a name. Everybody wanted something unique these days. What if they named the baby something like Pistachio or even a made-up word like "Maha"?)

She put down her cup and gave me the kind of look that made me feel marginalized and old. "Peter told me that you were some kind of Nancy Drew girl detective." She rethought her words. "Make that 'mature woman detective.' He was joking, wasn't he?"

Now I was the one keeping silent. What should I do? Lie and keep the peace or stir things up. She needed to know that G-ma was still in the thick of things. "I prefer to think of myself more like Sherlock Holmes."

* * *

"How did she react?" Dinah asked when I finished recounting the story.

"She looked horrified," I said, adding a laugh as I remembered how she'd almost dropped her cup. "Then she said she had to go, that she was meeting some people in Santa Monica to network. She asked me if I understood what that meant."

"Really?" Dinah said, wincing. "She sounds almost as bad as Commander's daughter." We were sitting in her She

193

Cave. I'd brought over sub sandwiches, with brownies for dessert, along with a bin of yarn and bags so we could work on the Serendipity kits.

"Enough about her," Dinah said. "What did you think about what Bitsy said?"

I laughed. "Good idea. We can play our Sherlock Holmes game." I put down my sandwich that oozed with more mayonnaise and dressing than I would have ever put on a sandwich that I made, which is why I'd given the job to Mark's Sub Shop. "I hope Commander doesn't object," I said.

She nodded. "It's no problem. He thinks it's great. Well, as long as we're just playing the game here and not going out and hunting down clues like we've done before."

"So, then, what do we know?" I began. "Bitsy and Darwin live in the house we named the All-American." I stopped myself as I thought for a moment. "He could be the one."

Dinah nodded, remembering him.

I got up and started to pace. "She said the neighbors are suspicious of each other now because they all think that one of them is responsible for the stinky seafood drop and the other vandalism that has ruined the idyllic peace of their cul-de-sac—before Miami has even rented one room. She said Darwin was more upset than she was. And we know he's into remote-control toys. And I was tormented by a remote-control SUV. How much of a jump is it from remote-control cars to a drone?"

"Sherlock would consider him a likely suspect," Dinah said. "But how do we find out for sure?" she said with a shrug. She finished her food and was now selecting yarn for the kits and putting them in the bags. "Maybe we should look at it another way. We've never considered where they got that garbage. It seemed to be mostly disgusting crab and lobster shells. I guess the why is obvious—the most stink for the buck."

We both cringed, thinking of the eyes of fish heads and the terrible stench of it all.

"I think it's safe to deduce that stuff came from a restaurant or market," I said. "I think I'll bring that up to Barry."

By the time I left, we had bagged a lot of yarn, and I had decided to break the rules and contact Barry first.

I knew he'd said he would call me, but what was he going to do, arrest me? I didn't wait until I got home but called when I was sitting in my car outside Dinah's.

It occurred to me that he might not even answer the call when he saw my number come up. It rang four times, then five, and I was about to hang up when he answered.

"Greenberg," he said in his professional voice. I knew he knew it was me since my cell number would have appeared on his screen. I was surprised when he reacted so distantly, but then I didn't know where I'd reached him and who else was around.

"I have something for you," I said, trying to be as cryptic as possible.

"Okay. I'll be in touch." And with that he hung up.

Okay, it must have been a really bad time for him to be that short. Maybe he and the nurse were just finishing a family evening.

I drove the short distance to my house. I could tell from the cars in the driveway that Peter and Gabby were home. No doubt Gabby had told him about teatime, and I'd probably hear some reprimand from him for talking about the shower.

I was sitting in the driveway, thinking about which door I should go in, when my cell phone rang. I didn't even look at the caller ID. I knew it was Barry.

"Molly Pink," I said in my version of a professional voice.

"Not funny," he said. "I told you I'd call you."

"Oh no, did I cause a problem?" I said in feigned distress.

"No," he said offering no more explanation. "I'm on my way. What door should I come to?"

"The Eagles have landed," I said in a vain attempt to be funny, "so we should keep it on the down low."

He said he'd meet me at the den door.

I went in through the kitchen, feeling there was no reason to sneak into my own house whether the eagles had landed or not. I was still glad that the kitchen was empty and even gladder when I heard the sound of a television and saw the door to their room closed. I really wasn't up for being treated like an intruder. There was the clatter of claws on the wood floor as Cosmo, Felix, Mr. Kitty, and Cat Woman came across the house to greet me. I gave them a round of treats and promised them some outside time when Barry left.

He was waiting by the den door when I opened it. "You can relax. They're out of the way for now." I glanced toward the living room. "But I can't predict what they'll do." I pointed at the door that led to the master suite.

The animals rushed in with us, and I closed the door, letting out a sigh of relief.

He went directly into my room, but he didn't sit. "Okay, let's have it," he said, holding out his hand.

"What do you mean?" I said, confused.

"You said you had something for me. It's Adele's video that is supposed to show the drone zeroing in on Sloan, right?"

I was stunned. I'd forgotten about the video once I knew she'd deleted it. What was I going to do? Stall, hoping he'd forget.

"Before we get to that, I want to ask you why I can't be the one to call when I have something to tell you." I stood in front of him with my arms crossed. "It's because you have to be the one to call all the shots, isn't it?"

"And here we go again," he said in a singsong voice. He let out a tired sigh and crossed his arms. He was out of his suit and tie uniform and wearing jeans that were soft and pale from washing, with a blue pocket T-shirt. Even though he was in his fifties, he could carry off jeans without them having the "dad" look. When we had dated, he'd kept fit using weights. I assumed he still did, especially now that he had Carol. I started to picture the two of them, side by side at the stove, but pushed away the image.

"What do you mean?" I asked.

"You don't know where you're reaching me. I could be in a car with a partner, or off duty with . . ." He seemed uneasy. "I could be with Carol." He cleared his throat. "I don't want any of them to hear my phone calls."

"In other words, just like I said, you want to be in control."

"But I *am* the one in charge. I'm the detective and you're my helper," he said. "Now how about that video?"

"About that," I said, "there's a little problem." I paused and took a breath, realizing my stall tactic hadn't worked. "Adele deleted it. But I'm telling you it really did show the drone going after Sloan."

Barry laughed and looked around at the assorted animals. "Really? That's right up there with 'the dog ate my homework.'"

I cringed, my worst fears having come to fruition. "It is not," I said defiantly. "The video really did exist."

"Even if it did, it's gone now. It's all good and well for you to give your opinion, but I'd need something to back it up in order to pursue it."

"Did you ever think about where all those seafood shells came from?" I said, trying to change the subject.

"That's what you called me about?"

"We never discussed it, so I thought you might have overlooked that detail," I said.

Barry leveled his gaze at me. "You can't be serious. Of course I checked it out."

"Are you going to share what you found out?" I asked.

When he hesitated, I jumped in. "Never mind. I'll figure it out for myself," I said. "I have resources. I've been making friends with the people who live in the cul-de-sac."

"So then you know the Yanas?"

"The who? I asked.

"The Yanas," he repeated. "They own the Seafood Cooker. It's in a strip mall on Ventura. Everything is served in plastic bags, and they dump the contents on the table."

"It sounds like you've been there," I said.

He seemed uncomfortable. "We're not here to talk about my restaurant visits."

"But you have been there, haven't you?" And the rest of my question was *with who?*—but I kept that part to myself.

He blew out his breath. "Yes, I've eaten there, but that's not the point. The Yanas said they knew nothing about anything and that the shells and residue from their restaurant go into a dumpster behind the restaurant that anyone has access to." He seemed to be considering something. "When I asked if I could look around their yard, they refused. I had to leave it at that. I didn't have enough to get a search warrant for them or any of the others on Starlight Court.

"They have all said that they had nothing to do with the drone attack, and I don't have anything to prove otherwise. I should correct that. I didn't speak to the people who live in the house on the end since they're on a cruise and weren't there when it happened."

He let his arms unfold. "That's why I brought you in. I figured they wouldn't see you as a threat and might drop something useful."

"So which was it? Were you with your partner or your nurse?

"You're not much of a detective if you have to ask," he said. "I'll give you a clue. Check out the clothes and footwear." He stuck out his foot, clad in a sneaker.

"Okay, so it was the nurse."

"Her name is Carol," Barry said. He'd leveled his gaze at me again. "If I didn't know that you're practically married to Mason already, I'd think you were jealous."

"Of course not. I'm glad you've found someone who fits in with your lifestyle." I didn't mean to, but there was an edge in my voice.

"You still haven't gotten over that I left you at a restaurant once," he said.

"You left in the middle of meals more than once. I never knew if you'd be around for dessert." I couldn't believe that I'd gone back to this old argument. There were others things too. A trip to Hawaii he had planned without discussing it with me. But why was I bringing any of this up, even if only in my mind?

There was a flash of emotion in his dark eyes, and he looked around the room. "I guess I hoped that when I was here with you, I made up for the times when I wasn't." The moment of heat disappeared behind his professional demeanor. "I think we got off the subject. The owners of the seafood place live in the fourth house from Holiday House. Their name is Yana. See what you can do."

"You actually gave me an assignment," I said.

He shrugged. "I guess I did."

He was getting ready to leave. I turned abruptly and almost lost my balance. He grabbed my elbow to steady me,

then let go without a hint of whether he'd had any reaction. It bugged me how he could just shut off his feelings.

Felix, Cosmo, Princess, and I walked Barry out into the yard. The dogs rushed off in the darkness to do their thing. Barry lingered for a moment, watching them. He seemed almost wistful as he stared out at the yard, and I imagined he was remembering times we'd spent there together. But when he turned back to me, he was all business again. "I'll be in touch. Remember, that's *I'll be in touch*."

*   *   *

It was almost midnight when Mason called. "Sorry for calling so late," he said. Despite the hour, his voice sounded animated. He'd gone back to Kansas on Monday.

"The plans are coming together. I arranged for the time off," I said, and I could almost hear him smile.

"It'll be so much nicer when you're here with me. We'll fly back to Topeka together on Tuesday."

"The She La La's tour ends this week, and Samuel will be home to take care of my animals," I said.

Mason noticed that my voice sounded a little warbly. "It'll be okay," he said in a reassuring tone. "I promise we'll have some fun too. You know I'm not an all-work kind of guy. I've already staked out some places to go, but the company is more important than the place."

"I agree," I said.

"I've been thinking that we could do this pro bono work for a few years. Hopefully we'll help a bunch of people get their lives back. Then," he said with a dramatic flourish, "it could be just you and me, off to see the world."

I didn't know what to say. It was so much a reminder that we were talking about more than a week.

"Are you still there?" he asked after a moment. "I'd hate to be making my offer to dead air."

"I'm here," I said. "Now you've given me even more to process. I have a lot going on here. There's the event at the bookstore, and I sort of got involved in trying to find out who was behind the drone drop. You know me—I hate to leave anything hanging. I heard all the neighbors denied having anything to do with it, and there's no way to prove who's lying." I told him my theory that it might have been something different, that Sloan might have been the target, and maybe it wasn't an accident after all.

"Is it just a hunch, or do you have any backup?" he asked. I mentioned Adele's video and what had happened to it.

"Leave it to The Adele to mess things up. But it might have just looked like the drone was after the woman who died. This could be one of those times when the obvious answer is the correct one. Someone created a nuisance, implying they'd do something again when she had the place up and running. Those rentals make it or break it based on reviews. The neighbors are all probably stonewalling the cops, and the only evidence is some stinking garbage since they don't seem to be able to track down the drone. The cops will realize they have nothing and put it on the back burner."

I didn't know what to say, and I heard him chuckle. "But I guess *you're* not putting it on the back burner."

"Right," I said.

"That's why I want you working with me. You never give up," he said.

"Neither do you."

"I guess that makes us made for each other," he said with a chuckle.

Chapter Twenty

I wasn't sure who would show up for the Hookers' social crocheting on Wednesday. Rhoda was already at the table when I entered the yarn department. Not that I was surprised. She was the most dependable of the group. Her skeins of yarn were already on the table, and her hook was moving. Sheila caught up with me and pulled out a chair. She worked almost next door, making it easy for her to come by.

"I'm glad I can depend on you two," I said. "I need to have as many finished scarves as possible to use as samples for the event."

"I've finished with the first skein," Rhoda said, holding up her work done in a royal blue. She looked over the skein of pale blue mohair and the one of a delft blue with a nubby texture she'd chosen for the project. "Any suggestions on which one I should go with next?" she asked.

"Have you thought about switching the mohair skein for one in orange?" I asked. "The contrast would be striking."

I had just gone over to the bins of yarn to see what I could find when I sensed someone walk in behind me. I looked up, hoping it was another Hooker, but it was Ms. Mayonnaise from the book club. I'd wanted to talk to her since I'd realized she lived in Starlight Court. The idea of remembering a name by associating it with something had really backfired. I had no problem remembering the *something*, but her name kept eluding me. The worst part was that she spent a lot of time at the bookstore.

She always seemed neatly dressed, but on the blah side.

She glanced at the table with interest. "What's going on?" she asked.

"Anastasia," I said, remembering her name a little too abruptly, yet again. To cover myself, I rushed to add something to it. "I guess you've never been in the bookstore around this time." I gestured toward the table just as Dinah and CeeCee arrived. "This is the crochet group, the Tarzana Hookers."

She laughed at the name, which was the usual reaction. "You're right, I'm usually here earlier or later." She turned to the crocheters at the table. "This place is my home away from home. I love to read and it's nice to have some place to go now that I'm retired. It used to be rush home from work to make dinner." She shrugged. "But my kids are on their own now, and my husband has decided that frozen meals are just the right portion for him. I overcooked his once, so now he insists on doing it himself. It leaves me with a lot of time to do what I want." The way she sighed at the end made me think she wasn't so happy about all the freedom. She looked over the yarn on the table. "What are you making?"

"They're called Serendipity scarves," Rhoda said.

"They're for an upcoming event we're having on Saturday," I said. "We're going to have kits to make these scarves. The crochet skills are very basic, and we'll have experts on hand to teach anyone to crochet who's interested. Tell your friends."

Her face lit up. "I will."

She seemed ready to leave, and I vowed not to let her get away this time. I got up and stood next to her. "What did your kids think about seeing you on the news?" I asked. The rest of the group had started talking among themselves and weren't paying any attention to our conversation.

"You saw me, then?" she said, and I nodded. "That reporter nabbed me before I could get away. I didn't want to say anything about anything, but she's relentless. She wanted to know if I had any idea who was behind the drone. Then she asked how we felt about that woman turning the house into a short-term rental." She shook her head with dismay, then leaned closer and dropped her voice. "We live in the house next door. My husband is livid about what that woman's doing, and it's all I hear about from him. Caleb tried to organize the neighbors to do something, but nobody wanted to get involved." She let out a sigh. "I didn't realize what a fussbudget he was until he retired and he was home all the time. I'm so relieved when he goes over to his friend's garage. He has a workshop set up, and they make models or something."

I swallowed and got ready to ask the big question. "What about that business with the drone?"

She looked horrified. "I'm sure whoever did it didn't intend to hurt that woman. My husband said he thought someone was trying to give her a taste of what might happen when she had guests."

"You probably know the other neighbors. Do you think one of them was behind it?" I asked.

"Probably, but I don't know which one. The police asked the same question."

"And what did you tell the police?" I asked.

She shrugged. "I said I didn't know anything." She paused for a moment, as if considering her words. "I wasn't going to say anything about the neighbors, well, unless I absolutely knew they sent the drone. But everyone was upset. Bitsy—she and Darwin live in the house next to mine—creates all the holiday parties and events for the cul-de-sac. They're just for the neighbors and some invited guests. She's sure Ms. Wintergarten will offer the events to the renters. Bitsy might have gone a little over the top in the kind of sleazy people she imagined renting the rooms, but really, none of us know what kind of people that young woman will rent to. The O'Malleys' house is right across from 'Holiday House,' as she calls it. They travel a lot and are worried that the renters will do things like treat their front yard like a park. It doesn't help that Ms. Wintergarten has refused to even talk to any of us."

For a moment she looked wistful. "We moved in when the houses on Starlight Court were all new. All the families had kids. We all did PTA together, and the whole cul-de-sac celebrated the kids' birthdays. We still know the neighbors, but not in the same way." She stopped and laughed nervously. "I didn't mean to go on so."

It seemed she was going to stop, so I threw out a question. "Didn't I hear the Yanas own a restaurant?"

Anastasia leaned closer and dropped her voice. "I heard that they tried to make a deal with Ms. Wintergarten. They wanted her to leave an advertisement with coupons for their seafood place in the rooms. My husband said the Yanas tried to sell her on it being the neighborly thing to do, but it didn't work."

She looked around the table. "Maybe I'll stay and watch. This could be something for me."

I'd barely had a chance to introduce her when her husband showed up. He was a tall, dull-looking guy and seemed impatient as he came up to the table. She started to explain who we were, but he just waved for her to leave.

"I'm going to come to your event," she said as she left. I heard him ask her in a grumbly tone what event she was talking about.

"What a pain," Rhoda said. "Thank heavens my Hal is nothing like that."

Dinah hung back with me while I did my usual cleanup. "What were you two talking about?" she asked.

I explained that Anastasia was one of the residents on the cul-de-sac who had plenty to say about the neighbors and who had specifically mentioned the Yanas.

"Wow, it doesn't sound too good for them," Dinah said. "Owning a restaurant means they had the means." She laughed at her own pun. "It sounds like they had an extra reason to be angry with Miami, so they had a motive too. All that's left is opportunity."

"Are you in the mood for seafood?" I asked.

* * *

"There's the Seafood Cooker," Dinah said as I steered the Greenmobile up Ventura Boulevard. It was the main street in the southern part of the San Fernando Valley and looped through all the communities along the base of the Santa Monica Mountains. I made a quick turn into the strip mall parking lot. "What's the plan?" Dinah asked as I pulled into a spot.

"We eat," I said with a laugh. "And it would help if we could somehow uncover that the Yanas have an illegal drone." On the way over, I'd explained what Barry had said about them.

"I doubt they'd keep it at the restaurant if they had one," Dinah countered.

The strip mall was L-shaped, and the Seafood Cooker was in the corner. There were umbrella tables outside around a fountain and more tables inside. The front was decorated with a giant lobster.

It was an informal eatery where you placed your order at the counter and the food was brought to you. As expected, the interior had a nautical theme, with the menu on a board over the counter.

While Dinah was looking at the menu, I was checking out the man and woman behind the counter, who gave off a vibe of being in charge. They weren't wearing name tags, but I was sure they must be Mr. and Mrs. Yana. They appeared to be in their forties and were both wearing white polo shirts.

"Are you ready to order?" the woman asked.

"It's our first time here," I said. "I haven't had a chance to check the menu."

"It's very easy. You pick what fish or seafood you want and then the sauce, spice level, and whatever you'd like with it."

I smiled and nodded and looked up at the board. I hadn't known what I was going to do until we got there. But now I had an idea. Dinah was an expert at picking up on what I was thinking and playing along.

"It all sounds so good, but it's hard to focus with all that going on," I said, making it seem I was speaking to Dinah but loud enough for the couple behind the counter to hear. "I can't believe the McPhersons signed up with that SleepOver App."

"You know it," Dinah said jumping in. "Great for them—they'll be raking in the cash—but terrible for us neighbors."

I seemed to be looking at the menu, but really I was giving it a moment for my words to sink in before I said what I hoped would get the Yanas talking. I caught a glimpse of them out of the corner of my eye, and they were both obviously listening. "There must be something we can do to stop them." I threw up my hands in mock frustration.

The words hung in the air for a moment before the man started to speak. "I feel your pain. The same thing happened on our block. But there's nothing legal you can do."

It seemed like he wanted to say more, but his wife gave him the evil eye and turned to us.

"If you're having trouble deciding, our crab legs are very popular," she said.

I took her suggestion and ordered the crab legs with mild garlic butter sauce, along with corn and veggies. Dinah ordered the shrimp with the same accompaniments.

"I just want you to know you'll have to peel the shrimp, eyes and all," Mr. Yana said. "I just like to remind our guests so there won't be any surprises."

"And now what?" I asked, looking around. "Do we wait for the food, or do you have a drone deliver it?" I tried to say it like it was a joke, but they both appeared unnerved by my comment.

"We'll bring the food to you. On a tray, by a human," Mr. Yana said.

Dinah and I took an umbrella table outside. The day was cooling off, and there was a nice breeze. A few minutes later, Mr. Yana came out and covered the table with paper, then poured the food on top of it. "Enjoy," he said. "Careful with the shrimp shells. Don't let them fall in your purse. They can make quite a stink."

Chapter
Twenty-One

I was tempted to call Barry and tell about how much I'd gotten from the Yanas. The way they'd reacted when I'd mentioned a drone, and then the comment about the shrimp shells stinking had to mean something. But he'd made such a fuss about my calling him before, I decided to wait.

After dinner, Dinah and I parted company, and I headed home. I picked up on the stormy vibe between Peter and Gabby before I'd even cleared my kitchen. I didn't hear any words, but the tone was definitely angry. As I crossed the house, I heard a door slam, and then someone stormed out.

Peter didn't have to worry about locking the animals in my room since they went there on their own. But as soon as they saw me, I got a happy welcome, and they all followed me back across the house, even Blondie and Princess. I fed them all and then let the dogs have some yard time. I felt bad not letting the cats out, but it was dark, and I was worried Cat Woman would find a "gift" for me.

I grabbed a cup of tea and took it outside with me. The temperature had dropped, and I was just short of needing a sweater. Even during the summer, evenings were cool. I sat for a long time enjoying the peace of my backyard and thinking of everything I had to do the next day. I was still sitting under the stars when Mason called on my cell phone. We did a little catch-up, then he said, "It will be so nice to have you with me. When everything is done for the day and it's just me in the hotel room, it gets pretty lonely."

"I understand, though at the moment I'm enjoying lonely, at least alone time. Living with Samuel is easy, but Peter and Gabby are a different story. They make it feel like *I'm* living with *them*."

"We'll have fun," he said. "I have one of those suites with a bedroom and a living room, complete with all the comforts like a microwave and refrigerator. We can make popcorn and watch a movie."

He asked about my day, and I told him about our trip to the Seafood Cooker. I had to pick and choose my words so as not to give away that Barry had asked me to see what I could find out.

I made it sound like it was all my idea to talk to the Yanas. "I keep calling them Mr. and Mrs. since I don't know their names." I heard some rustling come through the phone.

"It's Lucia and Massey Yana," he said. "And they have three teenage boys. Do you care about their names?

"I don't think so. What are you looking at?" I asked with a laugh.

"When you're here with me, you'll see we have all kinds of cool online information services available. Hmm . . . that's interesting."

"What? What did you find?"

"Apparently they've refinanced their house a number of times, and they're really in debt."

I heard him chuckle. "See, Sunshine, I can help you even when I'm far away."

I thanked him and then we signed off.

It was looking worse and worse for the Yanas.

I got to the bookstore early the next morning. There weren't many customers, and story time was in full swing. I caught a glimpse of Adele's outfit. She was wearing a big version of an old-fashioned little girl dress, complete with a sash tied at the back and a pair of Mary Jane's. I stopped outside to hear what she was reading and recognized "Rice Pudding," an A.A. Milne poem. Then I understood the outfit: she was a giant version of the little girl who was acting up. Clearly something Adele knew a lot about.

My house had been peaceful when I left that morning. Either Peter and Gabby were out somewhere or still asleep. I was just glad not to have to deal with them.

I went to my cubicle to finish up the computer file for the inserts for the kits and then printed up a stack of them. I snagged a Red Eye and a plateful of Bob's current cookie bar offering before heading back to the yarn department.

I'd put out the word that I needed help putting the kits together today. Eduardo had needed to beg off because he was supervising the placement of the glass cases at the new location of his store. Dinah had a summer school class and said she'd come afterward. CeeCee had a rehearsal and hoped to show up later. Sheila promised to spend her lunch break working with us, and who knew about Adele? Rhoda was already at the table. She held up two more of the scarves she'd already finished that we could use as samples. Elise came in behind me.

"I felt bad about letting you down," she said. "I figured I could give you an hour before I have a showing."

I put the snacks on the table and invited them to help themselves. "Here are the inserts," I said, putting the stack of sheets on the table. I showed how, when they were folded in half, they fit perfectly into a plastic bag. I put out a stack of hooks and uncovered the bin with the kits we'd already started. "Those just need the insert and the hooks, and then we'll be making the kits from scratch. It'll be your choice of yarn," I said. "You can use the samples as inspiration." I looked over the scarves on the table. "I love the mixture of textures and colors. These are beautiful. I'm sure that once people see them and understand how easy they are to make, we'll sell out."

"Music to my ears," Mrs. Shedd said, walking into the yarn department. "Thank you all for your help." She admired the scarves on the table. "I appreciate how you are all part of the bookstore family." Then she turned to me. "I need the list of titles the book club came up with for the next few months. You said you had it."

I took a few moments to think about it and remember I'd stuck it in my tote bag. I went to get it, thinking it was in my cubicle. When it wasn't there, a vision flashed in my mind of leaving it in Miami's guesthouse when I had gone for the yarn.

"I left it in my tote bag. I'll pick it up later and bring it you as soon as I can," I said.

"Good. I want to have everything in order before your time off," she said before going back to her office.

Dinah was the only one who knew all the details about my time off. I'd been rather vague about it to the rest of them and had said I was taking a trip with Mason. Nobody paid much attention anyway.

Elise pulled me aside. "Remember how Miami said Sloan was selling off some single items from the house? I found the list and the prices, but not where she'd placed them and whether they sold. All I know is the money certainly isn't in the account."

"Do you think Sloan was cheating her?"

Elise shrugged. "I don't know. But Miami seems very upset about it. The money is all mixed up."

"We better get to work," I said. I took a bunch of yarn and put it in the center of the table along with the other supplies.

Sheila did come during her lunch break, and Adele drifted in for a while as well. CeeCee dropped in after her rehearsal, but even with all the help, there was still a lot to be done when I stopped working on the kits in the late afternoon. I called Miami about picking up my tote bag.

She was just leaving, she said, but the guesthouse was open, and I could come by and get my bag.

I decided to stop in on my way home. It had been a long day, and when I finally got home, I wanted to take a hot bath and forget about everything.

This time, I pulled into the cul-de-sac with a different mindset. Now I knew who lived where. Anastasia and Caleb lived in the blue ranch house I'd named the Original. Bitsy and Darwin Jonquet lived in the All-American. Lucia and Massey Yanas' house was the one I called the Parking Lot. And I'd named the last house, which belonged to the O'Malleys, Colonel Mustard. It barely counted since they weren't home. A couple of teenage boys were playing basketball in the Yanas' driveway, but other than that, the short street was quiet.

I didn't worry about being seen. Everyone but the Yanas knew I had a connection to Miami's house, and I was sure the Yanas were probably at their restaurant, working on the dinner rush.

The sign for Holiday House seemed more secure now, no doubt thanks to Elise's efforts. Miami had told me to go through the gate on the side of the house. I felt a little uneasy about going in the yard when no one was there, but I had to get the tote bag.

Even though it was still August, the light reminded me of fall, and the yard was already cloaked in shadows The grass seemed freshly mowed, and the cutout section had been filled with dirt. There was no hint that anything bad had happened here. As Miami had promised, the guesthouse was unlocked, and the tote bag was just where I'd left it. I grabbed it quickly and went back outside.

I started to leave, but then I thought about that area I called the secret garden. I'd been so disoriented when Dinah and I had looked at it before, but now I thought I might be able to figure out what I was looking at. I walked behind the guesthouse and examined the wooden fence. When Dinah and I were putting away the stepladder, we had seen something that might have been a gate. I thought it had been an illusion, but as I went along the fence, I saw the hardware and realized it was real.

There was nothing to stop me from taking a quick peek back there. I left my purse and the tote bag on the ground next to the fence and pulled open the gate. It had a spring mechanism and closed behind me. Suddenly I was in an untamed world of tall grass and bushes. I looked around me, trying to orient myself. I saw some ivy-covered chain-link fencing off to my left, but then it disappeared behind tall, overgrown bushes. It was impossible to see where the wild area ended. Ahead, the bushes were in silhouette, and I imagined more growth beyond. The fence was clearly visible, and as I walked along the border of Miami's yard, the color of the wood planks changed to a darker shade, and I figured I'd reached Ms. Mayonnaise's yard. As I moved forward, I had to make my way over the uneven ground and through all the underbrush. I stepped on something that made a crunching noise. The last light of day was fading and I poked my way through the growth to see what I'd stepped on. I felt something hard and smooth, and when I lifted it above the grass, recognized a crab leg shell.

"Wow," I said out loud. The drone must have come from back here somewhere. I got close to the fence and jumped up and down, attempting to see over it into Ms. Mayonnaise's yard I got only a quick glimpse. Floodlights lit the rather plain landscaping of grass and some flowers alongside a dated-looking kidney-shaped pool.

I followed the fence, and when it changed from the dark wood to white vinyl, I knew I'd moved on to Bitsy's yard. I was able to boost myself up using one of the posts, but again only managed to stay up for a short time. I did a quick perusal, looking for the big black remote-control SUV that had chased me around my yard, but all I saw was that Bitsy had already pulled out her Halloween decorations in anticipation of decorating her front yard. A scarecrow was leaning against the back of the house, along with a bunch of tombstones. An inflatable ghost was on the ground, looking like a white puddle, near an all-season selection of remote-control cars and trucks. That was all I got before I lost my footing. The fencing changed again to a dark wood. This must be the Yanas' yard. I knew Barry would never approve of what I was doing, but would be very interested in whatever I found out. By now I'd developed a way to jump up, grab onto the top of the fence and then walk my feet up so I could pull myself up and have a look over.

Lights had come on in the Yanas' house, but the yard was still dark. There was a little daylight left in the sky, and I could just make out something in the yard. Suddenly a row of floodlights came on, and I was able to see clearly.

My mouth fell open as I looked at the line of drones on a long table. Bags of something were scattered among them. A short distance away, several tables and chairs were set up. Now I knew why the Yanas wouldn't agree to let Barry look around their house.

My hold didn't last long, and I was back on the ground now. The sky above was a translucent blue with only a hint of light, but the ground around me was all dark and mysterious. And a little creepy, as I heard something rustle in the bushes. I was going to skip the last yard since the people who lived there were away, but I'd come this far. They had more of the vinyl fencing, and I was able to use a post to hoist myself up and got a super-quick look over the top of the fence. Their sprinklers were on, making a big arc over the yard, but one of them was broken and was shooting out a stream instead of spray. It didn't register until too late, and as the sprinkler moved back over the yard, it shot water all over me.

I was sopping as I dropped down to the ground. Somehow the water had dripped into my slip-on shoes, and now my feet were sloshing around as I tried to retrace my steps. The sky was turning to a navy blue now, and the area was totally dark. I used the changes in fencing to find my way back to Miami's yard. Then I felt along the wood to find the gate. I found a slight space between the wood boards and let out a sigh of relief. I'd be out of there in no time. Except I realized with horror there was no way to open the gate from this side.

I felt a wave of panic and then willed myself to get it together. There had to be a way out somewhere.

I went back over all the fences and couldn't find an exit. I moved away from the fencing through the tangle of the open area. It was wild looking and disappeared into darkness. Finally, I saw a streetlight somewhere up ahead, glinting off something metal. I got closer and saw a large gate made out of chain link with barbed wire along the top. I let out a sigh of relief when I saw the street on the other side of it. The relief only lasted until I tried to pull open the gate and saw there was a padlock.

I felt a shiver as the breeze blew against my wet clothes. If I was panicked before, I was really freaking out now. Nobody knew where I was. I thought of how I'd been able to pull myself up to look over the fences for just a moment. Maybe if I did it again and yelled out, someone would hear me. The vinyl fence was a waste of time as it was too slick, particularly since I was wet. I found a wood fence. By now I was so disoriented, I didn't even know which one it was. I grabbed onto a post and tried to pull myself up as a sharp pain shot through my hand. I let go and fell backwards. I couldn't see it, but I knew I'd gotten a nasty splinter.

I went back over the fences again, checking for an exit, and it seemed they all had the same setup. A gate that only opened from the other side.

I was berating myself for not being one of those people whose phone was like an appendage. It hadn't occurred to me to grab mine before my adventure, and it was sitting in my purse . . . inside Miami's gate. I scrounged in my pocket to see if I'd left a piece of candy, thinking I was going to be stuck there for the night. I heard a noise in the distance.

It got louder and I recognized the thwack sound just as a bright line shone down on me. I heard a motor and metal clanking and a moment later a bunch of uniforms came at me. I was about to say thank you when one of them grabbed me and announced I was under arrest.

Of course, I tried to explain, but the cop wouldn't listen and put me in the back of a police car that smelled terrible. When we got to the station, another cop "helped me" to a metal bench and was attaching me to it.

"Hey, what about my phone call?" I said to the female officer doing the honors. She looked at me and seemed about to dismiss my request, but I guess I was such a mess she relented.

"I'm not supposed to do this," she said, pulling out her cell phone. "Give me the number. But I'll have to do the talking."

Nobody knows phone numbers anymore. You just click on something. I froze, realizing the only number I knew was my home. But did I really want Peter to bail me out? There was one other number I knew. This wasn't going to go well.

Chapter
Twenty-Two

"Arrested for being a peeping Tom?" Barry said, shaking his head as he approached the bench I was chained to. He plucked a twig from my hair and, judging from the way he looked at me, I gathered that wasn't the worst of it. A uniform came and unlocked the handcuffs, and I sat there, not sure what to do.

"You can leave," the officer said. "The person who reported you isn't pressing charges."

"Who was it?" I asked. "I bet that's who sent the drone."

Barry gave the uniform a look that I didn't quite see, but I'm assuming it implied that I was a little nutty. "C'mon Sherlock, you never ask questions when they tell you that you can go." He grabbed my hand, and I winced in pain, letting out a squeal as I pulled free.

"I have a splinter," I said. I held up my hand as evidence.

Barry turned to the uniform and asked for the first aid kit.

"You need tweezers," I said, looking over his shoulder as he examined the contents.

"Well, there aren't any," he said.

"You can't take it out without tweezers," I said.

"I'd hate to be lost in the wild with you," he said, shaking his head. "Now hold still." He grabbed my finger and pressed a piece of tape on it. I yelped with the stab of pain. He ripped the tape away and then examined the sticky side. "You're fixed," he said, showing me the piece of wood stuck to the tape.

Just to make sure, I touched the spot and sighed with relief when I felt nothing. "Let's go." He grabbed my hand again. It wasn't in any way a romantic gesture, more like dealing with an unruly teen.

He nodded to a few people he obviously knew as we headed to the door. I put my head down in embarrassment. He led the way to his Tahoe, glancing over at me. "You're soaking wet. What happened? Was the flood control ravine full of water?" He beeped open the SUV and retrieved a jacket from the back, draping it over me before I got in the passenger side.

"No. It's from a broken sprinkler," I said. "I think you might be right about the Yanas." Even with the jacket, I had a shivery feeling. It was probably the aftermath of what had happened.

"We'll get to that in a minute. First we get you home and out of those wet clothes."

"That sounds a little salacious," I said.

"You know what I mean. And by the way, your call got me in the middle of dinner. Aren't you glad I didn't insist on finishing first?"

"Okay, you got me. I'm sorry I got upset with you for leaving in the middle of a meal when we were . . . you know."

"Dating," he said with a laugh. He knew I thought it was a silly term for people our age. Just like I hadn't wanted to say he was my boyfriend.

"In a relationship," I said. Barry had pulled the Tahoe in front of my house, and I saw the car in my driveway.

"Oh, geez Louise, I forgot about Peter," I said. "I don't have my key. I can't ring the doorbell." I knew I was talking fast, but I didn't seem to be able to help it.

"Lucky for you I still have the key you gave me when Jeffrey was coming over to take care of Cosmo. "We can go in the door to the den, and your son will never have to know anything."

"But I have to get my stuff. I left my purse, phone, tote bag, and car at Miami's," I said a little franticly.

"None of it is going anywhere. Why don't you get out of those wet clothes, and then I'll take you to get your stuff.

"This is crazy, sneaking into my own house," I said as Barry silently unlocked the French door.

We slipped inside and then into the master suite. He waited in my room while I changed out of my wet clothes in the bathroom. I caught a look at myself in the mirror. I was right. The twig had been the least of it. There were dirt smudges all over my face, and my khaki pants were wet and stained with mud. I was pretty sure my white shirt was beyond saving.

I pulled on a pair of leggings and threw on a black T-shirt with the Mona Lisa on the front. I got all the guck out of my hair and pulled it back, stuffing it in a scrunchy.

We slipped back outside and Barry drove me to Starlight Court. Miami's house was still dark, so I went in the side gate and grabbed my things while Barry waited out front.

"Well, thanks for everything," I said as I unlocked the Greenmobile. "You can go home and finish your dinner now."

"Not yet," he said. "I want to make sure you get in safely." He was staring at me.

"What is it? Do I have something on my face?

He paused and seemed to be measuring his words. "You seem a little crazed."

"What do you mean? I'm fine." I looked around at the houses on the short street. "Which one of you called the cops on me? I bet it was the Yanas." I pointed accusingly at their house.

He put his fingers to his lips, shushing me, and urged me to get in my car.

It was a short drive to my place. I pulled into my driveway and he parked on the street. We both went in through the den door and back to my room.

"I'm good now," I said. Then I realized that all the animals needed their food and the dogs some outdoor time. "I have to take care of the animals. I don't want to keep you."

"No problem," he said. "I'll wait here."

I let the dogs have some yard time and made sure everyone had food. I heard the TV coming from Peter and

Gabby's room, and the door was shut. When I came back to my room, Barry was waiting.

"Okay, now can you tell me how you ended up trapped in the flood control space."

"It started because I left my tote bag at Miami's." I told him how Dinah and I had noticed the open space when we'd been there before. "I thought the drone had come from that direction and, well, there I was in the yard alone. It seemed like fate was telling me to have a look around."

He put his hand to his forehead in frustration. "Molly, you were just supposed to talk to people and listen."

"But you said there was nothing you could do, like get a warrant to look around the Yanas' place."

"You're just lucky that nobody wants to press charges."

"I'm sorry. I got carried away. I didn't stop and reason it out. I just went for it. It would have been fine if I'd realized the gate didn't open on the other side and I'd left it propped open," I said. "I'm not like you. I can't keep everything inside and be all logical and unemotional. Sometimes I just go for it." I knew I should stop talking, but somehow I couldn't, and the words kept falling out of my mouth.

We were standing staring at each other now. "I hope it works out with Carol. An ER nurse is probably just like you—a real cool cucumber with no flares of emotion."

"What are you talking about?" He seemed genuinely confused.

"Like right now. Here you are standing in my bedroom. A room with a lot of memories from our past, and you're totally unmoved. You keep it all shut down." I probably did sound a little crazed from all I'd just been through and the adrenaline rush, but once the genie was out of the bottle, I couldn't stop. "I admit I still feel a tiny spark when I see you. But for you the fire is all out."

"Molly, don't," Barry said in a warning voice. "I told you a long time ago that the way I deal with things that I can't have, like food when there's no time to eat, sleep when I have to keep going." He dropped his voice, "Or you." He blew out his breath. "I keep a lid on it. But that doesn't mean I don't feel anything. I just know how to handle it."

"Really?" I said.

"Yeah, really." For a moment he stared at me, and I thought he was going to turn to go, but he seemed to be fighting with himself. Then he rocked his head in capitulation and let his breath out as he muttered, "What am I doing?" Before I knew what was happening, he'd closed the space between us.

I was stunned. feeling his arm around me as I breathed in the scent of the citrus soap that he used. It was familiar and exciting, and then he leaned in to kiss me. Everything went swirling in my head, and when our lips met, it was like sparklers, rainbows, and rocket ships all going off at the same time and I felt myself melting. He pulled away so abruptly, I almost fell.

"I hope you're happy," he growled. "I gotta go." He rushed to the door before I could follow.

I sat a long time, trying to process what had just happened.

I finally left my room and went to make myself a cup of tea. I saw something slumped on the couch and didn't realize at first that it was Peter. He was always so upright and together, and suddenly he looked like all the starch had gone out of his body. Mother's instinct, I guess, but I immediately forgot about my own issues and focused on him.

"Is something wrong?"

"She left me," he said in a miserable tone.

I'd never seen my son so undone, and I wasn't sure how to proceed. Samuel had always cried on my shoulder when things didn't work out, but Peter never showed any vulnerability.

"Do you want to talk about it?" I asked, fully expecting him to suddenly straighten himself up and brush me off. But instead he nodded. "I was going to have some tea. Can I make you a cup?" He considered my offer for a moment, and I almost upped it to something alcoholic, but then he nodded again.

I brought the tea in with some cookies, thinking maybe the sugar would help.

"What happened?" I asked.

"She blamed me for everything falling apart. I should have known. I should have had a backup plan. Mostly, I should have figured out something besides living here." He stopped and drank some tea and gobbled a cookie. "She said she couldn't wait around for me to get it together. She got a job offer—to be a line producer on a film."

"What about the baby?" I asked.

"She doesn't see it as any reason to do anything differently. She moved back with her parents in the Palisades until she can get her own place." He slumped back against the couch. "It was fine when everything was going along as planned," he said, "but I thought there was something about for better or worse."

I didn't know what to say, so I said the only thing I could think of. "I'm sorry." And then he did something he hadn't done since he was four years old and couldn't find his Freddy Teddy bear: he threw himself against me and sobbed. I knew it was more than just Gabby leaving. It was everything—he'd lost his job, his lifestyle, the image he had of himself, and now the mother of his baby too.

I did the same thing I'd done for my younger son when he'd fallen apart. "It'll be okay," I said in a voice that sounded like I had some secret knowledge. Then I crossed my fingers, hoping I was right.

Chapter
Twenty-Three

"What am I going to do? It was all my fault," I said to Dinah. I'd skipped my morning coffee and dressed quickly before showing up at my best friend's door. Commander was already gone and we had the place to ourselves, but even so we went into her She Cave. She'd plied me with coffee and cinnamon toast, and I'd dumped the details of what had happened the previous day, ending with the moment with Barry. I felt like I had an emotional hangover, and only some girl time could help.

"Not exactly," my friend said. "He's the one who made the move."

"But I pushed him to it, going on about how locked down he was."

"But you were still stunned from all you'd gone through and were operating on nerve," Dinah said, trying to make me feel better.

"You're right. It was just a hiccup, a mistake after getting lost in the secret garden and arrested and all the adrenalin," I said, feeling a little calmer. "But what about Mason? Do I tell him?" I drank some more the coffee, hoping it would ease the burned-out feeling. Before she could answer, I did. "Maybe it is better to just leave it be. And then I won't have to explain what Barry was doing in my bedroom. I'm sure that will be the end of me helping Barry with this case anyway. I'll probably just get a curt phone call." I drained my cup and with a hug and a thank-you, I felt ready to face my day.

I'd left my car in the bookstore parking lot and walked to Dinah's. Now I retraced my steps and went into Shedd & Royal. After all the trouble it had caused, I'd made sure to bring in my tote bag with the list Mrs. Shedd had been so insistent about needing. My first stop was her office.

"Molly, you have it already? I hope it wasn't any trouble," she said. I wanted to laugh at how absurd her comment seemed, all things considered, but I didn't.

"No problem," I said, handing it to her.

I went directly to the yarn department after that. The Hookers had been a big help the day before, but there were still kits to make, as well as figuring out a way to display them. On top of it all, I was nervous. I'd pushed the idea of buying the yarn and making the kits. If nobody wanted them, it was a black mark for me.

I took a bunch of yarn and put the skeins on the table, along with the other supplies, and started putting together the kits. I was glad for the repetitive work as it took my mind off everything else for the moment.

"I wanted to be sure you had this," CeeCee said, coming up to the table. She laid one of the Serendipity scarves on the table with a flourish.

"Wow," I said. Seeing hers reminded me why I had fallen in love with the idea of mixing the yarns in the first place. She'd made hers in different shades of shades of pink with spring green running down the middle.

"I'll get it back after the event, won't I, dear?" She touched her work lovingly. "I've convinced the director to let me wear it in the play. If all else fails, at least *it* will get a good review." She punctuated it with her merry laugh, but there was a hint of worry in it.

"You'll be great," I said. "You're a professional."

"Yes, when I have a lot of takes and retakes. There's just one shot with live theater. It's not like when I played Ophelia in the Anthony movie." She'd gotten a faraway look, and I knew she was thinking back to the movie about the vampire who crocheted to contain his lust for blood, particularly that of his love interest. Suddenly, the actor snapped to attention. "Dear, how could I have forgotten that Sloan was one of the set designers on the movie." CeeCee'd had a supporting role in the movie, and not only had it given her career a huge boost, but she'd been nominated for an Academy Award. "She was the one who designed his lair." CeeCee glanced at the scarf that Rhoda had made. "Anthony would have loved that, all those shades of red."

Her face clouded. "It's so tragic that she was a victim of such a strange occurrence." She let out a sigh. "You haven't heard any more about it, have you?"

I considered whether to mention that I thought it might not have been an accident. In the past when I'd gotten involved with investigations, I'd always talked them over with the crochet group, but this time was different since no one but Dinah knew that I was involved with the case. I decided saying anything would lead to more explaining than I wanted to do. "The police are still investigating," I said before turning the subject back to her upcoming play and repeating my reassurance that she would be great.

"Join The Adele as we tour the Shedd & Royal yarn department." Adele came up to the table and pointed her phone at CeeCee. "We have a celebrity guest today, CeeCee Collins. Remember, she's in my group of crocheters. What's going on?" Adele looked at the table and figured it out. "CeeCee and a bookstore worker are in the midst of preparations for our big event tomorrow evening." She turned the camera on the table. If I was in the shot, it was only my hands. "It's your big chance to have a crochet lesson from The Adele herself. Then you can buy a kit and make one of these to remember the moment we met." She held up one of the samples and went on about what an amazing experience it was to get a lesson from her. I was usually annoyed by Adele, but this time I was glad she was pitching the event. She was livestreaming and, after giving the details of the bookstore location, signed off. She flopped in one of the chairs and let out a breath of relief.

"I hope that holds them for a while. My fans are like content monsters. They keep wanting more. I didn't know what I was going to give them, and then I saw you," she said to CeeCee.

"While you're sitting here, I could use some help making the kits," I said. CeeCee apologized for having to leave.

"I don't know. You *are* in charge of the department, so isn't it your responsibility?" Then she relented and joined me in putting the kits together.

All I could think to say was thank you.

By afternoon, we'd made as many as I was going to. If we sold half of the ones we had now, it would be a success. I headed to the café to get a another caffeine fix just as Barry came in the front door of the bookstore and looked around. I thought of trying to hide. I felt awkward about what had happened between us last night. And I was sure he was there to tell me that he didn't require my services anymore.

But he saw me before I could find a way to disappear. He was dressed in a dark suit and crisp light blue shirt and striped tie. I felt a thud in my stomach as I noted that he wasn't smiling.

"We need to talk," he said.

"I was going to get a coffee. Join me?" I gestured to the café.

"Right," he said in his detective tone.

Bob was pushing a party drink across the counter to a customer when we walked in. He started to smile at us but picked up on the uneasy vibe and just asked for the order. "I'll bring it to you," Bob said, giving me an understanding nod.

Barry led the way to the round wood table tucked in the corner by the front window. If we kept our voices low, it offered complete privacy, at least as far as sound was concerned. In typical cop fashion, he chose the seat that gave him a view of the whole place, and I took the one that put my back toward the entrance. He wanted to be able to see everything, while I didn't want anyone to see me.

"Okay," I said as soon as we sat down. "I'll save you the trouble. You don't want to work with me anymore. I was crazy and unprofessional, and I made you uncomfortable."

He listened to me say my piece without a flicker of reaction. Bob showed up with the drinks. He gave Barry a large coffee and pushed the other cup in front of me. "I threw in an extra shot of espresso." His eyes went sideways to Barry. "It seemed like you needed something extra."

Barry waited until Bob was all the way back at the counter before he spoke. "I know you're probably not going to want to hear this, but you're wrong."

"Huh," I said, surprised.

He took a slug of his coffee. "It probably would be better if we didn't work together anymore, but the problem is, I really need your help on this case. Because, since it seems like someone meant to create a nuisance and the homicide was accidental, the only way we'll find the guilty party is with your unorthodox methods." He put his hands over his eyes. "I can't believe I'm saying this, but I want to know what you found out last night. Did you get a look in any of the yards?"

"You really mean it?" I said. "I've got that and more."

"But first let me say something. We can't meet in your bedroom anymore."

"Right," I said. "Sorry if I made you lose your cool."

Barry looked uncomfortable. "I should have handled it better. You were a little crazy, probably from all that adrenalin. I shouldn't have reacted."

I wanted to ask him if the kiss had been all rainbows, sparklers, and rocket ships for him too, but I knew that would be a mistake and kept quiet. "We could talk here," I said, but he shook his head.

"I shouldn't even be talking to you now. You saw how Bob looked at us. It's hardly anonymous."

"Maybe we could talk in your detective car or the Tahoe. There's all that stuff like the gear shift and drink holders between the seats, keeping us at a respectful distance."

"I guess that will have to do," he said. He glanced toward the entrance, and his face collapsed. "I'm out of here."

I looked away for a second, and when I turned back, Barry and his coffee were gone.

I turned in my seat to survey the whole place and felt my breath catch. Mason was standing by the front counter, talking to Bob.

Chapter
Twenty-Four

"Mason," I squealed, getting up from the table and rushing to the front. "What are you doing here?" He was dressed in his fancy law firm work clothes—a perfectly tailored light-colored suit and a silky cotton off-white dress shirt, but no tie.

"I hope that means you're glad to see me," he said. His eyes flicked back toward the table where I'd been sitting. I knew he'd either seen Barry and figured out I'd been sitting with him, or Bob had told him. Barry was certainly right about it not being a good place to meet on the down low.

"Of course, I'm glad to see you. Just surprised." To demonstrate how glad I was, I gave him a hug. He put his arms around me and hugged me back. "It was a last-minute change of plans. It's the same clients. The good news is that it's finally winding down. There's the donation the family made to Worthington to set up the croquet program, but I'm sure I can make the judge see there was nothing illegal about it. It was done before their kids were admitted to Worthington. We're going to show him a film of the entire tournament that we made last weekend." Mason chuckled. "I needed those mallets to prop my eyes open. It's not a very exciting sport. But there will be no question that they are legitimate croquet athletes. But I'm not here to talk about lawn sports. Is there something you want to tell me?"

"Which was it? Did you see him or did Bob tell you?"

"How about both?" he said.

"Do you want to sit?" I asked.

"Not here. Whatever you have to say, I'd like a better backdrop."

"I have a lunch break coming. Just let me get my things and tell Mrs. Shedd I'm actually taking one today and it might go a little long."

He was waiting outside when I came through the door. "I want to whisk you away to someplace wonderful, but do you mind if we stop at my place first so I can change?"

"Sure," I said as I got into his Mercedes SUV. It was just a short drive to his place from the bookstore. Spike greeted us with wild yipping and followed me into the den while Mason went to change. He gave me a more thorough sniffing than usual. He probably smelled Princess. She was just his size, and I bet he would adore the little puffy white dog.

Mason returned dressed in jeans and a Hawaiian shirt with a bright floral pattern. "Do you want to talk here?" I asked.

He shook his head. "Location, location, location," he said with grin. "I'm probably not going to like what I hear. At least let it happen with a nice view."

Lunch with Mason was never a fast-food affair. All his buildup was making me nervous, and I wanted to get it out. Though I was still considering exactly what I was going to say. I was on the fence about whether to mention the kiss. He got on the 405 and headed toward the city, doing his usual move of keeping where we were headed a surprise.

When he got off at Getty Center Drive, the suspense was over. The art museum was perched on the side of a mountain and was as much of a draw as the art work displayed inside. There were courtyards and interesting water installations and a garden that was more unusual than pretty. We went directly to an airy patio that had a high covering to offer shade and a view of the ocean and the planes taking off from LAX. My stomach was in knots by now, and I barely picked at the chopped salad and cheese plate Mason had gotten for us to share.

"Are you finally ready to hear?" I asked.

He nodded. Then he put his hand up. "Let me say something first. I know I put pressure on you about running off with me and, well, getting married." He took a breath. "That's what I'd like in my heart of hearts, but if that doesn't work for you . . ."

"It is a bit much to deal with," I said.

"How about we leave it that you come with me on this trip and we see how it goes?" He chuckled. "Of course, I expect you'll be so wowed that you'll be willing to go to the ends of the earth with me. But no pressure."

I got it, he was pleading his case with the idea that it would affect what I said about Barry. Mason was all about winning, and I was the prize.

"That works for me," I said. I watched a plane take off and fly out over the ocean as it got higher and higher. It was really only a speck from here, but I imagined the view that I'd be seeing soon with Mason. I knew that as it kept ascending, it would turn and fly along Catalina, still low enough to pick out Two Harbors and maybe get a glimpse of Avalon before a turn eastward. The trip would be the beginning of something. The real start of "us."

"Okay, I'm waiting," Mason said with a smile.

"I think you've made this into so much more than it is," I said. "Here's the big story. I'm working with Barry. Because of the kind of case it is—according to him, someone being in the wrong place at the wrong time rather than being the intended victim, and I was already sort of in the middle of it, and he thought that I might hear useful information. I didn't say anything to you because Barry asked me to keep it quiet." I put my hands up. "And that's it."

"There's only one thing wrong with that story," Mason said. "If it was so hush-hush, why were you meeting in the café where Bob could pass along that you were there together?"

That was the reason why Mason got the big bucks as an attorney. He knew the right questions to ask. Right for him, not for me.

"Fine, I'll tell you everything. I don't like keeping anything from you anyway. I just didn't want to upset you for no reason."

"Do I need to get a glass of wine to hear this?" he asked. His tone was light, but there was something in his dark eyes that looked worried.

"I just want to get it over with. You can get the wine afterward if you want it." I paused to psych myself up for what I was about to tell him. "Because of everything going on at my house, Barry and I have been meeting in my bedroom."

I heard a squeak from Mason, and when I checked his expression, he was doing his best to keep cool. "And, well, there was a moment when we sort of lost it." I had to take a breath. "It came after I got arrested—really detained since the people who called it in refused to press charges and I used my one phone call to call Barry." I looked at Mason. "I would have called you, but you were in Kansas. There was all this adrenalin from the whole episode. I was emotional. And—well, there was a kiss. But it didn't mean anything. It was a mistake. I don't know if I told you, but he's seeing someone, an ER nurse, and it sounds like it's really serious. And we're not going to meet in my bedroom anymore." I was talking too fast, a dead giveaway that I was trying to make less of what had happened.

"Just a kiss?" Mason said, looking intently at my face.

"Yes. So, now you know. Go get your wine if you need it."

He reached over and squeezed my hand. "I should have let you talk sooner. I imagined far worse. Coffee will do," Mason said, getting up. "By the way, you could have called me. I would have arranged to get you sprung."

He came back with cappuccinos for both of us. "Why don't you tell me what's going on, and maybe we can wrap this up quickly. Then you won't have to meet Barry anymore."

"What if it isn't as it seems?" I said. "I keep thinking that Sloan was the intended victim. I wish I had Adele's video. Then you'd see what I mean."

"Sunshine, it's gone. Nick Charles would tell you that, from an outside observer's perspective, the other idea seems more likely," he said, referring to the fictional detective.

"It was easy for Nick and Nora Charles. Their cases weren't real, and I think they were soaked in martinis most of the time."

"But sober enough to tell you probably never to depend on The Adele for evidence or anything else. And then they'd go dancing. He'd be in a tuxedo and she in a slinky gown. They'd call each other darling and take the elevator to a set decorator's idea of what their apartment should look like," Mason said.

"Sloan could have been the one to do it, if they'd decided to do a remake," I said.

"You're back to her. She sounds like a really nice person. Why would somebody have a drone chase her?"

"She had her fingers in a lot of pots, doing similar but different things. She was even designing backdrops for people's online group meetings."

"Why did she do so many different things?" he asked.

"You know the entertainment business. There were probably a lot of gaps between her set design jobs. Gaps with no pay. She lived relatively modestly. Her house is adorable, but not a mansion. But her sister is in bad health, and she was either supporting her completely or helping her out."

"I get it, Nora, dear, you're saying that she took jobs just for the money."

"It gets worse," I said. I told him how Elise was concerned that money from some sold items was supposed to go into an account and might have made a detour.

"So, you think that Sloan was on the take? What was the account for?" Mason asked.

"To furnish the rental rooms. The other person on the account was Miami."

"Aha. She could have been upset with Sloan embezzling funds and set up the whole drone attack as revenge."

"There's something missing there, Nick, I said. "She would have needed an accomplice. I was with Miami when it happened."

"You have a point, my dear," Mason said.

"My head is swimming."

"Backstroke or doggy paddle?"

"That absolutely sounds like something Nick Charles would have said. But seriously, I have to go back to my real life now. There's an event tomorrow at the bookstore, and I have things to take care of. I really want it to be a big success. It'll ease my guilt about taking the time off."

Mason reached over and put his hand on mine. "The bookstore will survive without you."

"But will I survive without the bookstore?"

"Do you think I'm making you give it up?" he asked. "I'm willing to work with you. Whatever makes you happy."

"Really?" I said surprised.

"Of course. We'll figure it out."

"You know I come with baggage," I said, thinking of my family and menagerie of pets, with one more than he even knew about.

"No problem, Nora dear. I'll call a porter," he said with a grin.

Chapter
Twenty-Five

B efore I went back to the bookstore, I stopped in at Luxe, the lifestyle store down the street. "Lifestyle store" was a loose term, but in the case of Luxe it meant it covered the whole spectrum of things for the home and the self. The inventory was always changing and always interesting.

Sheila had worked her way up to manager of the place, and I'd stopped by to pick up the scarf she'd made that I wanted to include in a display advertising the event. It stood out because it wasn't in her usual pallet of greens, blues and lavenders. She'd used yellow, a rusty orange, and gold. It was so cheery that I knew it would draw attention.

She was behind the glass counter, dealing with a customer, and I took the opportunity to check out their offerings. There was a legal bookcase with the glass doors all up. It was for sale and was being used to display Sheila's pieces. I went from there to a display of fragrant handmade soaps. I picked up a block of lemon yellow wrapped in cellophane. I could already smell the citrusy scent, which instantly reminded me of Barry. For just a second I was back with him in my room, experiencing the sparklers, rainbow, and rocket ship moment. I felt my face grow hot as I dropped the soap like it was a burning coal.

I was relieved when Sheila finished with the customer and beckoned me over. She knew what I was there for and said she had the scarf in the back.

"It was fun to try something different," she said with a shy smile. "It's been wonderful how people seem to like what I've been making. But these colors just spoke to me."

While she went to get the sample for me, I looked down at the counter of jewelry and admired a silver cuff set with an oval of rose quartz.

"Here it is," she said, holding the scarf up. The colors made me think of a sunrise.

"It's beautiful," I said. "It will certainly help move the kits when people realize they could make something like this."

She saw me admiring the jewelry. "Can I take anything out for you? We'd be happy to get it inscribed." She gestured around the store. "We have some new pieces. She pointed to a lamp with a beautiful glass shade painted an iridescent green. "It's authentic, signed by Tiffany," she said.

"Not today," I said. I looked at my watch. "I didn't realize how late it was. I went out to lunch with Mason." She smiled knowingly. All the Hookers new that lunch with Mason was never a sub sandwich on a park bench.

As I walked into the bookstore, I realized I should have called Mrs. Shedd to let her know I was delayed. But Mason and I had gotten into playing Nick and Nora on the way home, and I sort of forgot about everything else, which had of course been his plan.

The bookstore owner was by the door when I came in and gave me a worried look. "It's okay," I said, quickly. "Mason took me to the Getty for lunch."

"That man knows the best spots," she said. "I'll have to remind Joshua about the Getty. It's the perfect place for us to go next time we want a little getaway."

I held out the scarf I'd just picked up. "Sheila made it. Isn't it beautiful?"

"It is. If she wants to sell it, I think I'll buy it for myself," Mrs. Shedd said with almost a swoon in her voice. "Be sure and put it where everyone can see it."

"I will, but all the scarves the group has made are wonderful. Do you want to go over the plans for the event?" I asked.

"It would help put my mind at ease," she said. "What are we going to do with the kits if they don't move?" She let out a little sigh. "You don't think the yarn has bad vibes after what happened?"

"Yarn is just yarn, and I really think the kits are stunning, with a broad appeal. The signs are up, and Mr. Royal got the word out on social media. Adele mentioned it a number of times on her vlog. I don't think anybody is going to fly in from Alaska, but she has a lot of local followers, and they might show up."

"I hope we get some benefit out of that frightful thing of hers. Every time I look at her, she's talking to her phone and calling herself 'The Adele.'"

I assured her that we had plenty of kits and that some of the Hookers would be there to give lessons. I'd arranged with Bob to have drinks and some snacks. That also drew extra people in. I hoped they'd come for the treats but end up excited about the kits.

"I do think it was brilliant of you to figure out how to make it appeal to people who don't know how to crochet."

She went off to help a customer, and I went back to the yarn department to straighten up and create a display for the front of the store. I decided to use a glass case we used for expensive items. I put Sheila's scarf in it with several of the kits and a sheet listing the details of the event. I placed it near the door so everyone walking in couldn't miss it. I located some free-standing cardboard display cases we had for books, and realized they'd be perfect for the kits. I filled them and left them in the storage room to be brought out the next day.

Mason had a dinner meeting that night. Peter texted me that he was meeting some people for a round of golf and then they'd be coming back to the house, which I took to mean I ought to make myself scarce. He said he'd attended to the animals and even played fetch with them. Maybe our moment the night before had somehow transformed him into a better version of himself.

I had a greeting committee watching me as I came across the patio to the kitchen door when I got home. Although Peter had said he'd attended to them, I wasn't sure whether he meant all of them. I dropped my things and headed across the house. Blondie was in her chair with Princess nestled next to her. I got them both to come with me and let them into the yard. I gave the whole crew an extra dinner just in case.

My lunch with Mason had been so emotionally charged I hadn't eaten much, and now I was hungry. But I also had limited time. I considered my options while my mind went back over the afternoon. I was glad that I'd told Mason everything since he'd imagined far worse. Everything I'd said was true. The moment with Barry had come out of the events that led up to it.

I thought back to the secret garden now known by the much less romantic name of Flood Control Location 23. I'd learned the hard way that next time I went exploring, I'd make sure I had an exit.

The quickest thing to make was an omelet. I sautéed a handful of fresh baby spinach with some white mushrooms and set them aside while I made the eggs. I'd mastered how to shake the pan and push the edges of the cooked eggs, letting the raw part get to the heat. When it was perfect I poured on the filling and flipped it in half. It always gave me a sense of satisfaction to make a perfect omelet. Glad to have the whole place to myself for the moment, I sat at the kitchen table and ate. True, I kept glancing outside for any signs of Peter's return with his golf people.

As it got dark, they're arrival became more imminent. I finished up, grabbed my infamous tote bag, and went to my room. I didn't have to worry about the animals; the cats and dogs followed me like a parade. I had brought home some work. I still needed to add the fringe to the scarves I'd made.

I had purposely not been thinking about
now, when I was sitting in my room, cutting
different yarn to add to the scarves, I began to w
ever hear from him again. I was sure the whole
had unnerved him. He was so good at keepin
collected, it must have upset him to have lost
want to even consider what feelings were behind

I heard cars in the driveway and voices as Pe
guests arrived.

Even if I never heard from Barry, it wouldn
from getting to the bottom of what happened,
with a shrug.

I glanced down at the phone next to me in
to make sure I hadn't missed a call. Thanks to Pe
ing in, I'd become dependent on my cell phone an
myself to carry it around, but even so it still got l
purse a lot of the time. No one had called. I finis
ting on the fringe and packed up the scarves to t
me the next day.

The phone rang, startling me. "Rang" wasn
the right word—my ringer was set to harp sounds
always made me feel like heaven was calling.

"Hello," I said.

"Sunshine, you sound funny. Did I wake you?"
said.

"No, no. The phone startled me," I said. I'd for
that he'd said he would call.

"I was hoping to be able to see you," he said and I
him yawn. "I hate to admit that my body remember

251

wasn't in my twenties, thirties, geez forties either anymore. Tomorrow for sure."

"I have the event at the bookstore," I said.

"We can do something afterward," he said with a
chuckle. He let out another yawn as he said goodbye.

When the phone rang again, I thought he'd called back
see if he could get me to come to his place.

"I thought you were too tired," I said in a flirty voice.

"Too tired for what?" Barry said.

"Oh, it's you," I said, surprised and uncomfortable. It
was going to be the last time I answered the phone without
checking the screen, no matter how sure I was that I knew
who was calling.

"Sorry it's so late," he said. "I was tied up. I realized we
never got to talk about what you found out during your
snooping expedition. It'll probably be the last time we
meet. Could you do it now?" He sounded all business.

I figured it was probably best to get it over with, so I agreed.

"We're talking in the Tahoe, right?" he said.

"Sure," I said. He explained he was parked down the
street, away from the street lamps.

I grabbed a sweater and slipped out the den door.

I got into the passenger side and almost laughed when I
saw a pile of stuff on the console between the seats.

"Thanks for coming," he said. There was an awkward-
ness in the way he was looking out the front window instead
of at me as he spoke. I suppose it could have been a cop
thing, like the way he always sat with a view of the room,
but I sensed it was something else.

"We can't really sit here," he said. "One of your neighbors could look out their window and decide we look suspicious." He waited until I put on my seat belt and he put the car in gear. He turned onto Wells Drive. The road curved around the base of the hills. The houses were all big and behind tall fences. As we passed a side street, I saw the side of Miami's house in the streetlight. Funny, I hadn't realized how close it was to the corner estate on the curving street.

"We should really get right to it," he began. "Did you find out anything about the Yanas?" I glanced over at Barry, who had his eyes on the road. At least now he had an excuse for not looking at me as he spoke.

"The food is really good at their place," I said, hoping to lighten things up. I could see him shaking his head in reproach.

"I suppose you told Mason all about it," he said.

"All about what?" I asked.

"Molly," he said with a touch of annoyance, "don't play games with me. You know what I mean, and it's not the crab legs."

"Did you tell Carol?" I asked.

"Can't you just answer a question without another question?"

"Can you begin by answering mine?"

He blew out his breath. "I didn't know how to tell her. It would have required explaining too much. It sounds idiotic to be using your ex as an informant you're meeting in her bedroom." He finally stole a quick glance my way. "Did you tell Mason where we'd been talking?"

"Don't worry, he's not going to demand you have a duel at dawn. He'd imagined far worse than it was. When I explained the events of the evening, he got that there was just an overflow of emotion. All my fault because I started bugging you about being so collected. I'm sure you just meant to put an arm around me to help me calm down," I said.

"Right," he said, keeping his eyes on the road ahead. "Can we get to what I'm here for?"

For a moment I toyed with answering with another question, but it seemed better to give him the information he wanted and get out of there. We were separated, but it was still close enough to catch the scent of the lemon soap and something more that I was trying to ignore. I began by telling him about stepping on the seafood shell behind Miami's fence.

"You do realize what that means?" I hadn't been paying attention to where we were going and finally glanced out the window as we went up and down a steep hill. It took a moment for me to orient myself to what street we were on. He'd taken Wells until it became Serrania and then turned onto Dumetz.

"Why don't you tell me what you think it means," he said.

"I think the drone was loaded with the shells and took off from there. Unfortunately, that doesn't narrow it down. I spent a lot of time looking at those fences, and all of them had a gate to that back area. I got the splinter to prove it." I held up my hand as the SUV glided to a stop at the traffic light for Topanga Canyon Boulevard.

I was surprised when he grabbed it and used the flashlight on his phone to check the wound.

"You're not going to kiss it and make it better?" I joked, and he scowled. The light changed and he turned onto the cross street. I thought at any moment he'd make a U-turn and head back the way we came.

"I'll leave that up to Mason," he said. "You're still planning to go off and be his legal sidekick, aren't you?" Not only had Barry not turned to go back the way we'd come, but we'd passed the level part of the street and begun the winding ascent up through the canyon.

"Yes," I said, finally.

"And then you'll probably marry him."

"That hasn't been decided. I'm not sure."

"If you go with him, you will. He'll wow you with rose petals floating in a tub surrounded by candles and glasses of champagne."

I laughed. "Where did that come from?"

"I don't know. Forget I said that." He let out an exasperated breath. "We're getting off the subject. Back to the case—you were going to check on the Yanas," he said.

I was relieved that he'd changed the subject. It was getting a little too personal. "When Dinah and I ate at their restaurant, I made a joke about drones, and they freaked. And Massey Yana told Dinah to be careful not to get any shrimp shells in her purse because they stink."

255

"What about the yards? You said you looked in all of them."

"I was getting to that. I didn't get a long look at any of the yards, but the Yanas have practically a drone airport in their yard. They were all sitting on a long table with bags of stuff next to them. They wanted Miami to let them leave coupons for their restaurant in the rental rooms and weren't happy when she said no. Plus I have it on good authority that they're having financial problems. It looks pretty bad for them, but you can't really discount the others, except the O'Malleys since they're not home." I laughed to myself and told him how I'd named the houses and called theirs Colonel Mustard.

"Not something I would do, but cute," he said. "Continue."

"The Jonquets have a lot of remote toys. A drone isn't too far from that, and the remote-control SUV is even closer. The husband was worried about their property value. The people in the blue ranch house have lived there since the houses were built. The man seems like a cranky engineer type. He's livid about the short-term rentals, and he hangs out with a friend in his workshop. They probably build things, like maybe a drone."

"Thanks. I'm impressed at all the information you got. And more impressed that you just told it to me instead of making me pull it out of you. I knew you'd get better stuff than I would because they'd let their guard down with you. Sometimes it's harder when you're dealing with an average Joe who made a mistake rather than a premeditating killer."

"About that," I said. "I really think you should consider that Sloan was the target."

"Are we back to Adele's video again?"

"If you'd seen it, you'd know what I mean." I'd been too involved in our conversation to keep track of where we were. As we came to a stop at a traffic light, I was surprised to see an expanse of dark ocean ahead of us. The view always mesmerized me. The sky was midnight blue, with a few stars visible, and the quarter moon was a lonely shade of yellow that barely reflected in the dark water.

"What are we doing here?" I asked.

Barry didn't say anything, but I could tell he was upset with himself. "I don't know. I must have been on automatic pilot." He kept his gaze on the road. "As long as we're here—there's an all-night donut stand up ahead."

We had donuts and coffee, sitting in the parking lot, looking across the highway to the beach. I didn't know what to say, and I guess he didn't either because he was silent too. It was a relief when he turned on the radio for the ride back.

He dropped me off where he'd picked me up. I was expecting a speech thanking me for whatever I'd done, but letting me know that he didn't need my help anymore. It would be his way of controlling an uncomfortable situation.

"Good night," I said, opening it up for him to give me my swan song.

But instead he said, "If you get any proof that Sloan was the intended victim, let me know."

"Then you listened to what I said." I was surprised and pleased.

"Why would I go to all this trouble to meet up with you if I wasn't going to listen to you? But remember, I said proof or evidence, not a disappearing video."

Chapter
Twenty-Six

I made a point of slipping in through the den door when I got home, but it wasn't necessary. The house was quiet, and the door to Peter's room was shut. When I checked the house phone, there was a message from Samuel. He offered the usual update from the concert tour, telling me my mother's group the She La Las was still "killing it." He said they were doing their last show and gave details about when they'd be home over the weekend. I'd kept them all in the dark about everything. They didn't know Peter had moved in, had a pregnant girlfriend who'd moved out, or that Mason had proposed. I'd only said that I was going out of town for a short time.

I was glad that Samuel would be back in time to take care of everything while I was gone. But I knew there'd be chaos and a power struggle. I doubted Samuel would be as agreeable as I was to making himself scarce for his brother.

It was all too much to think about right now.

* * *

I awoke after a restless night. Princess had decided to leave Blondie's side and joined the other two dogs and cats in bed with me. Felix and Cosmo weren't so sure about having to share the space. I was the one who really should have been upset, since it left even less room for me.

It was going to be a long day at the bookstore since the event was scheduled for the evening. We didn't usually have events on weekend nights, but since I was leaving and we'd arranged it for Saturday, I had my fingers crossed that we'd get a good turnout.

In the back of my mind I was thinking this might be the last event I put on at the bookstore. If I was going to be away traveling with Mason a lot, I'd have to give up being assistant manager and events coordinator and become just a bookstore associate, which was a nice way of saying sales help. Adele would grab my old position. I let out a groan, imagining her running the events and the yarn department.

Dinah and Mrs. Shedd were the only ones who knew I was taking a week off. And Dinah was the only one who knew what it might mean.

Mason had sent me a long text, wishing me the best for my day and reminding me we were getting together after the event was over. There was a lot of sweet stuff about how he couldn't wait to see me. He seemed to understand that I was feeling emotional about the changes in store and he wanted to be supportive. His last line was assuring me that I would see that what I was getting was far more than what I was giving up.

Mason came with a lot. He was fun and had the ability to make anything into a special occurrence. He was interesting and always up for an experience. The idea of working with him seemed appealing since it was literally giving people new lives. It had always been casual between us, fun with no strings. Then he had started wanting strings, which we decided was like going steady.

That had been about as serious as I had wanted it. When Charlie died, I'd had to restart my life. I'd never lived on my own and hadn't had a job beyond working with him in his public relation firm for years. I'd gotten the job at the bookstore, met the Hookers, and learned to crochet. I'd made friends and created a whole life of my own.

Maybe it was time for another new chapter, this time as a committed part of a couple.

I pushed the thoughts from my mind as I went into the bookstore.

At the last minute, I thought we should talk over how the event would go. Rhoda was going to be the main crochet teacher for the demonstration. She had grabbed a coffee and come to the back table in the yarn department. Sheila came in during her break from her duties at Luxe. Dinah lived just a block away. They were both going to be available as crochet teachers as well.

"The plan is that Mrs. Shedd will hand out tickets to people as they come in. They'll keep half and deposit the other half in a bowl—in other words, standard raffle procedure. When we're ready to start, I'll pick one of the tickets. The winner gets their choice of one of the kits and then Rhoda will help them start it as the audience watches. If the winner is a non-crocheter, Rhoda will teach them enough crochet to make the scarf. We'll have refreshments. People can watch the lesson and hopefully be inspired to buy one of the kits. I will announce that we have lessons available during the evening or they can come back. I gave a nod to Sheila. We'll set up some chairs and small tables for the lessons."

Mrs. Shedd walked in as I was speaking. She glanced around the yarn department. "Are you sure that you want to hold it here? We could still set up chairs in the event space."

"I'd like to keep it here," I said. "It makes it feel a little more informal, and if people are standing, it's easier for them to see what's happening at the table." The real truth was, I wasn't sure what the turnout would be. I worried there would be a lot of empty chairs. The way I was doing it, no matter how few people showed up, it would still look good.

"I'm sure you know what you're doing," she said.

"Kits are all the rage now," Rhoda said. "This is even better because we're going to have a demonstration of how to use one."

Mrs. Shedd lowered her voice. "What about Adele? What part does she have?"

I laughed to myself, remembering her reaction when I'd reminded her about helping. "She prefers to stay as a crochet advisor-at-large so she can be free to be adored by her followers."

"I hope her followers are also buyers," Mrs. Shedd said. "It seems you have things under control." She started to leave and then turned back. "The list for the book club seems to be missing a page. Could you see if you have it?"

That book club list had become a real pain. First Mrs. Shedd had seemed in a hurry to get it, which was why I'd ended stuck in the secret garden. And when I gave it to her, it was suddenly not so urgent. Now it was obvious she hadn't even looked at it until now. I promised to check. I stopped what I was doing and went to get the tote bag out of the cabinet.

I turned it upside down, hoping the sheet she wanted would fall out. It did and something else fell out with it and hit the floor. "I forgot all about this silver bracelet I found the other day." I turned to Mrs. Shedd. "Has anybody said they lost one?"

"Let me see it," Sheila said, reaching out her hand. She looked it over and nodded. "This is from Luxe. I remember selling it. Remember, I said that we do inscriptions," she said to me as she pointed to the inside of it.

I took it back and checked the inner portion. It said: "Allergy Alert Shellfish." I asked Sheila who had bought it, but I already knew the answer.

"It was Sloan. I didn't pay a lot of attention at the time, but I think she said she wanted something more stylish than the typical alert bracelet." Sheila's expression crumpled. "If only she'd been wearing it, maybe they could have saved her."

I didn't say anything to Sheila, but I looked at Dinah and gave her a little nod. What I'd told Barry was correct.

It wasn't a random nuisance prank. It was premeditated murder.

"I bet you can't wait to tell Barry," Dinah said. She'd stayed after when the rehearsal ended, and we'd gone to the café to sample the refreshments we were going to provide. Coffee and tea along with some of Bob's milk-chocolate-chip cookie bars. I hadn't said anything to the others. The Hookers all knew what had happened to Sloan, but I hadn't told anyone I was investigating. Only Dinah knew everything.

"Yes," I said, "but it's going to have to wait. I can't do anything that will distract me from the event. You heard Mrs. Shedd. She's nervous about the outcome. And so am I. I keep thinking we should have advertised more. I put something on our Facebook page. I'm hoping that we can start offering more kits, with events in conjunction. But this one has to work first."

"It may not be your concern anymore," Dinah said, looking at me directly.

"You thought of that too," I said. "It makes me too upset to even consider it." I ate a piece of cookie bar and washed it down with a slug of coffee.

"Yes, but on the other side, you'll have a whole new exciting beginning. You and Mason springing the innocent from jail while being stylish and having fun."

"He said we'll be like Nick and Nora Charles. I have to say that the timing is good for me to go off with him. My mother's tour is ending, and Samuel is coming home. He doesn't even know that his brother is living in his room. My

mother is probably expecting to use my living room so she and the girls can keep sharp for their next tour. And Barry is claiming Cosmo. The ER nurse suggested it."

"Oh," Dinah said. "And I suppose he'll give you your key back." I nodded. "And that will be that. You'll both get on with your lives." She dipped her cookie bar in the coffee. "So when are you going to tell Barry?" she asked.

"What, that I want my key back?" I said, confused.

"No. Tell him that Sloan was the intended victim."

Someone walked past our table, and I looked to see if they'd heard what Dinah said. No way, the man was too involved with the carrier full of whipped-cream-covered frozen coffee drinks. "I'll wait until he gets in touch. He got all upset when I contacted him." I finished my coffee and cookie bar. "But for right now, all I'm worried about is tonight."

* * *

By seven o'clock I had transformed the yarn department into the backdrop for the gathering. There were cases with the kits so that the bags could be examined to see the selection of yarn. Some had shades of the same color with a skein of something contrasting. Some were hodgepodges of colors and textures. If I said so myself, the packaging looked great.

Rhoda was at the table, ready for our winner. Sheila and Dinah would go to their stations once I'd done the presentation. There was a nice crowd around the table, and I'd already had to send Dinah to the café for more refreshments.

"Hello, everybody," I began. I felt a little self-conscious with the microphone, but it was worth using it because I didn't have to worry about everyone hearing me. "Usually this sort of thing ends with a raffle, but we're going to begin with ours. The lucky winner will get to pick one of the scarf kits and will have the expert help of one the Tarzana Hookers, Rhoda Klein. No problem if the winner doesn't know how to crochet. Rhoda will have them up and running in no time while we watch. Tonight's event is all about introducing our scarf kits. Everything you need to make a one-of-a-kind scarf. The pattern is easy enough for a beginner. The combinations of yarn have been picked by the Tarzana Hookers, some of whom are here tonight. Dinah Lyons and Sheila Altman will be glad to help anyone start their scarf or teach them how to crochet, and as a bonus, if you purchase one of the kits, you can always come into the bookstore for help or just to hang out for social crocheting."

I reached deep in the bowl and pulled out a ticket. As I read the number, I heard a squeal from the crowd. I scanned the assembled group until I saw an arm waving wildly as a woman stepped forward. I recognized her right away, and I almost called her Mayonnaise. That's one of the problems of using something to remind you of someone's name. You remember the something more than the name. "Lucky you, Anastasia," I said as she reached me. "She's a member of one of our book clubs," I said to the crowd, but to myself I was adding that she was a homeowner in the cul-du-sac.

"I can't wait to tell the rest of the book club that I won," she said.

I took off the microphone and took her over to the display of kits. I showed her how she could see the yarn through the back of the bag. She looked at a number of them and then turned to me. "What if I wanted to make the whole thing in the same yarn?"

I tried to explain the point was that no two scarves would be alike, but then I just told her we'd bought the yarn in a special way and the skeins were all different.

"This is the yarn from the house on the corner. That Sloan was telling you about when book club met," she said, suddenly figuring it out.

"Then you knew Sloan?" I asked.

"I wouldn't say I knew her. She came around periodically, dropping off a pumpkin for Halloween, or an American flag for the Fourth. There'd always be one of her cards attached, reminding everyone that she could do so much more than just list a house. All her experience as a set designer gave her skills to turn every house into something that would spark a buyer's imagination."

Anastasia's expression had gone from the excitement of winning to troubled. "She tried to present herself as someone who knew the area and cared about it. But obviously she didn't, or she wouldn't have been helping bring a short-term rental property to our street." She shook her head in annoyance. "There was more trouble. Someone was creeping around the flood control area, looking over fences. The land is actually owned by all the neighbors, but it can't be used because it floods in the rainy season. "There were cops and a helicopter. I was relieved that TV reporter didn't show up that time."

You and me both. I pictured Peter's face if Kimberly Wang Diaz had gotten a shot of me being taken away in handcuffs. "Were you the one who called the police?"

"No," she said. "We were just getting home when the police cars were pulling away. Bitsy is the one who told me what happened, but she said she didn't call the cops, and the Yanas said they didn't either. It couldn't have been the O'Malleys because they're out of town. Maybe it was neighbors on the other side." I was going to ask for a name, but I heard Adele's voice announcing her arrival. She moved through the crowd doing a royal wave.

"Welcome to all my followers. The Adele is here," she said, taking a bow. The crowd reorganized themselves around her and began reaching out to touch her.

Then I heard someone squeal, "I got one." A hand waved above the crowd holding one of the crocheted flowers that had been on Adele's sweater. Someone else said something about wanting a piece of The Adele too.

"You said if we came we'd get a souvenir to remember meeting you," someone else said. "We love you The Adele!" another voice cried.

"Pink, save me," Adele cried, surrounded by fans that loved her too much. I grabbed the microphone and put it back on before pushing my way through the crowd. When I reached her, I put my arms out to hold the crowd back from their idol. Was I really acting as her bodyguard now? I looked toward the front and saw Mrs. Shedd watching what was happening with a worried expression. And then I had an idea.

"The Adele will sign any kits you purchase and you'll each get a moment with her." I heard Adele let out a whine, and I whispered to her, "It's that or I step away and let them have their way with you."

"I'll do it," she said. "But I need someone to guard me. I thought it was bad when they demanded content, but now they're actually taking a piece of me." She looked at her sleeve and a dangling piece of pink yarn that had anchored a crocheted flower in place.

I was never so glad to see Eric Humphries arrive. The barrel-chested super-tall motorcycle officer was only too glad to act as his wife's bodyguard. And I was only too glad to let him.

Then Rhoda gave Anastasia her lesson while Sheila and Dinah helped some of the purchasers start their scarves. The refreshments had to be refilled again. Adele was besieged with one fan after another telling her their life story, but they all bought kits.

When the last of them cleared the yarn department, I saw that Mason had been hanging at the back.

"You had quite a night, Sunshine," Mason said, coming up to me and giving me a warm hug. "Can I help you with that?" He pointed to the overfull tray of empty cups and the remnants of the refreshments. He grabbed the things that were about to fall off before I could say a weary yes.

"You were here. I didn't see you."

He pointed at a post. "I wanted to stay out of your way. Nobody can say your events are dull," he said, adding a chuckle. We dropped everything off in the café. "It's

Saturday night," he said. "I finished with my clients and, like I promised, the rest of the evening is ours."

Mrs. Shedd let the last of the shoppers out the door and then locked it, letting out a sigh of relief. Adele insisted that Eric bring the car around to the back door so she wouldn't be accosted in the parking lot. I would have laughed at her request before, but after what I'd seen, she might have been right.

Dinah smiled at Mason as she and Sheila walked to the front. "Have fun, you two."

Mason put his arm around my shoulder and gave it a squeeze. "We will," he said.

Mrs. Shedd and Mr. Royal looked over the bins of kits that were now largely empty. "Good job," Mr. Royal said. "You can leave everything. Pamela and I will clear up."

I didn't argue and let Mason lead the way to the door.

"I had thought of doing something splashy, but honestly I'm pretty tired," he said. "What do you say we get a pizza from Paoli's and take it home?"

"I'd say yes, and be sure to get the half red sauce and half white sauce." He opened the passenger door of his Mercedes SUV for me. Some women complained it was an old-fashioned custom that was demeaning, but I thought it was gallant. He called in the pizza order, and by the time we got there, it was ready. My mouth was watering from the smell all the way to his place.

Spike gave me a big welcome and followed us as we walked down the hall. "I can't wait for Princess and Spike to have a playdate," I said, looking at the tiny dog.

We went into Mason's den and he put the pizza on the coffee table. I got plates and silverware. Then we both flopped on the couch and took our shoes off.

The pizza was the best, with a thick crust and oozing with toping. The white sauce was insanely rich, but worth every calorie, and the red sauce added a contrast to the thick layer of cheese.

"I'm afraid that wasn't exactly a Nick and Nora Charles meal," Mason said, putting his empty plate on the table.

"Maybe if we'd had martinis," I said.

"We still can. I can whip some up."

"Are you kidding?" I said.

"Maybe," he said with a grin. I was known for my lack of tolerance for alcohol. I could smell it and get tipsy.

We opted for cappuccinos, and he went off to make them while I enjoyed doing nothing for a while. He came back with the foamy drinks and set them down. "I finally, finally finished with my clients. The whole issue has been dropped, and the DA is not going to bother with the rest of the team. It's not my concern, but they're probably relieved since I think some ringers slipped in. At least it's over with."

"Are you talking about the croquet players?" I said. "It sounds like much ado about nothing."

"I'll second that," he said. "Except that the stakes were really high. In that Varsity Blue scandal, some wealthy, powerful people got jail time and big fines. But it's over with. Let's talk about you. Anything new about the woman hit by the drone?"

"Well, actually there is," I said. "I thought all along there was the possibility that it wasn't a random accident and that someone was after Sloan. And I found out I was right," I said. I told him about the bracelet with the allergy alert.

"Any meetings with Barry to share the information?" he asked. His tone had changed and seemed tinged with worry.

"I haven't had time."

"You could just phone it in," he said.

"Good idea, maybe I will."

"And now," he said, "the perfect end for the evening."

He took my hand and led me back through the house to an enclosed patio off the master suite. The whirlpool spa was surrounded by candles, and there were rose petals floating on the water. I choked. It was almost what Barry had described, only there was no champagne and we wore bathing suits.

Chapter Twenty-Seven

I awoke by falling out of bed. For a moment I was disoriented, and then I recognized the crocheted cover on my bed and realized I was in my own room—I was just seeing it from a different perspective.

I pulled myself off the floor, and when I checked out my bed, I immediately understood what had happened. Three dogs and two cats were happily asleep, taking up most of my bed. There was just a sliver along the side where I must have been sleeping before I rolled too far.

Mason had wanted me to stay, but I said I couldn't depend on Peter to take care of the menagerie overnight. It was really an excuse. Mason kept referring to his place as "home," meaning for both of us, but I wasn't quite ready for that yet. I was sure I'd feel different after our week together. I could only imagine what would happen at my house. Samuel would want his room back, and with me gone for a week, Peter would probably take over my room.

But for now I needed coffee. With Gabby gone, I was back to having coffee in my kitchen. Peter had said nothing about anything since that first night. I didn't know how he'd react if I asked, so for now I left it to him to come to me. I did hope they were at least talking. Whatever their differences, they were going to be parents. And I was going to be a grandparent. For a moment I thought of Charlie and how sad it was that he wasn't there to be called Pops and spoil the little girl with pink unicorns and ice-cream cones.

It took two cups of coffee that morning for me to really be alert. I had the tote bag with me and took out the silver bracelet. Before I said anything to Barry, I wanted to get some more information.

Peter had passed me on his way out the door. He was meeting someone for golf. "It's business," he said. "I don't want you to think that I moved in here and am slacking off."

"I never thought you were," I said. The moment we'd had seemed to have changed him. Before he'd been annoyed at me for embarrassing him by doing anything. His comments were usually curt and meant to shut me up and remind me that I was in a different world than he was. It was crazy, because I was only in my fifties, not closing in on one hundred. But now he seemed to be talking *to* me instead of *at* me, which was an improvement.

"What about breakfast?" I said, reverting to the role I'd played when he was a kid.

"We'll get something at the club. It'll be a chance to talk business."

I wished him luck and considered giving him a hug, but I knew that was pushing it.

With him gone I didn't have to worry about him walking in on a call. I dialed Donna's number, and the caretaker, Marge, answered. As soon as she heard it was me, she handed the phone to Donna.

"It isn't about Princess, is it? I was hoping you could keep her," Donna said.

"No worries. She has a forever home with me."

"That's a relief," she said. "There's something else. I know you said you'd be willing to help out, and I wonder if you'd just have a look at my sister's place and make sure everything is okay. And take in the mail."

"Of course," I said. "What would you like me to do with it?" I asked.

"If you wouldn't mind, could you go through it and separate anything like a bill. Just put them on her desk for now." She seemed like she was going to sign off but realized I'd made the call. "Sorry. What did you call about?"

"I found a bracelet I believe was your sister's. It's a regular silver bangle with an allergy alert inscription on the inside."

"Yes, she was allergic to shellfish. That didn't have anything to do with what happened, did it?" she asked.

"Then the detective that called didn't tell you?" I asked.

"Tell me what? All they said was that Sloan had been hit in the head with a drone."

"The drone had a payload of crab, lobster, and shrimp shells."

"Oh no," Donna said, "Sloan was so allergic, the smell of cooking shellfish alone would give her a reaction and she'd need to use an epi pen, but if the shells touched her it would be a disaster."

"Did your sister have any enemies?" I asked, and I heard her gasp.

"Then you think it wasn't a freak accident? I can't imagine anyone wanting to hurt my sister. She was always looking out for me. The reason she was such a jack-of-all trades was so she could pay for my medicine or my rent. She was so good to me." Donna sounded so sad, it broke my heart. Bad enough to lose her sister, but then to think it was deliberate. "They have to find out who did it," she said.

"I'm doing my best to figure out what happened," I said.

"Bless you," she said before she hung up.

I wondered if the bracelet and what Donna had told me would be enough to convince Barry that someone had deliberately killed Sloan while trying to make it look like a prank.

I went into the bookstore early on Sunday to clean up any mess from the previous night. Mrs. Shedd and Mr. Royal had gotten rid of all the stray trash, but the yarn department needed attention. I was amazed at how many of the kits were gone. I put all the ones that were left in one display and set the other cardboard case aside to put back in the storage room. Mrs. Shedd came by as I was straightening the chairs around the table.

"There was a message for you," she said. "One of the associates took it." She handed me a piece of paper and I read it over.

"It's from the woman we bought the yarn from," I said. "She said she found still another box of yarn in a closet and said that I can pick it up from the guesthouse, hopefully today."

"By all means get it," my boss said. "We want to have as many kits as possible together before you leave." She picked up Rhoda's blood-red sample scarf and compared it with one in shades of green and blue with a blast of textured yarn running through it. "They are exactly as advertised. Each one is unique and stunning."

She put down the scarf and glanced around the bookstore. "You'll make sure everything else is in order before you leave for your trip?"

I assured her I would.

"This kit idea seems like a winner. When you come back, we should discuss ways to offer more of them," Mrs. Shedd said.

I agreed, but I wondered what my mindset would be when I returned. She was just looking at it as a week away, but to me it felt like a dividing point in my life.

* * *

Sometimes weekend days were slow, but this week they were busy. Mick Byrd brought in a box of books he'd taken home for Merry to sign. Anastasia came in with the kit she'd won, asking for help. I took her back to the yarn department, and we were soon joined by some other kit purchasers who needed help. Adele saw me assisting the group and couldn't help herself. The Adele swooped in and took over. "Pink, I'm so much better at this than you are."

I was actually relieved by her comment, knowing she'd be there to offer the help we'd promised would be available. When I left the area, Anastasia was busy telling the others that the yarn was infamous and had been part of a crime scene, before going on about the short-term rental business, which she seemed to think was going to fizzle now that the house was connected to a death.

I helped customers, got the newsletter together, and was in and out of the yarn department as people came in asking about the scarf kits. Before I knew it, it was time to leave.

I went directly home to take care of the animals. Then I would go to Sloan's and take care of things, as I'd promised her sister. The last stop would be to pick up the yarn from Miami's since it didn't matter if she was there or not.

Peter was off somewhere, and my house was peaceful. I soaked up the moment of aloneness, knowing it was all going to change with Samuel's return, along with my parents'. They had their own place, but all family gatherings were at my house, and my mother treated my living room as a rehearsal hall.

I fed everybody and gave them all some outdoor time while it was still light. Princess had become part of the crew and was running with Felix and Cosmo. I had no idea how Blondie felt about sharing her pal. The cats did their usual thing. Mr. Kitty found a last spot of sunlight to lie in, and Cat Woman prowled the bushes.

I got them all back inside and left for my errands.

It was a short drive to Sloan's. Her garbage cans were the only ones still at the curb. I dragged them into the backyard. It was already evening, and the yard was in the shadows. I hadn't noticed it before but now admired how she had created a park-like feeling, making the small space seem much larger.

I remembered Donna's request and went back to the street to get the mail out of the box by the curb. The key was just where Donna had said, and I let myself in.

I felt less like an intruder this time and took the mail into the bedroom that Sloan had used as an office. I sat down at the desk and began to sort through the mail. When I went to move the keyboard of her computer, I accidentally hit a key and the screen came on.

She had left a bunch of programs open, and out of curiosity, I began clicking around. As various files opened, I figured they were projects she'd been working on. Bitsy had described the backdrop Sloan had created for her parents, and I recognized the shelving and blue-gray color of the wall. It was the perfect backdrop for Zoom meetings. Another file had photos of the rental rooms at Miami's with mockups of how they might look with various furniture arrangements. The next file had a montage of photographs that confused me, and the last one totally surprised me. As I went through them a second time, I suddenly understood what they were. It was mind-boggling, but a bunch of puzzle pieces fell into place, and I finally had an idea of who had killed Sloan. I just needed to make sure.

Chapter Twenty-Eight

I thought about calling Barry and just dropping it all in his lap, but at the last minute I reconsidered. This was my last hurrah with him, and I didn't want to go halfway. I'd make sure he had enough to get a search warrant. And there was always the possibility I was wrong. Better check everything out myself.

I drove to the cul-de-sac and parked in front of Miami's. Her place was dark, and I assumed she wasn't home, so I didn't bother to announce myself. If anything, I think she preferred that I just went through the yard to the guesthouse for the yarn, without contacting her.

I knew my way well enough to be able to move through the yard in the semi-darkness. I'd get the yarn on the way back. For now I was on a hunt to check something out.

This time when I opened the gate to go into the secret garden, I made sure to lodge something in the gate to keep it open. I left my purse by the fence but took my phone. Now back in the open green space, I had to get my bearings. When I looked back at the fencing along Miami's yard, I realized what I'd missed before. It was something that Anastasia had said before that I hadn't understood. I had only considered the neighbors on the cul-de-sac, but there was a property on the other side of the wild area that faced another street.

I found the chain-link fence, even though it was almost completely covered in ivy. I pushed away some of the big pointy leaves to peer through the opening. I couldn't see much beyond the wall of a building. I ran my hand along the ivy-covered metal fencing until I felt a gate. I tore away at vines until the lock mechanism was visible. The fence seemed long forgotten, and it took a lot of pushing, but I was able to release what held the gate shut. I pulled it toward me until it was open enough to squeeze through. I made sure it stayed open so I'd be able to make an easy exit.

I figured that I was at the back of the property and did a quick perusal, determining that the yard was much bigger than the ones on Starlight Court. It sloped up toward a grand-looking Spanish style house. The yard was illuminated with landscape lighting. The wall I'd seen belonged to a building that seemed like a garage. I had a feeling it housed what I was looking for. Staying in the shadows, I searched for an entrance. There were no windows, and the front had a pull-up door that was far too obvious for me to use. I toured the final side of it and discovered a normal-size door. When I tried the handle, it didn't turn, but years of weather and earthquakes had shifted the frame, and when I pulled on the handle, the door reluctantly opened while the handle stayed locked.

A smell like an aquarium that needed to be cleaned hit me as I walked in. I felt along the wall and found a light switch. A row of lights in the ceiling came on, illuminating one side of the large interior. It seemed like an oversized garage that was being used as a workshop. I stepped closer to the shelving on the wall to get a better view of what was on them. There were a number of drones and remote-control vehicles that weren't meant to be toys. I recognized the black SUV that had chased me. I pulled out my phone and began taking pictures. I'd give them to Barry and let him figure out what to do with them.

I knew I should probably get out of there, but I'd noticed something in the shadows. It appeared to be an aboveground swimming pool, but on steroids. It was too tall for me to see over the top, and I went up the metal stairway on the side of it. When I got to the top, I saw there was what looked like a diving board that went halfway across the water. I tested it with my foot, and it seemed to be anchored on the other end. I was considering what it was for when suddenly the whole interior was bathed in bright light. I tried to back down the stairway, but someone was blocking it. Mick Byrd stood on the bottom step.

A message flashed in my mind that I needed to get out of there. "Sorry for being in here," I said, trying to keep my voice level. "I'm the one who got stuck in that drainage area before. I dropped something and I came back looking for it. I should have learned my lesson, but I got stuck in here again. I came in here hoping I could use a phone to call the owner of the house next door so she could open the gate." It sounded pretty lame, but I hope he'd go for it. I saw his eye go to the phone sticking out of my slacks. "It's dead," I said. "Too much texting, not enough charging." I was trying to sound a little daffy, hoping he'd fall for it.

"You can't leave without meeting Fred and Ginger," he said. He came up behind me on the stairway, forcing me to go to the top just before the plank that went across the water. I looked down and saw two long, black, snake-like fish swimming around in the tank.

"Electric eels are fascinating creatures. Everybody calls them eels, but they're really knifefish. After all these years they're making a sequel to *Eels*. Of course, Merry won't be in it this time. A horror film hardly goes with her image and brand now." I remembered now that at that book club meeting Merry had mentioned she'd met Mick on that movie.

He looked down at the swimming pair. "I'm doing the special effects again. The mechanical eels I made before would never pass muster now. That's why I have Fred and Ginger, so I can study everything about them before I create the fakes. I spend hours on the plank, watching how they move."

"That's all very interesting," I said, doing my best to sound casual, "but I really need to go." I tried to back up, but he held his position, and I felt something sharp poking me in the back.

"I always carry a pocket knife," he said. "You never know when it will come in handy. More interesting stuff about Fred and Ginger—their bodies are like six-foot-long

283

batteries. They carry quite a charge and can give off enough to stun a person if they're bothered. And they keep stunning the intruder until their charge runs out. It's kind of like being shot with a stun gun fish style. Then, well, unless someone rescues the person, they drown."

"So, you're still working special effects while being your wife's manager," I said, hoping to keep him talking.

"I'm mostly out of it now, but I couldn't turn down *Eels Two*. It's my shot for an Academy Award. I've done a great job of keeping Merry's brand going. Not many actors have managed the career she has. She was never the lead but has become a fixture as the mom or best friend. Everybody knows who she is and what she stands for. Now it's my turn for a little of the spotlight." I could feel his breath on my back. "I know you've been snooping around. What do you think you know?" he demanded.

A whole lot came to mind, but I wasn't about to say anything. I just wanted to get out of there.

"I was taking pictures of the interior. This is just the kind of building I'd like to add to my property. My son has moved in." I was on a roll, thinking I'd be so annoying he'd let me go to get me out of there.

"Shut up. Nobody's going to buy that story. I don't know how you know it, but you know too much," a woman's voice said. I turned and saw that Merry had joined us. Gone was the cheery upbeat voice she'd used at the book club. Her face seemed different without her perpetual smile. She looked older and harder. "Will you just do it." She handed him a long pole with a brush at the end used for cleaning a pool.

"I'll take care of it," he said with an annoyed grunt.

She looked at me again and at him holding the pole. "What are you waiting for?" She threw up her hands. "It's got to seem like she's a busybody who snooped one time too many and fell in the pool."

When Mick didn't make a move, she continued, "Do I have to do everything? You wimped out, and I had to fly the drone," Merry said in an impatient voice.

"I'll do it," he said angrily. He poked the knife a little harder. "Okay then, time to walk the plank." I couldn't believe he really said that, but I reluctantly took a step out on the wooden board. I looked back and Merry had joined him on the platform at the top of the metal stairs. He was still holding the pool cleaning pole, and I figured when I got out far enough, he'd use it to knock me off. Unless I could do something first. Though at the moment I was coming up empty.

"This is taking too long," Merry said. She grabbed the other end of the pole and tried to pull it away, but he held on, and as they struggled, she started to lose her balance and, with a scream, fell over the side into the deep pool.

She was thrashing around, trying to get to the side, but there was a flash in the water followed by a loud crack as the eels found her. Her body went limp and floated up to the surface facedown. Mick was too busy trying to save her to pay attention to me. It was my chance to escape, and I backed off the plank and down the stairs until I felt someone grab me.

Chapter
Twenty-Nine

"Barry!" I said—well, actually, shrieked. "What are you doing here?"

"Maybe the better question is what are *you* doing here?" he said, pulling out his phone as he looked around, taking in the scene.

Mick was in panic mode and had tossed aside the pole as Merry's body convulsed again, and I shuddered, imagining the serpentine creatures attacking her. Mick rushed to the shelving, and a moment later a heavy-duty drone took off and flew over the tank. A long hook hung from its bottom. The drone lowered with precision, and the hook slipped under Merry's arm before the drone rose up. It barely made it outside the tank and lowered before the hook broke loose, and she slipped to the ground. The craft landed next to her, and Mick rushed to tend to her. Finally, I heard some coughing and sputtering as Merry moved, and he helped her sit up. He looked over and saw Barry for the first time.

"Who are you?" Mick demanded.

Barry pulled out his badge.

Not missing a beat, Mick pointed at me. "Good. Arrest her for trespassing," he said.

"They tried to kill me," I protested.

"It was self-defense," Mick said to Barry. "I was protecting myself against an intruder."

"I don't think that quite flies," Barry said. "She has no weapon, and you have security cameras in here and by the fence, so you knew she was here before you confronted her. You could have just called us." I looked up at the ceiling and saw the tiny camera he was referring to.

Mick seemed stumped for a moment before he said, "Well, she pushed my wife in the water."

]Merry glanced around the room, looking a little confused. Her expression had gone back to the girl-next-door look and she had her usual sunny smile.

"What happened?" she said. "I feel a little strange." She looked at her husband. "But what she said is true. We were trying to kill her." We all looked at her in surprise.

"Shut up," Mick said.

"No, you shut up," she said. "Molly had become a problem to get rid of, just like Sloan." She turned back to Mick. "If you hadn't dawdled and had pushed her in, our problem would have been solved."

"What's wrong with you?" Mick demanded. "You're supposed to get amnesia from a shock."

She shook her head with the smile still plastered on her face. "I just can't seem to help telling the truth."

I heard the loud thwack of a police helicopter starting to circle above just as EMTs and officers flooded in.

The EMTs checked her out and determined she didn't need any medical attention. Then, while Mick watched in horror, she started to talk as she looked around at all of us.

"I had to find a way for my twins to go to Worthington. It went along with the image that we were the perfect family." She made a face. "I hired a college consultant, but it was a waste of money. The only thing she did was tell me that Worthington had a croquet team. I got in touch with the coach on my own. Lucky for me, she turned out to be a fan and took my word that the twins were croquet champions—as long as we provided photographic proof that they'd been in a championship—and she 'suggested' we include a donation to the equipment fund."

"So you hired Sloan to create the illusion," I said.

"It's was Mick's idea to use her," Merry said. "She created a tournament, set the whole thing up in her backyard. She knew just how to take close-up photos so it appeared a tournament was going on, complete with the twins getting trophies, and then she created a montage to give to the coach. The montage and generous donation we made worked. And they got admittance to Worthington as recruits for the croquet team." She stopped and took a breath. "The plan was they would claim they sprained their ankles right after school started and would have to quit the team."

"Would you listen to what you're saying?" Mick pleaded.

She seemed unmoved and went on talking. "It all would have been fine, but Sloan heard that the district attorney was asking questions about the kids who'd gotten admission as croquet athletes, and she lost her cool. I knew she was going to go directly to the DA and presumptively make a deal to save herself and bury us. I saw what happened to those people in that other college admission scandal. Overnight they lost their careers and got jail time. I wasn't going to let that happen to me," she said in an angry tone.

Mick hit his forehead with his hand in frustration and tried to stop her from talking, but she kept on.

"We had to stop Sloan. I was the one who remembered Sloan was allergic to shellfish, from a lobster boil wrap party for the movie we all worked on. Just smelling them cooking was enough for her to need an epi pen. I was the one who found out all the neighbors were upset about that woman setting her house up for short-term rentals. Mick monkeyed with the sign out in front of her house and put the posters on the street signs. I discovered that one of the neighbors owned a seafood restaurant, but I let Mick do the dirty work of getting the stinky garbage. It was a perfect plan. There were rocks in the bottom of the bag hanging off the drone. On the first pass, the bag hit Sloan in the head, knocking her out, and then the drone flew over her again, and I opened the bag, letting all the shells pour over her. Then I used the drone to keep you away," Merry said to me. "Before you or anyone could get to her, she'd gone into anaphylactic shock, closing up her throat, and she was dead. Everyone bought that Sloan got hit by accident, and it was just part of a protest against the short-term rentals." Merry seemed to be almost proud of her accomplishment.

"It'll be inadmissible," Mick said when she finished. "You had no right to come in here." He glared at Barry. "Where's your warrant?"

Barry was totally in his controlled detective mode. "I didn't need one. I heard a scream and entered to protect the safety of someone inside." The officers swarmed the couple as he told them both that they were under arrest. Merry let out a protest about being wet, and there was a brief negotiation before Barry agreed to let her change her clothes, with a female officer accompanying her.

I followed Barry as he checked out the drones on the shelf, noting that a piece of a crab shell was stuck to one of them. Barry marked it as evidence. I understood why there'd been no record of nearby large drones when I saw that they all had plaques showing they were property of Winkle Brothers Studio.

"Am I free to go?" I asked. Somehow I'd kept my cool this time and stayed rational.

Barry turned toward me. "The fact you were trespassing seems like a moot point now. But I am going to need a statement from you." He looked at the tank. "I never did get a look." He went up the stairs and gazed down in the water before returning to me. "Drones, seafood shells, electric eels—" He shook his head. "What a case." He went to talk to one of the officers who seemed in charge and came back to me.

"We can talk in the car." We went back into the yard and through the open space back into Miami's yard. "How did you find me?" I asked as I grabbed my purse off the ground where I'd left it.

He held out his phone. "You pocket-dialed me." I stared at his phone and remembered that I'd considered calling him and must have left the screen on his number. "I happened to be near the bookstore, and Mrs. Shedd told me about you going back for more yarn. I figured you might be in trouble again. Your car was parked out in front of the Holiday House. I saw your purse by the fence, and then I followed the breadcrumbs. All I heard were muffled sounds from the call until Merry screamed."

The side gate from Miami's yard was open, and as we approached, I saw there was a crowd in the short street. The news van from Channel 3 was there, and Kimberly Wang Diaz was interviewing people. Both the Greenmobile and Barry's black Crown Victoria were in the middle of it.

"How do we get out of here?" I said.

"I got this," Barry said, his voice full of authority as he grabbed my hand and led the way. As we reached the circus in the street, the reporter stuck her microphone in my face, and I uttered, "No comment."

She pointed the microphone at Barry, asking if I was a suspect.

"No," he said. "She's an important witness." I couldn't see his face, and I wondered if he'd rolled his eyes as he said it. We got through the crowd, and he opened the passenger door to the Crown Vic for me to get in. "You'll have to get your car later."

He got us out of the crowded cul-de-sac and pulled over to the curb. "I didn't think to ask. Are you all right? No damages this time, no splinters or eel bites? I have a first aid kit."

"Nope, but thanks for asking," I said.

"It seems like you kept it together pretty well, but you probably need something after what you've been through. You want some coffee while we talk?" I gave him a hearty nod as I felt my inner starch giving way.

He pulled into the parking lot of a coffee place and went in to get the drinks.

He came back a few minutes later, beverages in hand. "I got you an extra shot of espresso, and I figured you probably needed a little sugar," I looked into the carrier, and there were two bright pink cake pops. "It's the end of the day and it was all they had."

Once everything was sorted out, I saw he had taken out a note pad and pen. "Now can we finally get to it? What possessed you to go there?" He looked over at me. "And no games or questions answered with questions this time."

"Don't worry. I don't have it in me." I looked over at him. "Your suit has no wrinkles, your shirt is still crisp, even your tie is pulled tight. How do you manage it?"

"Practice in keeping it all together—the thing that seems to bother you so much—and clothing made out of iron." He managed a smile.

I took a moment to eat my cake pop and collect my thoughts. He was right about the sugar. I felt an instant pick-me-up.

I told him about the bracelet with the allergy warning. "There was no way that it was a coincidence that she was allergic to seafood and that was what the drone dropped."

"Why didn't you tell me about that?" he said.

"I would have, but you got so upset the time I contacted you and told me not to do it again."

"Sorry, my bad," he said. He offered me the second cake pop. "You need this more than I do."

"One's my limit," I said, pushing it on him. "Once I knew she was the intended victim, I wondered why." He was staring at the cake pop, probably trying to figure out how to eat it without looking silly. Finally, he pulled it off the stick and popped it in his mouth whole.

"I thought that it could be because the neighbors blamed her for setting Miami up with the idea of turning the place into a short-term rental spot, but then something happened." I stopped and let the suspense build up.

"Hey, I thought we agreed no games," he said, feeling around his mouth for pink icing residue.

"*My* bad. I guess I can't help myself," I said, offering a sheepish smile. "I went by Sloan's," I said. Barry's expression darkened, and I knew what he was thinking. "It wasn't breaking and entering or sneaking in a window. Sloan's sister told me where a key was hidden and gave me permission to go inside." I explained putting the mail on her desk. "I accidentally turned on her computer, and that's when I saw a montage of photographs. It didn't make sense at first. I could tell it was Sloan's backyard, but it appeared to be set up for a croquet match. There were two players in the shots, with a hint of a crowd watching, which was probably photoshopped in. The final shot showed the two players with their trophies and their proud parents." I left a dramatic pause. "The parents were Merry Riley and Mick Byrd." I took a sip of the strong coffee drink, which added to the boost the cake pop had given me. "I put it together with something Mason told me." Even in the semi-darkness, I picked up Barry's prickly expression at the mention of Mason.

"He kept coming back to town because the DA was harassing some clients of his. Mason said it was because the DA was upset that his kid didn't get into Worthington University, but the client's kid did, and he was looking for some kind of scam like that Varsity Blues scandal that happened before. Some high-profile parents had made their kids out to be athletes to get them into prominent schools. Mason told me his clients were legit, but he couldn't vouch for the rest of the team. Sloan was a set designer. She designed the perfect setting of a fake croquet championship."

"Croquet? Not what I think of when I hear college sports," he said. "I get it—Riley thought Sloan would talk."

"The final piece was when I remembered that one of the book club members made an offhand remark that Merry was a neighbor. I didn't know at the time that the woman lived in one of the houses on the cul-de-sac. I didn't put it all together until she said something about a neighbor on the other side of the wild area, and I remembered seeing a bit of chain-link fence near Miami's fence and put it together with what else I knew."

"I think I know the rest," he said, putting away his notebook.

"What's going to happen to them?" I asked.

"Do you really have to ask, hot shot?" he said.

"Okay, I guess I know. Their worst nightmare. All the deals Merry had will end. Their kids will be un-admitted to Worthington and will be angry at their parents for ruining their lives, which for once is actually true. And Merry and Mick will be charged with murder. Thanks to Merry's truth-serum reaction to getting shocked by the fish, I'm guessing they will plead guilty and try to make a deal. Oh, and the coach who accepted their generous gift will probably be replaced."

"Sounds right," he said, starting the engine. "By the way, I did follow up on the Yanas and the drones in their yard. They're trying to come up with a way to use drones to deliver the bags of seafood to the tables at their restaurant."

"Good luck on that," I said picturing drones crashing into each other and dropping bags of seafood all over the place.

He pulled up to the curb in front of my house. There were cars in the driveway and out front. I could see people moving around in my living room.

"Is Peter entertaining again?" he asked.

"No, it's all family."

We sat for a moment in silence before he finally spoke. "I'll give it to you that your gut was right about Sloan being the victim."

I gasped. "Did you really just say that I was right?"

"Don't let it go to your head, though. You broke all kinds of rules. You were supposed to just give me the information, not go poking around on your own. You could have ended up swimming with the eels. It's lucky I heard that scream." He glanced toward the front window, where it looked like a party was going on. "You probably want to get in there."

"I should. There's probably chaos. My mother just came back from her tour. Samuel is just finding out that Peter has taken over his room."

"Do you need backup?" he asked.

"Thanks, but I can manage."

Well then, I guess we're done," he said. "When are you leaving on your grand adventure with Mason?"

"About that," I said, "if you're going to take Cosmo, that's probably the time to do it."

"Right," he said. "I'll bring your key."

"Right," I said.

"It was an experience working with you," he said. "Good luck in your future endeavors." It felt so strange and formal, but then what else was there for him to say?

"Same to you," I said as I got out of the car.

Chapter Thirty

"There you are," Mason said when I came into my kitchen. I'd made a pit stop in the garage to make sure my shirt was tucked in and there weren't any ivy leaves stuck anywhere. "I tried calling you and kept getting your voicemail." He looked over my face with concern. "I was worried."

I pulled out my phone and saw that it was still connected to Barry's, and I clicked it off. Mason and my father were unloading shopping bags of take-out food. I gave my father a welcome-home hug and went into the living room. I was the center of attention just long enough to say hello. Peter and Samuel went back to talking about something, probably negotiating rooms. My mother and the other two members of her singing group had moved some of the furniture and were already practicing some new dance moves.

The animals were probably hiding from the commotion, in my room.

"You look a little frazzled," Mason said when I went back into the kitchen to help with the food. "Want to tell me about your day."

"A little frazzled," I repeated with a laugh. "Let me explain." I gave him a short version of the whole story. "But I never would have figured it out if you hadn't told me about your clients."

"We're a good team," he said. "Eels?" He shook his head with disbelief. "Nobody can say you don't have an interesting life. I'm glad you got it all tied up, and now you're free to go off. I settled in as he wrapped his arms around me in a warm hug. "It sounds like you're finished dealing with Barry too." There was just the slightest question in his voice.

"He's going to pick up Cosmo and drop off his key before we leave," I said. I was doing my best to sound cheerful about it, but the truth was I hated to give up Cosmo. I loved how he looked so much like a little black mop that it was hard to tell which end was which. He'd been the cuddler that Blondie had never been. I thought of how he slept next to me with his feet in the air.

Mason seemed to be reading my mind. "I'm sure they'll give him a good home, and he *is* Barry and Jeffrey's dog. I know he was the one who slept next to you. But now you'll have me." He chuckled at his comment. "Sorry, you bring out the corny in me."

Mason took me to get my car before we went back into the kitchen to deal with the food. I was surprised to see Peter talking to Gabby in the yard, but she seemed to be on her way out. Later Peter told me she'd just come to pick something up, but she'd been friendly, so maybe there was hope. I was going to leave it to him to tell the family about their relationship and his impending fatherhood.

Mason helped me set the food up buffet style in the dining room. Everybody served themselves and spread out around the living room and den to eat. I said nothing about my day or the solution to Sloan's murder.

I thought I was home free, but somebody turned on the eleven o'clock news. Kimberly Wang Diaz was doing a remote report in front of Merry and Mick's house. Samuel looked at the screen. "That's just a few blocks from here," he said. When the newscaster went to an earlier tape as she tried to explain what had happened, I heard Peter groan.

"Isn't that you?" he said accusingly. "And not that detective again. What have you done now?"

I had no choice but to tell them. They all listened in silence as I told the whole story, including that I'd been helping Barry with the case. There were groans all around except for Mason and Samuel, who both gave me a thumbs-up.

Peter started to fuss at me, but then it got through to him who the guilty party was, and I heard him let out a "Whew. Lucky they didn't take the deal with me."

My mother pulled me aside. "You were playing detective again," she said with a discouraging shake of her head. "I thought you were done with all that. And with that cop."

"He has a name," I said.

"Okay, I thought you were done with Barry," my mother said, doing her best to make his name sound odious. "Mason told us that you're going to be away for a week and that you're working with him. He implied there might me something more." She looked at me for a comment.

"Nothing to talk about now," I said, walking away.

Mason helped me clear up, and then I walked him to his car. "I bet going off to Topeka with me is looking pretty good about now. Just you and me in a mini suite with a view of Pizza Joe's," Mason said.

"Sounds good to me. I'm really looking forward to that microwave popcorn you promised."

"And just think, we won't be saying goodbye anymore. It will be good night instead," he said, taking me in his arms and giving me a kiss I felt down to my toes.

Chapter Thirty-One

As it was the last day before I left, I'd hoped for a regular Monday at the bookstore, but of course it wasn't. The news about Merry Riley, the croquet scandal, and the eel attack that had temporarily left her unable to tell a lie was already everywhere.

Before we'd even gotten our drinks, Dinah was grilling me about it when we met for coffee. "I feel so left out of this one," she said as we went to let Bob know we wanted our regulars. "But I guess this time Barry was your sidekick."

I laughed. "I'm sure he'd see it the other way around."

Then we talked about my upcoming trip. "I know how persuasive Mason can be, but don't let him talk you into eloping. I want to be there for your wedding."

"We're going to Topeka and back, with no detours. And it's just for a week," I said.

"Maybe that's what you think, but he's probably betting on it being the beginning of happily ever after," she said. We finished our drinks and went back to the yarn department, where we took out our crochet projects.

We joined the others at the long table. I barely got a chance to remind them that I'd be gone for a week, before they started asking for details about Sloan's death, having heard that I was involved. I'd told the story so many times now, I had it down to a short explanation.

"What is wrong with Merry Riley?" CeeCee said. "I know I said her career was on the boring side, but she certainly blew it. It's made me feel better about doing live theater," she said. "I think I'd rather keep the eye of the tiger rather than rest on my laurels. I may bomb in this play, but at least I'm still putting myself out there."

Adele was leaning on her arm, looking at the dark screen of her phone as it sat on the table. It was as if she'd ignored the whole conversation I'd had with the others. "I know I've been a little upset with how my fans all want a piece of me. I was thinking of giving up being an influencer, but I can't do that to my people. They need their Adele fix to get through the day." She looked at me. "Next week will be fun for them. They can watch as I make changes to the yarn department while you're gone. Hint: we'll be playing hide the knitting needles."

Elise was a late arrival and was practically buzzing with excitement when she came up to the table and dropped a box of yarn. "Miami said this is yours." She slid into one of the chairs. "I've been with Miami all morning. There's just so much going on." Her wispy voice sounded a little frantic. "A production company already wants to do something about Miami's house. She's upset because they seem more interested in the house than her. They already have a pitch:

'What happens when one of the houses on a tight-knit cul-de-sac starts offering rooms as a short-term rental? Every group of guests has a story.' They aren't sure what it's going to be yet—a reality show, a sitcom, or a drama. They signed up Miami, the house, and all the neighbors. And in addition to everything else I'm doing for Miami, the production company wants me to be the real estate advisor." She paused for a moment and struck a cocky pose. "So much to do. I have to get new business cards and so much else. I can't wait until I tell Logan," she said, referring to her husband. She pulled out the afghan she was working on and started crocheting like a runaway train.

Sheila listened to it all with a tense expression and urged Elise to take some deep breaths and slow down her hook. It made Sheila so nervous, she had to take out her emergency ball of cotton yarn and do some mindful crocheting. Her face began to even out after a few moments, and she let out a long sigh. "You're probably who my boss should talk to. He just told me that the vintage pieces he'd taken on consignment were brought in by Sloan. The only piece left is the Tiffany lamp. He's holding all the money," she said to Elise. I blanked out for a moment and then remembered that I'd heard some concern that Sloan might have been cheating Miami on some pieces that were sold on consignment. It had never occurred to me that they were at Luxe. Elise had calmed a little and said she'd stop into the store.

Eduardo was stunned with everything that had gone on. "I've been so involved with my new place, I missed out on a lot." He looked to me. "I'm sorry you won't be around for the grand opening of Apothecary II."

Rhoda patted my hand. "We're going to miss you," she said.

"Dear, you won't be here for the debut of my play," CeeCee said, sounding worried. Rhoda reassured her they'd still fill the first row.

"It's only a week," I said. "I'm sure I can make up for everything when I come back."

When the group broke up, Dinah stayed behind while I put away the box of yarn, saying I'd deal with making the kits when I came back.

"Remember I'm counting on being your matron of honor."

I laughed at the image of myself in an elaborate wedding dress at a chapel in Vegas. "Don't worry. It's not going to happen."

Mrs. Shedd and Mr. Royal came out of their office when I was packing up to go. I took a few minutes to go over things with them. And then Dinah and I walked to the front door.

"We could do a girls' night," she said. "Commander is off with his daughter."

I said I'd have to pass. I had loose ends to take care of, and Barry was coming for Cosmo.

"I've resigned myself to the fact that it's just going to be difficult dealing with Cassandra," Dinah said. "No matter what I say or do, I'm going to be the intruder. But I can live with it." She gave me a long hug. "Don't do anything I wouldn't do," she joked.

It was dark when I pulled into my driveway, and the house was quiet. Now that Samuel was home, I knew the animals had all been cared for. He'd already gone back to his barista day job and was spending his evening waiting for his turn to perform at an open mic night. Peter was having dinner with Gabby's family, which seemed like a good sign. I'd heard my two sons fussing about sleeping arrangements, and I was pretty sure Peter had called dibs on my room while I was gone. There'd also been an email from my father, requesting my living room for my mother's rehearsals before they went on their next tour.

Mason had called, wanting to get dinner, but I'd begged off.

I'd barely turned the lights on when my cell phone rang. I knew it was Barry without looking at the screen. I felt a lump in my throat as I told him to come to the front door.

Cosmo put on his usual show when Barry came in. He jumped up and put his paws on Barry's knee. Only this time there would be no reverting back to being my dog when Barry left.

Barry looked at my suitcase sitting by the door. "It looks like you're all set to go," he said.

I nodded. "I'll get Cosmo's things."

Barry stood in the entrance hall while I gathered the dog's leash and some cans of food to start out with, along with a bag of his preferred treats. I grabbed his favorite toy and put everything in a red striped Target bag. When I came back, I saw that he'd put the key on the old treadle sewing machine cabinet that sat by the entrance.

"Well, I guess this is it," I said. I held out the Target bag. The leash was still balled up in my hand. I was waiting for the final moment to give it to Barry because I knew the dog would go crazy.

Barry was dressed in his work clothes, but his tie was pulled loose. When I looked up at his face, his gaze was off to the corner, and he looked haggard.

"I don't want to keep you," I said. "I'm sure Carol and her kids are anxious to meet Cosmo."

Barry was still avoiding my gaze. I wanted this to be over with, like a Band-Aid ripped off quickly.

"I can't do this," he said more to himself than to me. "I thought I could, but I can't."

"Do what?" I asked.

"Just pick up the dog and leave the key," he answered. I wasn't exactly sure what was going on with him. I'd never seen him like this before, looking so undone. "The thing is," he began in a low voice. Then he blew out his breath. "I'm no good at this." He stopped, and blew out his breath again. "You've always told me I hold everything in." He was still looking away, and it was making me uncomfortable. "You're right," he said, letting the phrase come out in a rush, as if it was hard for him to say. "But I can't say goodbye to you without telling you this." There was a long pause, and I felt like I was going to pass out from the suspense.

"I know I said you should go with Mason. That he could offer you the life you wanted and was the kind of person you ought to be with. I'm always going to be married to my job, and I'm not very good at letting other people have control, but . . ." He finally turned his gaze directly on me. His eyes flared with all the emotion he was so good at keeping under wraps, and I felt my breath stop.

"You are the love of my life." The words hung in the air, and he seemed relieved that he'd gotten them out. "So I'm asking you not to go. Please stay here—with me."

I felt my head spinning as I considered what to say. But there was only one word that kept coming up.

And then I took a deep breath.

"Yes," I said softly and fell into his arms.

Serendipity Scarf

This is a good project for leftover yarn or orphan skeins. The length and width depend on the yarn used, but it's approximately 3 in. (7.5 cm) wide and 88 in. (224 cm) long. It's a very easy pattern and works up quickly. It helps to mark the first stitch in each row.

Supplies

3 skeins of different yarns, each skein approximately 100 yd (91 m)

Size L (8 mm) hook

Smaller crochet hook for fringe

Stitches used: chain (ch) and half double crochet (hdc)

With color A chain 182

Row 1: Hdc in the second chain from hook, hdc across

Row 2: Turn, ch 2 (doesn't count as first stitch) hdc across until the last stitch. When there are 3 loops on the hook, pull through with color B.

Row 3: Turn, ch 2 (doesn't count as first stitch) with color B, hdc across

Row 4: Turn, ch 2 (doesn't count as first stitch) hdc across until the last stitch. When there are three loops on the hook, pull through with color C.

Row 5: Turn, ch 2 (doesn't count as first stitch) with color C, hdc across

Row 6: Turn, ch2 (doesn't count as first stitch), hdc across, fasten off; hanging strands can be incorporated into fringe.

Cut 5 pieces of each yarn approximately 10 in. long. Taking one of each yarn, fold in half and use smaller hook to poke the fold through the bottom of the scarf and then pull the strands through. Start by putting fringe at edges, then middle and on either side of middle. The ends can be trimmed or left uneven, depending on taste.

Molly's Spaghetti Sauce

Ingredients
1 can (28 oz, 794 g) peeled tomatoes
1 can (14.5 oz, 411 g) diced tomatoes
2 T. olive oil
1 onion peeled and quartered
1½ T. minced garlic
2 tsp. oregano
2 tsp. basil
2 tsp. sugar
2 tsp. balsamic vinegar
Salt to taste
1 lb (454 g) spaghetti noodles

Pour the whole tomatoes and juice into a medium saucepan. Crush with a spoon and add chopped tomatoes followed by rest of ingredients except the spaghetti. Simmer for approx. 45 minutes, stirring occasionally.

Prepare spaghetti noodles according to package directions, drain. Pour the sauce over the spaghetti . Garnish with grated parmesan/Romano cheese.

Molly's Spaghetti Sauce

Ingredients
1 can (28 oz, 794 g) peeled tomatoes
1 can (14.5 oz, 411 g) diced tomatoes
2 T. olive oil
1 onion peeled and quartered
1½ T. minced garlic
2 tsp. oregano
2 tsp. basil
2 tsp. sugar
2 tsp. balsamic vinegar
Salt to taste
1 lb (454 g) spaghetti noodles

Pour the whole tomatoes and juice into a medium saucepan. Crush with a spoon and add chopped tomatoes followed by rest of ingredients except the spaghetti. Simmer for approx. 45 minutes, stirring occasionally.

Prepare spaghetti noodles according to package directions, drain. Pour the sauce over the spaghetti . Garnish with grated parmesan/Romano cheese.

Acknowledgments

I would like to thank my editor, Faith Black Ross, for her help with the book and her understanding when I needed extra time. It's been a difficult time for everyone, and I had a few extras thrown in to deal with. Jessica Faust always has my back. And I want to thank the whole crew at Crooked Lane for the great book cover and all the support.

I managed to get a surprised laugh from my son when I bought a drone and started flying it around the backyard. When you read the book, you'll understand the importance of my drone flying.

The pandemic made it hard to shop for yarn, so I looked to my stash and came up with a project that made use of stray skeins of yarn. Thanks to the pandemic I rediscovered my stove, and instead of microwaving everything, started cooking from scratch again. It was a big time for pasta at my house, and Molly's spaghetti sauce recipe came out of my endeavors.

Everything in Molly's world is normal; in other words, no pandemic. It was a pleasure to escape into life that way, and my hope is that we all have "normal" again soon. Though I think my cooking is here to stay.

Thanks to Rene Biederman, Diane Carver, Terry Cohen, Sonia Flaum, Winnie Hinson, Reva Mallon, Elayne Moschin, Charlotte Newman, Vicki Stotsman, Paula Tesler, and Anne Thomeson for the friendship and yarn help over the years. I know Linda Hopkins and Roberta Martia are here in spirit. I miss them both.

My brother, David Jacobson, was the one who told me that going from typing to using a word processing program on a computer was like going from doing the dog paddle to flying. He helped me into the computer age when the screens were gray and the memory was in the kilobytes. He was also my backup real-life memory. It is hard to realize that he's gone.

I'd like to thank Burl and Max—somehow we have managed to spend so much time together and still get along.